A BROTHER'S BEST FRIEND HOLIDAY ROMANCE

MISTLE Ho

A BROTHER'S BEST FRIEND RUGBY ROMANCE

MISTLE Ho

JANICE WHITEAKER WRITING AS
JOSIE WATTS

First printing, 2024
Illustration: Courtney Whitworth at Romance and Rosemary
Cover design: Janice Whiteaker
Editing: Michelle Fewer

1

The Night's Young #1

Alexis

AS I CLIMB the stairs leading to the porch of my parents' stucco two-story, my already bad mood sours further. The heavy chords of "Jingle Bell Rock" thump against my brain like the beginning of a migraine. Through the glowing windows I can see that the place is packed to the gills. I've done this enough times to know that by now, ninety percent of the friends and neighbors filling my childhood home are shit-faced, so they'll be loud and chatty and huggy. It's a lot for me to handle on a good day, and today has not been a good day.

I'm turning on the heel of my red ribboned stilettos, preparing to go back to my car and claim uncontrollable diarrhea, when the front door flies open. My mother smiles out at me. Her small but curvy frame is covered with enough red and green flashing lights that she should come with a warning label, and there's tinsel stuck in her blonde hair.

"There you are." She grabs my arm, pulling me into the eggnog-fueled fold as she announces my arrival at the top of her lungs. "*Alexis is finally here.*"

Hell's bells.

I attempt to tug free of her grip, hoping to flee to some other—less peopley—area of the house before I get swarmed by the masses, but she holds firm as everyone greets me, dishing out overtight hugs and blurry smiles. It's almost like my mom has no clue how much I hate this party. Honestly, she probably doesn't. It's never occurred to my parents that not everyone loves to hang out with a houseful of people who've been chugging mulled wine and Christmas punch, spending hours fending off meddling questions from people invading your personal space.

"How was your work thing? Do you want a drink?" My mother reaches up with her free hand, adjusting the battery powered antlers glowing brightly against her blonde hair as she continues firing off questions. "Or something to eat? I made those meatballs you like. Want me to get you some?"

I manage a small smile. "No, thanks." I wasn't lying when I told her I'd be late, but I might have stretched the truth about the reason. While I technically wasn't on the clock for my dinner at The Providence, a coworker *was* there. And boy was that a mistake. I should have realized going out with a guy I would have to see every day was a terrible fucking idea.

To be fair, I'm starting to think going out with *any* guy is a terrible fucking idea.

"Finally." The single, deeply-boomed word is my only warning as my older brother comes out of nowhere. He expertly extricates me from our mother's grip, so she can get back to her beloved party, before pulling me into a bear hug that smashes my face against his muscly chest.

While I got our mother's shorter, softer stature, Leo takes after our dad, which means he's well over six feet tall and built like a bull. It makes him an amazing rugby player, but next to impossible to wiggle away from.

He leans into my ear as he squeezes the air from my lungs, ignoring my attempts to free myself from his hold. "I was about to come find you and drag you here myself. No way am I suffering through this thing alone."

I roll my eyes. "Don't try to feed me that bullshit. You love this party as much as they do." I might look like our mother, but Leo acts like her. He inherited her outgoing personality and love of socializing.

After a few more seconds of unwanted affection, he finally releases me. One big paw moves in the direction of my head and I lean back, shooting him a glare as I lower my voice. "If you touch my hair, I'll shove Cookie Clause off the counter and tell mom you're the one who did it."

Leo's eyes widen like he doesn't already know I'm the more vicious sibling, regardless of what our careers might suggest. "You monster."

Melting from the crowd like a specter, my brother's best friend suddenly appears on my other side, his arrival proving he's worth every penny the Cape Coral Swamp Cats pay him. He gives me a smirk. "She's a monster all right."

For fuck's sake. I'm not even out of the entryway and I already have to deal with him? I knew Gavin would be here, but part of me hoped I'd get lucky and be able to avoid him all night. God knows I could use a little luck after spending an hour and a half listening to yet another idiot with an over-inflated ego drone on about himself.

I thought scheduling a date tonight to reduce the amount of time I had to spend surrounded by my loud family and their loud friends was a stroke of brilliance. It was not. It left me even more pissy than normal, which is saying something.

I pull in a deep breath, trying to temper my aggravation. "Hello, Gavin."

I've known the towering giant of a man for almost fifteen years. And for almost fifteen years he's teased me mercilessly. Every time our paths cross, Gavin pretends to flirt with me, dishing out easy smiles and smooth lines like a lunch lady on pizza day.

When I was younger, I was dumb enough to think maybe it was real. That he genuinely had an interest in me. I spent more than a few teenage nights expecting something to develop between us, and sulking in disappointment when it didn't.

Then I grew up and figured out it was all fake. To Gavin, I was just his friend's little sister. There to be teased and annoyed.

He still holds the same opinion, and tonight I'm not sure how that's going to go for him. Based on the way my evening's played out so far, there's a good chance he could end up with Cookie Clause shoved up his crapper.

That would be more difficult to blame on Leo though...

"I was starting to worry you weren't coming, Al." Right out of the gate, Gavin pisses me off, using the nickname he gave me the first time we met. "I thought the party was going to be ruined."

I tip my head with a smile. "It might still be ruined. The night's young."

As usual, Gavin isn't deterred by my bad attitude. Amusement flares in his caramel-colored eyes as he grins at me over a glass of eggnog that looks comically small in his enormous hand. "Promises, promises."

I almost shift in my stilettos at the way he's looking at me. If I didn't know better, it would be easy to mistake his intense focus and unwavering attention for interest. But I do know better. And what I know is, Gavin's fucking with me.

I'm not foolish enough to think I'm the only woman he does this with. The man is a notorious fuckboy with a reputation that would ruin anyone else. Not him. If anything, it's almost made him more desirable to the female population of coastal Florida.

Maybe it's because, from a strictly observational standpoint, he's gorgeous. The quintessential tall, dark, and handsome, but not in a classic way. He has more of a caveman esthetic going on. His extreme height is only amplified by his equally extreme width. His chest would fill more than one barrel, and I swear his shoulders look like they shouldn't fit through a doorway. The thick, rich brown wave of his hair nearly reaches those barbarically broad shoulders. A stubborn piece of it insists on always falling over one eye, adding to an unexplainably boyish charm that has probably disarmed more than a few females.

Oh. And he's the most popular—and highest paid—rugby player in the US. Can't forget that.

Objectively speaking, I can see why women throw themselves at him. And good for them, I guess. At this point, I've got no room to judge anyone for their romantic choices. Mine sure as hell leave a lot to be desired.

"I'm going to get a drink." I elbow away from Gavin and Leo, dodging the wobbly bodies of my parents' friends on my way to the kitchen. Reaching the drink station set up down the marble countertop of the island they added when they renovated last year, I barely hesitate before snatching up a plastic poinsettia-print cup and scooping in a healthy dose of my mother's infamous Christmas punch. Checking the clock so I know when I'll be safe to make my exit, I chug it down, the familiar burn warming me from the inside out.

Once the cup is empty, I slam it down and go to work unlacing the threadbare scarf looped around my neck, muttering 'Holy shit it's hot in here,' to myself as I detangle the red and white stripes.

"That's just you."

Frustration has me ready to yank at the delicate knit of the accessory, so I force myself to stop and breathe, counting backwards from ten before I spin to face the man behind me. I shoot Gavin a scowl that would send most people scurrying. "Funny."

"What can I say?" He shrugs, eyes staying on mine. "I'm a funny guy." The smile on his face almost seems to slip before coming back full force. "You look good tonight." He reaches out to finger the scarf cooking into my skin. "Red is your color."

I cross both arms over my chest, resisting the urge to fan my face as I get warmer and warmer thanks to whatever my mom laces her punch with. "Can I do something for you, Gavin?"

His smile tilts into a smirk. "I guess that depends on what you're offering." His tone is low and silky and it sends the warmth I'm wrestling lower.

That... Unexpected.

He leans closer, bringing a hint of cedar and surf into the personal bubble I try to protect at all costs.

I'm used to feeling short. Between my brother and my father, I'm accustomed to people towering over me. But this is different. Gavin's presence feels less like an imposition and more like a barrier. The substantial

width of him blocks out a little of the noise and conges-
tion that's the equivalent of nails on a chalkboard to me.

It's almost... Nice. Probably because of all that
punch I just guzzled.

His eyes stay fixed on mine as he continues closing
the distance between us. "For now, you can move so I
can get something to drink."

All the warmth sliding under my skin flashes to a
flame of embarrassment. I can't believe I almost fell for
his bullshit. Again.

"You're such a dick." I shove at his chest, shoul-
dering him back enough I can slip away. "Enjoy your
punch. I hope you choke on it."

2

Don't Let Babs Punch You

"YOU PISSED HER off already?" Leo clicks his tongue, head shaking as he joins me in the kitchen where I stand watching Alexis stomp away. "That might be a record for you."

"Probably." I pass him the cup in my hand. I wasn't really thirsty, I was just looking for an excuse to be where Alexis was. "But to be fair, I think I piss her off by breathing."

It hasn't always been that way. Leo's little sister and I got along when we were younger, but about five years ago, something changed. Our easy, comfortable interactions became tense, scowling exchanges that almost always end with her glaring at me before storming off.

Just like she is now. And damned if I can stop myself from watching her go. That dress Al's wearing should be illegal. There's technically nothing revealing about the red plaid garment. It doesn't cling to her curves or dip low on her substantial tits. Even the skirt of it is a perfectly respectable length.

And yet...

"At least one woman in this world has sense enough not to worship you." Leo dumps a ladle of the deep red, overly alcoholed punch Babs makes into his cup. "You need to be humbled now and then." My best friend turns to lean back against the counter, wincing a little as he tips back some of the drink that will be responsible for more than a few rough mornings tomorrow. "I wouldn't worry about it too much. I doubt she'll be here long. She always skips out early."

I shake my head when he offers me a sip. I learned the hard way to avoid that punch at all costs. "She skips out early because she hates this thing."

Leo's sandy brows pinch tightly together, creating a crease between them. "What? No she doesn't. This is our family's favorite night of the year."

I almost laugh, but when his expression doesn't change, I realize he's serious, and it sends a pang of sympathy for the woman who just left searing through my gut. "It might be your and your parents' favorite night, but it's not your sister's."

Leo stares at me a second before his face splits into a smile and he barks out a laugh, slapping me on the back. "Dude, you almost had me there." He turns to scoop out another serving of the punch I've puked more times than I can count. "Top off your drink and I'll introduce you to the Millers' daughter. I haven't seen her in years, and she's looking pretty damn good tonight."

I turn down both the drink and the introduction. "Maybe later." I don't have any interest in meeting some random chick, no matter how good Leo thinks she looks. All my thoughts are on finding Alexis and apologizing for whatever I did to upset her.

Leo studies me a second. "You need to get back into the swing of things, man. I can't stand you when you're not getting laid."

"You can't stand me when I *am* getting laid." I give him a grin. "And maybe you should introduce *yourself* to Miss Miller, because I'm pretty sure you've got a little dry spell of your own going on."

Leo tips his head from side to side as he considers. "That's not a bad idea." He straightens off the counter, drinking down more of the Devil's Kool-Aid. "I'm going to tell her I make more money than you, and you better fucking back me up."

"I have lied to your own mother for you." I lift one hand, holding up two fingers. "Twice."

Leo gives me the lopsided smile that makes him seem unthreatening despite his size. "And I expect you to lie to her again when she asks if you saw me talking to Miss Miller."

"Fuck, Leo." I rake one hand through my hair. "Your mom told you to stay away from her and you were going to throw me under the bus?"

"Hell yeah, I was." He smooths down the front of

the green T-shirt stretched across his chest. "But you missed your chance, so now I'm the one who'll be under the bus." Leo gives me a wink as he backs away. "And maybe under Miss Miller."

I angle a brow as I look pointedly at his shirt. "You sure you want to shoot your shot wearing a 'Balls Deep in Christmas' shirt?"

Leo's eyes drop to the white print scrolled over his pecs. "Shit."

Forcing away any trace of a smile, I ask in my most serious tone, "You want to trade?"

My best friend scoffs. "Yours says 'Wanna See My Sack?,' dick. It's fucking worse." Leo looks around, like a less offensive shirt will appear out of thin air, as he slides his empty cup onto the counter. "I need to go raid my dad's closet. Entertain yourself for a while."

As he stalks off, I collect his cup and chuck it in the trash then send a few others to the same fate, killing time until he's out of sight. Then I go on a little search of my own.

Making a quick stop at the enormous Christmas tree positioned in front of the windows spanning the back of the house, I crouch down. Picking through the brightly colored packages stacked beneath the ornament laden evergreen branches, I retrieve the small gift tucked at the very back. I always get presents for Leo's parents, but this year I bought an additional gift. One that was too perfect to pass up. I didn't want to make shit weird by bringing it here Christmas morning, so I snuck it in with me tonight, hoping I'd have the chance to deliver it.

Tucking the item close, I duck off to the side of the tree, using it as cover to slip out the back door unnoticed. Stepping silently onto the dark deck, it takes my eyes a second to adjust to the change in brightness. Between the tree, the string lights, and the illuminated decorations stacked on every available surface, the interior of the house is like being under a spotlight. Out here, there's just the glow of the windows to break up the night, and I'm blinded by the sudden shift.

After a few blinks, the woman I'm seeking comes into view. As I expected, Alexis has retreated to the darkest corner of the deck. She's got both elbows propped on the railing, her clasped hands supporting her chin as she stares across the backyard that still sports the swing set and treehouse she played in as a kid.

"Hey." I keep my voice low so I don't startle her. I don't want her to think I'm sneaking up on her. Trying to steal the peace she came here to claim.

Alexis sucks in a breath as she turns my way. Her eyes narrow when they land on me. "Am I in your way of enjoying the deck now?"

Shit. I knew she was gonna take that wrong. Sometimes I forget I can't tease Al. Not the way I used to. I don't know why things changed between us, but I'm hoping my peace offering will change them back.

"You weren't in my way earlier." I cross the distance between us. "I was just trying to joke around."

Her blue eyes remain cool. "It was hilarious."

I wince a little. "That's why I'm out here. I want to apologize." I hold out the box, watching her reaction. The sage green paper taped around it feels almost like velvet. An evergreen sprig and two small gold pinecones dangle from the deep green bow tied at the center. I thought it was a little much, but the chick at the gift-wrapping counter assured me a woman as stylish as Alexis would love it. "I got you something."

Al's eyes drop to the package before coming back to mine, still narrowed but now also filled with suspicion. "What is it?"

"Open it and find out." I tip it from side to side, trying to entice her to take it. "Unless you're scared."

Al's brows lift. "Should I be?"

I shake my head. "Not of me."

For a second, her expression softens, but then it snaps right back to the mask of irritation she wears whenever I'm around. "Somehow I don't believe you."

She takes the present anyway, giving me one more look before going to work unwrapping it. I don't miss how careful she is to not tear the paper or how gently she slips the bow off one side. Guess the wrapping lady was right.

Once the box is free, Alexis cautiously lifts the lid and pulls back the tissue paper to reveal what's inside.

The seconds tick by and I start to think I missed the

mark. That maybe I don't know the woman in front of me any better than her brother does.

So I start explaining.

"Last Christmas, I noticed the scarf you always wear was starting to look a little rough. I saw this one when I was out shopping and it looked just like it, so I thought maybe..."

My words slow as she frowns down at the soft cashmere knit. I don't know what else to say, so I accidentally fall back on what usually works best for me. "It was either that or lingerie."

Al's eyes snap to mine. "Stop it."

The venom in her tone almost sends me back a step. "Stop, what?"

"You know, *what*," she snarls at me, looking way more dangerous than any man I've faced down on the pitch. "It's not fucking funny when you pretend to flirt with me."

I'm surprised at her reaction and it throws me off even more. Making me confess something I know better than to admit. "I'm not pretending."

She stares at me for a second, the silence stretching out between us. Then she starts to laugh. But not in an amused way. This laugh is a little unhinged, and I'm starting to fear for my life.

Funny thing is, the idea of Alexis having at me isn't nearly as unappealing as it should be.

"Right." She squares her shoulders and steps close enough we'd be nose-to-nose if she wasn't so short. "All the bullshit you say to me is completely serious." The words drip with sarcasm.

I manage to keep my dumbass mouth shut like I should have earlier, which she takes as an admission of guilt.

Al snorts. "That's what I thought." After slamming the scarf box onto the railing, she starts to storm away. "Stay the fuck away from me, Gavin."

Something about her snapped request makes me react, and before I know what I'm doing, my hand is holding her arm, stopping her escape. "I'm not pretending, Al."

Warning lights and sirens are going off in my head, but I ignore them the way I've never been able to ignore the woman now shooting daggers from her eyes.

Alexis pulls her arm free, but instead of continuing her earlier path, she comes back toward me, bringing the lush curves I know are hiding under that dress right against me. "Yeah? Prove it."

She thinks she's calling my bluff. Expects me to back down and admit my guilt.

I should. Acting on how fucking appealing I find every inch of her won't end well for me. But, yet again, I find myself saying something I shouldn't.

"Fine. Treehouse. Fifteen minutes."

3

That Was Fast

Alexis

"FINE. TREEHOUSE. Fifteen minutes."

My jaw drops and words fail me. Gavin takes full advantage, using that time to stalk back into the house, leaving me alone on the deck with nothing but an odd flipping in my belly to keep me company.

For just a second, my punch-punched brain skips its way into a place I haven't allowed it to go in years. Things have definitely changed since I was there last. I'm older. Wiser. Somewhat more experienced.

As a teenager, I imagined kissing him. Cuddling with him. We might have even made it to fictional first base. Now I'm rounding those things like a home run champion, flashes of scandalous scenarios my youthful brain never would have concocted pulling my nipples tight and making my clit beat like a tiny tambourine.

The problem is, it's all bullshit. Gavin isn't really interested in me. Never has been. Never will be.

And I'm not interested in him. Not really. I have zero desire to be with someone as outgoing and social as my parents. Spending my adult life suffering through frequent get-togethers and nights out sounds like a complete nightmare.

Plus the man is famous. Everywhere Gavin goes, people fawn all over him, taking photos and wanting autographs.

No fucking thank you.

Smoothing down my hair, I take a deep breath and smile, feeling better now that the unwanted detour my filthy little mind tried to take has been diverted back to the straight and narrow.

And my straight and narrow is irritated.

"Fucking prick."

I snatch up the scarf, getting angrier as I look down at the item. It's flipping gorgeous and feels like butter under my fingers. I also looks remarkably similar to the one looped around my neck. I don't know why he would remember something like that, or what in the hell would possess him to get this for me, but I don't want it.

Even though I kinda want it.

I carry it along with me as I march down the steps leading off the deck and across the yard. Pausing at the bottom of the ladder leading to the stilted wood structure my dad built over twenty years ago, I decide not to attempt it in my shoes. After taking a second to work them off, I clutch the heels in one hand, the scarf box in the other, and start to climb, using my wrists and elbows to grip. Reaching the top, I shimmy my way onto the platform before getting to my bare feet and slinging open the door.

In the years since I moved out on my own, the tree-house has changed pretty significantly. My mom has turned it from a simple sort of structure with bare wood floors and open-air windows to a fully decked out she-shed, complete with a pillow-stacked daybed, a plush area rug, and a glittering chandelier. It also sports double-hung windows, a salvaged antique door, and an air-conditioning unit.

The place is way nicer than when I was a kid, but I'm not complaining. I've taken advantage of its rustic luxury every Christmas for the past few years, spending the night of the annual party piled on the bed in comfort, scrolling on my phone while I run down the clock.

And that's what I'm going to do again tonight. Because I know, without a shadow of a doubt, Gavin won't be putting his money where his mouth is.

Dropping my shoes to the carpet, I take a guilty second to run the tips of my fingers over the luxurious scarf he gave me, scowling at how silky soft it is. Maybe I can wear it a couple times before I send it off in a garbage bag of clothes destined for the local women's shelter.

"Ugh." Disgusted with myself and my weakness for

29

nice things, I sling the box onto one of the small tables flanking the daybed.

"You're early."

My stomach drops and I nearly choke on my spit as I gasp in shock at Gavin's voice behind me. Spinning, I find his hulking form taking up the entirety of the doorway. "What are you doing here?"

Gavin ducks his head so he can clear the low frame, but straightens to his full height once he's inside, the sheer bulk of him making my mouth dry. A man his size could throw a woman around without breaking a freaking sweat—an assumption that has me feeling hot all over again.

He grips the edge of the door and swings it closed, the move just as silent as his ascent into the treehouse had been. "You asked me to prove something and I'm here to do it." His face is shadowed, making it impossible to read his expression. "Unless you've changed your mind."

Is he trying to turn this around on me? Make *me* take the blame for *his* bullshit? Like fucking hell he will.

I stand taller, even though it still only brings me up to his mid chest now that I'm without my shoes. "I haven't changed my mind." Lifting my chin, I square my shoulders, still certain he's going to back down and admit this is all exactly what I think it is.

Gavin acting like I'm still a little girl he can tease and taunt.

He shifts on his feet, hands restless at his sides,

fisting tight a second before his long fingers stretch and twitch. When his shoulders drop, I nearly smile in victory, but the expression is stalled by a twinge of disappointment I'm going to ignore and deny until my dying breath.

Then he steps toward me and my heart stutters to a stop. I'm frozen in place, bare feet fused to the rug as he closes in, crowding me in a way that makes me want to run almost as much as it makes me want to stay put.

Just to see what happens.

When he reaches for me, my lungs join my heart, abandoning their task as every cell in my body zeroes in on the tip of his pointer as it meets the front of my throat, sliding like a whisper down my skin, tracing the dip between my collarbones. His voice is just as gentle when he says, "You're so soft, Al."

I must have chugged more punch than I thought, because I think I'm going to pass out. "I moisturize." My brain barely registers how dumb of a response that was because Gavin's wandering finger is now sliding under the neckline of my dress to skim over the swell of one boob. As if I'm possessed by some lust-driven entity, I arch my back, encouraging him to touch more of me.

My sex life has been incredibly lackluster thanks to my shining personality and engaging temperament. I'm not the girl men approach at bars, and my chances of catching their romantic attention drop even lower when they meet me without the influence of alcohol.

I can't fake interest. Even when I can make myself

say all the right words, my face gives me away. I don't like small talk and I can't flirt, so my body count is in the single digits.

More accurately, one single digit.

"Can I touch you?" Gavin's deep voice is a little hesitant, which is weird because, based on what I've heard, the man has enough experience for both of us.

And probably a few of his friends.

"You are touching me." My own voice is breathy and filled with need, which is also weird because... No. It's not weird. I *am* filled with need and struggling to breathe.

Gavin moves in a little more, that taunting touch still steering clear of anything worthwhile. "I mean *really* touch you."

The urge to continue arguing even though I know what he means is strong, but not as strong as the desire to see how far he's willing to take this. "You can touch me however you want." My eyes dip down the front of his well-muscled frame. "Can I touch you?"

"*No.*" The word is harsh. Gavin closes his eyes, going still for a second before opening them to meet mine, quietly repeating the single word. "No."

I'm not sure how to take that, but it becomes irrelevant when the finger toying with my neckline hooks into the flannel fabric, dragging that side of my wrap dress down, along with the bra beneath it, to bare my entire tit.

I could swear Gavin's breath catches, but that's got

to be my imagination. He's seen enough boobs that my ample—and God given—DD-cups shouldn't even faze him. That's probably why I don't feel shy over the focused way he's staring as he palms one, the size of his hand easily scooping up every bit of my flesh. When the rough pad of his thumb skims across my tight nipple, a whimper slips from my lips.

Gavin's eyes snap to my face, his gaze simmering with intensity as he repeats the motion, this time adding his finger so he can roll the sensitive peak until it's so hard it almost aches. I'm about to crawl out of my skin with need when his head dips, the long line of his big body nearly folding in half as his mouth closes over my nipple, drawing on it in a pulse that shoots straight between my thighs.

When he tugs down the other side of my dress and pulls that already beaded tip past his lips, I go a little feral, hands fumbling around in search of his fly, desperate to get more. To get all I can. It's been so long since I've been filled, and even then it left a lot to be desired.

A *lot*.

But so far Gavin is proving his skill set, and I want to know what it's like to have someone else get me off. Preferably while his thick cock pistons in and out of me.

And holy hell is his cock thick.

I free it from the prison of his jeans, peeking down as I wrap my hand around the base. Squeezing tight, I give the length a pump, dragging the pad of my thumb through a drop of wetness that sneaks out to greet me.

Gavin's mouth pulls off my boob with a pop, his hands going to my hips, fingers sinking into their curving softness as he groans into my hair. He shudders as I give his cock another tug, and feminine power surges through my veins, riding the back of arousal and excitement.

I can't believe I have my hand on Gavin's cock. His very big, very hard, very heavy cock.

"Al, you've got to stop." Gavin's voice is as strained and tight as the hold he has on me. "I can't—" His voice breaks, chest heaving with raspy breaths. "Fuck, that feels so good." His hands move to my ass, gripping each cheek tight as he pulls me closer. "So fucking perfect."

The only guy I've ever been with never made a peep during sex. Not a moan. Not a whisper of dirty talk. Not even a grunt.

Gavin doesn't seem to be like that. At all. And I love it. I love hearing how into this he is. How much he likes my hand on him. How—

"Shit. *No.*" Gavin tries to pull away from me, but I got caught up in the moment and managed to tangle around him. A leg's hooked at his thigh and one hand is fisted in his shirt. The other's... Well...

His dick flexes against my palm as his body goes rigid.

Oh shit. Am I doing something wrong? Has he realized how little I know about this and now has yet another thing to tease me about? "Gavin? Are you ok—"

One hand leaves my ass to tangle in my hair, pinning my front to his as a rumbling moan vibrates through his chest. There's a sudden warmth against my belly and my hand starts to feel wet.

Uhh…

Gavin releases me, dick pulling from my grip. The move is so sudden and unexpected I wobble a little as I look down my front, trying to make sense of what just happened.

Pinching at the fabric clinging to my middle, I pull it away from my skin, staring at the spot a second longer before shooting the wide-eyed rugby player in front of me an accusing glare. "Did you just Bill Clinton me?"

4

There's a First Time for Everything

Gavin

I STARE DOWN in shock at the mess soaking into the front of Al's dress. This has never happened to me. Ever. Not even when I was young and inexperienced and could jack off in under thirty seconds.

Alexis tries to pull the clinging fabric from her skin, looking grossed out and a little horrified at what I've done. "I just bought this dress."

"Here." I strip off my shirt, peeling it over my head. "Change into this."

She only hesitates a second, then she's loosening the tie at her middle and peeling away the soiled dress to reveal a body that is every bit as amazing as I expected. I'm not going to deny having a very specific type, and Al fits it to a T. She's small but thick. Tiny enough to appeal to the part of me that loves being the biggest, strongest guy in the room, but is filled out enough that I don't feel like I'll break her. She's got full hips and thighs, fucking majestic tits, and a curved belly I want to bury my face in.

I swallow hard, not even trying to hide the way I'm looking at her as the dress I violated falls to the floor, leaving her in just a red lace bra and matching panties.

Wait.

"Why the fuck do your panties and bra match?" I frown as she pulls my shirt over her head, both because she's obscuring my view and because I know what matching underwear means. "Where are you going after this?"

Alexis shoves both arms through their respective holes and the hem of the shirt hits her knees. "Clubbing." She flings both arms out, scowling at the shirt hanging off her body before turning the expression on me. "Can't you tell?"

I study her for a second. "You were late tonight. Where did you go before you got here?"

She bristles, standing taller as she tosses one side of her long blonde hair back. "That's none of your business."

Alexis is right. It is none of my business. But that doesn't mean I don't still want to know. "Tell me anyway."

I haven't felt the bite of jealousy in years, but that shit is just as ugly and painful as it was back then. Maybe worse. Because back then it was over a girl who didn't deserve my time, let alone my suffering.

The woman in front of me though... Alexis is different. She always has been. But up until tonight she was also securely slotted in the off-limits tab of my brain. I don't know what the fuck happened, but suddenly my filing system has gone all the way off the goddamned rails.

She steps around where I stand, shirtless with my spent dick still hanging out of my pants, and huffs out, "I don't have to tell you anything." Crouching down, she collects her dress and shoes, along with a tiny matching red purse, then makes a beeline for the door. "And you should put that thing away before you go back inside."

"Where are you going?" I don't want her to leave. Not like this. I need—

I don't honestly know what I need. Normally, getting off is the end of interactions like this, but tonight I don't like the way it feels. Maybe because I'm the only one who got anything out of it.

Yeah. That's got to be it.

"I'm going home because I need to stain stick my dress." Alexis doesn't look at me as she yanks the door open and darts onto the narrow deck.

I hurry after her, one hand cramming my still half-hard cock back into place as I scramble to think of a way to get her to come back. "I can take it to the cleaners for you."

"I'm good." She's halfway down the ladder already. "You should get back in there before someone notices you're missing."

"What about you?"

Her bare feet hit the ground and she finally looks up at me, pretty face illuminated in the moonlight. "No one's going to notice I'm gone."

And then she is. Running in the shadows of the yard to duck up the side of the house. A minute later, the headlights of her car cut through the night as she speeds down the street, taking her wrong opinion with her.

Raking one hand through my hair, I let out a curse, swearing a few more times as I pace along the small platform flanking the front of the structure. What did I just do?

Not the part where I embarrassed the fuck out of myself by nutting the second Alexis touched me—the part where I lost my mind and crossed every line there is with my best friend's little sister.

And now I've got to go back into the party—shirtless —like nothing happened.

"Stupid, stupid, stupid." I collect the scarf and packaging she abandoned and descend the ladder, being careful not to throw my weight against it just in case it's not as solid as it seems. Babs will kill me if I break the entrance to her little hideaway.

Hopefully she never finds out I've done way worse than that in it.

I'm still berating myself as I move along the back of the house, trying the doors that lead inside, hoping I can sneak into one of the less crowded areas. A six-five, long- haired, shirtless man is a proven attention grabber, and I want to fly under the radar. The universe must take pity on me, because the handle leading into the master bedroom twists in my hand.

Letting out a sigh of relief, I push it open and rush in, silently closing it behind me before turning to get my bearings in the dimly lit room. It's the only spot on the first floor that stays closed off during parties, so I'm a little surprised—and dismayed—to hear the murmur of voices.

I wasn't looking forward to having witnesses to my walk of shame.

Since I've been outside, my eyes are used to the darkness, so it doesn't take me long to identify the source of the voices. The sight that greets me sends me flattening back against the wall like I've forgotten I'm not the kind of guy who's capable of hiding in plain sight.

Leo is on his knees at the side of the bed, his face between the thighs of who I'm thinking might be Miss Miller. She's got one hand on the back of his head and the other bracing herself upright on the mattress, head thrown back, face blissed out, hips working her cunt against his mouth.

That ugly emotion I never planned to feel again stabs through me as I'm reminded I should be in a similar situation right now. Instead, I'm hiding like a fucking creeper while my best friend enjoys the best kind of meal.

Miss Miller starts to twitch, the sounds she's making

getting louder, and I slide deeper into the shadows, resolved to the fact that I've got to suffer through whatever happens because I can't escape this room without being caught.

When my shoulder bumps the adjoining wall, it moves. I peek that way, discovering the closet door.

Thank fucking god.

Silently, I ease it open and duck in just as Miss Miller hits her peak, coming loudly as Leo groans against her flesh.

As carefully as I can, I close the closet door. Digging into my pocket, I find my phone, pulling it out and switching on the flashlight. Hopefully the minor glow it offers won't be noticeable through the gap at the bottom of the door. Working quickly and quietly, I flip through Leo's dad's shirts, choosing a T-shirt from the back that looks like it's never been worn. After turning off the flashlight on my phone, I work the shirt over my head, settling it into place as the voices on the other side of the door indicate Leo and Miss Miller have finished up their meet-and-greet and are heading back to the party.

I wait for a few minutes, counting down the silence before cracking the door open and peering out to make sure the coast is clear. When it is, I follow the same path that brought me here, going back out onto the deck before letting myself in the door hidden beside the gigantic tree. The level of inebriation at this time of night works in my favor, and I'm able to easily blend back into the crowd as if I'd never left.

I probably shouldn't have. *Definitely* shouldn't have. It was the worst thing I could have done.

Because now when I see Babs coming my way, I don't bask in the warmth of her motherly glow. All I can think of is that I just defiled her daughter in her beloved she-shed.

"Gavin." Babs stops in front of me, her hands coming to rest on my arms. "Tell me you're coming over Christmas morning for breakfast. I just gave Dolly Start'n a nice feed, so I'll have plenty of discard to make those sourdough cinnamon rolls you love so much."

I manage a smile. "I'll be here."

And I'll have to sit across the table from Alexis, eating those cinnamon rolls, acting like I didn't just embarrass the fuck out of myself and leave her driving home in nothing but a crass Christmas T-shirt.

"I'll make an extra pan to send home with you." Her sharp gaze snaps to where Leo is tucked into the corner, talking quietly with Miss Miller. "None for my son though, since he doesn't know how to listen."

She has no idea.

"Is that one of my shirts?" Leo's dad moves in at his wife's side, tucking her much smaller body against his. "Looks better on you than it ever has on me."

I smooth one hand down the front, shifting on my feet. "I spilled punch down mine."

Leo's dad slaps me on the shoulder. "It sounds like you need more punch then." He grips me tight, using his hold to twist me toward the kitchen. "I wanted to talk to you anyway."

My stomach drops, caught in a twisted net of dread. "Sure."

Did he see me go into the treehouse? Worse, did he see the condition his daughter left it in?

My misery over the situation compounds as the full scope of what I've done settles around me. If Babs and Dan find out I pawed all over Alexis, everything will change. The way they see me. The way they treat me. The way they welcome me into their home and their lives.

And I can't lose that. I can't lose them.

They're all I really have.

Dan leads me through the house, his hand staying on my shoulder. "I got a new tablet and I can't get the darn thing to hook up to the internet. You think you can take a look at it before you go?"

A little of the tension collecting in my chest eases. "Sure thing." I try to sound normal. Like I didn't just have his daughter's nipples in my mouth. "I'm sure I can figure it out."

Dan gives me a wide smile and another shoulder slap as we reach the kitchen island. "I knew you could." His eyes move around the room, like he's looking for something.

Or someone.

Probably the daughter I just felt up and jizzed on.

Dan's brows pinch together. "Have you seen—"

I brace to hear Al's name, ready to keep my reaction from giving me away.

"Leo?" Dan steps back, craning his neck to peer out into the dining room. "I haven't heard his big mouth in a while."

I grab a cup and go to work filling it with the punch I rejected earlier. Puking pink no longer sounds like the worst thing that could happen to me. "He's over by the Christmas tree."

Normally I'd try to keep the heat off him and send Dan in a different direction, but if Leo's parents are pissed at him, they won't notice I'm drowning in guilt and regret.

But now, thanks to Dan, I'm also pissed.

He asked where Leo was, but not Alexis. It digs under my skin because that's the kind of shit that makes her think no one cares when she's gone.

She's still wrong though. Someone *does* notice when she leaves.

Always.

5

Girl Dinner for the Win

MY FRIEND HAZEL'S house isn't nearly as decked out as my parents' place is this time of year, but it's still festive and bright for our Christmas girls' night. She's got a cute evergreen wreath hanging on the door and a small tree glowing in the front window. There's even a string of multi-colored twinkle lights draped around the set of small palms planted in the bed next to the stoop.

Skipping up the steps, I peck out a quick knock as my stomach growls in anticipation of what's coming. Girl dinner is one of my most favorite things, and the dishes my friends craft are epic.

Hazel whips the door open, greeting me with a big smile. "Merry Christmas." She grabs me in a tight squeeze and I laugh, rolling my eyes a little as she rocks us from side to side.

I ride out the embrace even though it makes me

twitchy. "Merry Christmas. Just so we're clear, this hug is your gift."

Hazel doesn't let me go, just keeps squishing our bodies together. "Listen, I get one a year and I'm taking full advantage of the opportunity." She leans back, her smile still just as wide. "Thank you. That should tide me over until next Christmas."

I lean against the wall, letting out a resigned sigh as I reach down to hook a finger into the back of my pumps. "I could maybe be convinced to give you a birthday hug too."

Hazel's eyes widen behind her thick-rimmed glasses. "Really?" Her smile turns a little misty. "I'm honored you would suffer twice in one year for me."

Letting one shoe fall to the floor, I switch feet, flashing her a smile. "That's what friends are for." After kicking off my heels, I pass her the bottles of wine I brought since, unlike my friends, I am not a cook. As Hazel inspects the labels, I look around, taking everything in. "This place looks amazing."

The last time I was here, Hazel had just closed on the new build and it was still pretty bare bones. In the month since she moved in, my childhood friend has made amazing headway, filling out the sleek and modern two-story with her trademark color and quirk. The formal living room on my left now houses bright red sofas stacked with pillows in varying shades of teal and turquoise. Large, hammered copper panels hang on the walls, along with a variety of thrifted paintings. To the right, a dark wood table sits at the center of the dining room, surrounded by lime green chairs. A line of paint swatches is taped down the wall, each option bright and showy. Her style is totally different from mine, but I love it and can't wait to see which one she picks.

"Thanks." Hazel's honey blonde hair is still pulled up into the messy bun she sports at work, but she's changed out of her scrubs and into a cropped T-shirt and flowing lounge pants, looking both like the brainiac she is and the laid back friend I love. "It's been a huge pain in the ass trying to get my shit together." She tucks the wine into the crook of one arm, reaching up to push her glasses higher on the narrow bridge of her nose. "Especially with how busy I've been at the lab."

"I bet." Hazel works for a company that produces THC and CBD edibles, and, now that it's legal for everyone, her bosses want to expand their product line. And of course they want it done yesterday. "I still think it's hilarious that their lead formulation chemist has never been high."

"I don't know that I'd call it hilarious." Hazel gives me a little grin. "Ironic, maybe."

She leads me from the entryway to the kitchen and adjoining great room that make up the back of the house. Everyone else in our group has already arrived and they're collected around the island, looking gorgeous and only a little drunk. They all turn when I walk in, a chorus of Merry Christmases greeting me as

49

they plow through a countertop's worth of hors d'oeu-vres and bottles of wine.

"You're late." Isla, the loudest and most outspoken of our group, frowns at me over the rim of her glass. "Did Dillon accost you after work and try to convince you to go out with him again?"

I release a suffering sigh. "Of course he did." I take my spot at the counter, accepting a filled wine glass from Hazel. "I should never have gone out with him. Worst idea I've had in a long time."

Wren leans my way, her dark bob shining in the overhead light as she reaches out to squeeze my hand. "It's not your fault, babes. They all put their best foot forward until they think they've got you." She rolls her dark eyes. "It's hilarious that he thought he had you after one date, though."

He really did. Dillon thought one dinner of listening to him drone on about his awesomeness was all it would take for me to fall all over his dick.

And now I've got to face him every day at work.

"I was hoping I could just tell him I thought it over and decided it's not smart for us to get entangled since we work in such a small office, but he doesn't seem to be getting it." I down a few gulps of my wine. "So now I'm going to have to be a bitch, which is going to royally fuck my workdays up."

"*And* your dry spell continues." Lola sighs like going without sex is the worst thing she could imagine.

It's really not that bad. I've been as single as it gets

since we graduated college, so I'm used to it. Plus, I have a whole drawer of dry spell devices to take the edge off.

And recently my desert hasn't been *completely* dry.

"Wait." Isla points at me across a tray of tiny rye bread squares topped with cream cheese, cucumber, and dill. "Why did your face just do that thing?" Her eyes widen and she starts to bounce a little, her accusing finger wagging with the movement. "Something happened and you think you're going to get away without telling us."

There are lots of perks to having a tight-knit group of friends. There's always someone to talk to. Always someone to go out to lunch with. We've known each other for over a decade, so I don't have to dig into backstory when shit goes down, because they lived it right next to me. These girls have my back and are always ready to saddle up when I need sidekicks. And if I ever have to be bailed out of jail in the middle of the night, I have a whole list of options.

But they also know me really well. Well enough they can tell when I've got a secret.

"Oh, shit." Wren's lips curve into a smile, white teeth flashing against her dark skin. "You're blushing. This must be really fucking juicy."

I didn't plan to tell them about what happened with Gavin. I didn't plan to tell *anyone* what happened with Gavin. But I'm fighting myself over the whole thing, and I need someone to fight along with me, so a confession comes spilling out.

"I accidentally jacked Gavin off in the treehouse during my parents' Christmas party."

Silence.

My friends stare at me, mouths agape, as the seconds stretch out.

Unsurprisingly, Isla is the first to speak. "I'm going to need you to repeat that, because it sounded like you said you gave your brother's best friend," she pauses, sucking in a breath and lifting that same damn finger, "and the guy you had the biggest crush on all through high school, a holiday hand job in your mom's she-shed."

I roll my lips inward, immediately regretting my decision to share my story with the rest of the class. They're clearly going to make a bigger deal of this than they should. Time for some damage control.

"I didn't have a crush on him *all* through high school."

I'd figured out Gavin wasn't genuinely into me by spring of our senior year and the embarrassment of how stupid I was to think he liked me murdered any warm feelings I had toward him.

Lola presses both palms to her softly curved cheeks, heavily lashed eyes wide as she asks, "Does he have a big dick?"

Isla bumps Lola's plush hip with her own bony one.

"You can't ask that." Isla focuses on me, lifting her brows. "Is his body proportionate?"

Hazel smashes a hand into the center of Isla's face, pushing the wild redhead back a step. "Don't answer them. Studies have shown penis size is practically irrelevant to female pleasure." She squares up to me before firing off her own question. "Which is why I want to know if he returned the favor."

I chew my lower lip, because the answer isn't going to go over well with my friends. "I kind of ran away before he got the chance."

They all gasp at once and Wren's hand flutters to her chest like she's appalled at my behavior.

"You didn't stick around and demand yours?" Isla shakes her head at me, full lips pressed into a deep frown. "Have you learned nothing since Hugo?"

"Ugh." Lola's head falls back, her long, dark curls spilling around her shoulders. "You just had to say his name, didn't you? Now we're all going to be pissy for the rest of the night."

"We can remedy that. It's not too late to hunt him down and fuck him up a little." Isla pitches the same idea she does every time my college boyfriend comes up. "Give his house a nice Christmas egging."

"Egging houses is a waste." Hazel sips her wine. "If you want to fuck someone up, you throw bologna on their car. The acidity eats into the paint." She pauses before adding on, "It takes a little while though, so you've got to stick it in spots where they won't notice it right away."

'We're getting sidetracked here." Wren points at me. "We need to talk about why Alexis is still avoiding letting a guy get her off."

I laugh, the sound sudden and sharp. "I'm not *avoiding* it." I down some of my wine, needing the alcohol to help me through the mess I've walked myself into. "My dress was covered in jizz. What did you want me to do?"

"We want you to get your kitty worshiped until you can't walk straight." Isla purses her lips thoughtfully. "You think he's any good at going downtown?" She squints her eyes. "He seems like the kind of guy who eats like he's starving every single time."

"If he's not good at it, he should be ashamed." Hazel snorts. "He's certainly had enough opportunity to perfect his technique."

"Is that why you didn't stay and let him sex you?" Lola's voice drops, like the next bit is a secret we all don't already know. "Because he's a fuckboy?"

"No." The answer comes easily. I actually don't give a shit about how many women Gavin's been with. I wouldn't judge him for that the same way I don't want to be judged for my own lack of partners. "I didn't stay and let him sex me because I came to my senses and realized it was a terrible idea to mess around with him."

I down the rest of my wine, setting the glass on the counter as my friends go back to staring at me in silence. "He's not at all what I'm looking for, so there's no reason to make shit weird between us."

"I hate to break it to you, but giving him a handy during your parents' party probably already made shit weird." Isla's expression is stern as she continues lecturing me. "You might as well have gotten something out of it too."

"Well, it's too late for that now." I grab the open bottle of white wine and spill the rest into my glass. "And I highly doubt the opportunity for reciprocation will present itself anytime soon, so I'm going to forget it even happened."

I'm sure Gavin already has. No doubt he quickly focused his interest elsewhere. There's probably a whole line of women begging for his attention. And when I have to face him down Christmas morning, things will be the way they always were.

He'll give me shit and I'll hate him for it.

6

Three Times is Three Times Too Many

Gavin

I SHOULD HAVE found a way to make Alexis stay the night of the party. Should have stopped her when she started to leave and done all the things I can't stop thinking about doing now.

Instead, I've spent the days since watching her run across the yard in my T-shirt, imagining what it would have been like if I'd popped my head out of my ass and gotten to touch her the way I'm desperate to now.

"What's wrong?" My dad scowls at me across the table, a forkful of steak dinner hanging in front of his mouth.

"Nothing." I lean back in my seat and stab at my own filet.

Our yearly Christmas dinner is going about as well as it always does. He spends the whole meal bitching about my mother and downing top-shelf bourbon, and I do my best not to roll my eyes at having to listen to the same bitter story for the millionth time.

I get why he's upset, I do, but I'd fucking love it if we could talk about something else for once.

"You sure as hell don't have anything to be pissy about." My old man chews his mouthful. "You're good-looking, rich, and you don't have a woman fucking up your life." He points the tines of his fork at my face. "And you should keep it that way. The only thing a woman will do is take your money and break your fucking heart."

His bitterness has only grown since he and my mother finally divorced after years of infidelity—hers—and misery—his. I see where he's coming from. In his mind, he loved the shit out of her and it was never enough.

I'm still sick of hearing about it, though, so I try to shift the topic. "How's work going? They keeping you busy?"

My dad shrugs. "They always keep me busy." He downs what's left of his drink, looking around for our server so he can order another. "But what else have I got to do?" He snorts, the sound lacking any amusement. "It's not like I've got women beating down my door like you do." He catches our waiter's eye and lifts his glass. "Take full advantage of it while you can."

I shift in my seat, not any happier with the turn the conversation has taken. Not long ago I *was* taking full advantage of the opportunities being thrown my way, but—like things with Alexis—that changed, and I can't seem to get back where I was.

"Have fun while you can so you have the memories when you can't." My dad continues on, barreling into the same lecture he's given me every time I've seen him for the past ten years. "But never trust a single one of them, and make sure as hell you don't fall in love." His creased eyes narrow when they meet mine. "You remember what happened the last time you let a girl make a fool of you."

"I remember." And even if I didn't, he wouldn't let me forget. It's the event that defined our relationship and brought us together. The common ground every interaction we have always ends up centering around.

My dad's scowl morphs into a smirk. "I bet that girl's kicking herself now for what she did to you." His eyes drift to one side, lighting up as they fix on a spot over my right shoulder. "Don't look now, but you're getting some attention from a couple tables over." He jerks his chin in the direction he's looking. "Pretty little thing with a big smile. You can go talk to her. I don't mind."

My tri-annual dinners with my dad have gotten less and less enjoyable the past few years. Time has only made him angrier, and the glee in his gaze over the thought of me sleeping with some random woman and cutting her loose turns my stomach. "I don't want to go talk to her."

I know what my dad thinks of me, but while I have made my way into more than a few beds, I always told them the truth. That I wasn't looking for anything more. I wouldn't be calling them. We wouldn't be going out to dinner or movies. And nearly all of them were fine with it. The ones who weren't, walked away, so I never felt bad about what I was doing. It wasn't about punishing every woman I met for what one of them did to me.

In spite of what my dad obviously thinks.

"Fine." He smiles wide, waving one hand in a beckoning motion. "Then I'll bring her over here."

"Don't—" I clamp my mouth shut as a brunette bounces up next to our table. She beams at me as she rocks up onto her toes.

"Have you met my son Gavin?" My dad lays on the charm he's capable of in spite of his normally shitty temperament. "He plays for the Cape Coral Swamp Cats."

"You're The Wall." The woman looks to be a couple years younger than me—probably Al's age, but she's way more bubbly and smiley than my best friend's little sister. "I'm Betsy."

I only give her half a smile because I don't want her getting any wrong ideas. "Nice to meet you." That's all I offer her before standing from my seat. "If you'll excuse me." I don't say where I'm going because I'm not going to lie. If they think I'm heading to the bathroom, that's on them.

Cutting across the restaurant, I find our waiter and pay the bill before ducking out into the night, leaving my dad to deal with the mess he created. Over the years,

I've done my best to keep some sort of relationship with him so I'd at least have one parent in my life, but the time I can stomach him has dwindled more every time I see his face.

And might have just dropped to zero.

My mood keeps dropping as I climb behind the wheel of my new Hummer SUV. It's a little too flashy for my taste, but after wasting hours of my life trying to shoehorn myself into cars with no legroom, I got over it. Thank God, because at least I'm comfortable while I stew over my dad and how badly I fucked up with Al.

By the time I get home, I'm pissed as hell, so instead of going to my own door, I stop at the one next to it and knock. Fynn, my friend and neighbor, opens it after a few seconds. The wealthy businessman whose condo takes up the other half of our floor of the ocean-view building is normally perfectly groomed, but tonight his button-up shirt is open at the neck and his dark hair is sticking out in all directions.

I take a step back, realizing I've interrupted an evening of marital bliss... Again. "I'll come back later."

"It's fine." Fynn's new wife Val ducks under his arm, giving me a smile. "He was pacing around because he found out his mother decided to start another business."

Warmth and envy hit my gut in almost equal proportions. "If anyone can juggle it, she can."

Fynn's mother is just coming out of a cancer battle and she's never been one to sit idly, so I can imagine she's gunning to get back to normal. For her, that equals brainstorming and creating new business ventures.

"She needs to give herself time to recover." Fynn rakes one hand through his hair, explaining its current state. "It's bad enough she insists on hosting a party to celebrate our marriage and the baby."

Party makes it sound like Helena's organizing a small get-together for friends and family. Like the one Babs and Dan hosted last week. But that's not Helena's style. Her style will be in the ballroom of a hotel with a caterer and a florist and gold-foiled invitations.

As Fynn paces away, Val grabs my arm, pulling me into their condo before closing the door. "Your mother would be miserable if she did what you want her to do. And you know that." She goes to the fridge, taking out a beer and passing it off to me while staying focused on her husband. "And I'm helping her, so it's not like she's doing it all on her own."

Fynn turns to his wife, hands out at his sides. His voice pitches so quickly I can almost hear his blood pressure rise. "You're pregnant. *You* shouldn't be doing it either."

Val lets out a long sigh, eyes rolling my way. "You talk to him." She walks past Fynn, pausing to push up onto her toes so she can press a kiss against her husband's cheek. "Listen to your friend. He's a smart guy."

Fynn grabs her before she can leave, pulling his wife close and burying his face in her dark hair. He murmurs something I can't hear before releasing her, then watches as she walks down the hall.

That pang of envy hits me again at the easy show of affection and the expression on his face. It's pure, unfiltered and unrestrained adoration. Offered like a man who's unafraid of letting someone have that kind of power over his heart and his life.

Once she's out of sight, my friend turns to me, raking his hand through his hair once more. "She's going to make me bloody gray before the baby comes."

I hold out my untouched beer. "Don't worry too much. It'll make you look distinguished."

Fynn takes the bottle and drinks some down as he goes to flop onto the sofa. "Tell me you came here to talk about something besides my mother and wife teaming up to make me lose my mind."

I take a seat in one of the armchairs I used to spend a decent amount of time occupying before Val came into my neighbor's life. "I'm not sure hearing about my bullshit will make you feel any better."

"It most certainly will." He slides the half empty beer onto the coffee table. "How was dinner with your dad?"

I sigh, shaking my head. "I don't even know why I try, man. He's fucking miserable, and he loves it." I pause before admitting something I've been avoiding for years. "I think he wants me to end up just like him."

Fynn stares at me for a few long seconds before blowing out a breath. "I'm afraid I'd have to agree with you on that one." He picks his beer back up, taking a sip. "From what you've said, he seems to love imagining you out in the world, punishing the female population for what your mother did to him."

"That's not what I was doing." My response is swift and sharp. "I never led a single woman on. I never let any of them think it was more than it was."

"I know that, and you know that, but *he* doesn't know that." Fynn pauses, leaning forward, his voice softening. "Did you tell him you've been celibate for six months?"

I don't respond immediately, because technically, I broke that streak a few nights ago. I might not have had sex with Alexis, but I'm not sure I can still claim I've been living like a monk. "It's none of his business."

Again, my friend studies me, and it takes everything I have not to shift in my seat. For the bulk of our friendship, it was me offering Fynn advice as his world crumbled around him. I'm starting to discover it's not as fun to be on the other side.

"What do you think he'd say if he knew?"

I let the question marinate for a second, and the answer I come up with surprises me. "I don't think I care." I've tried to ignore how shitty my dad is for years because I hated the thought of not having a parent in my life.

Like so much else in the past six months, it seems that's changed as well.

I don't want to spend my life dealing with more incidents like tonight. I don't want to tolerate his fucked-up opinions or be forced to wallow alongside him in his misery. I understand what it's like to have your heart broken. I also understand it changes you. But you can't let it ruin you forever.

And you can't let it affect other people.

Which means I have to figure out how to fix what happened between Alexis and me. She didn't deserve for me to take without giving, and she sure as hell didn't deserve for me to make everything weird between us.

But my desire to right the wrong I created isn't just for her benefit. I have some purely selfish reasons to smooth this whole thing over.

Without my dad, her family is the only family I have. And while the thought of leaving my dad behind doesn't sit as uncomfortably as I thought it would, the thought of losing them makes me sick to my stomach.

I've got to fix this. And I've got to do it before I have to face her—and them—Christmas morning.

7

The Do-Over

Alexis

I'VE JUST CHANGED into a pair of knit joggers and an off-the-shoulder T-shirt before getting cuddled up under my favorite blanket on the couch, when someone knocks on my door. "Ugh." I let my head fall back against the plush cushions as the opening credits of *It's A Wonderful Life* play across the television. "You have got to be kidding me."

I thought I was finally done fielding visits from my neighbors for the day, and my brain races through the faces I've already seen, trying to figure out who I missed. Whoever it is, they're going to have to deal with seeing me in my pajamas.

I love my apartment. It's in a great location and has fantastic closet space, but the friendliness of the people on my floor is a little much.

At least I was prepared for it this year. Last year I felt

like a total ass when they brought me all sorts of little gifts and I had nothing for them.

After sliding my bowl of freshly popped corn onto the coffee table, I toss the super soft plush covering to one side, trying my best to work on some semblance of a smile as I pad barefoot across the floor. I pause to grab one of the small boxes of cookies I picked up at the bakery around the corner, before unlocking the deadbolt and flinging it open, bracing for another of the overexcited Christmas greetings I've been dealing with all day while trying to wrap presents for tomorrow.

Instead of the expected smiling neighbor, it's Gavin standing on my doorstep. And I nearly swallow my tongue.

His honey brown eyes hold mine for a second before dropping to the box of cookies in my hand. "Those for me?"

I open my mouth, but nothing comes out. I was planning to spend the evening watching movies while hyping myself up to face him tomorrow at Christmas breakfast, and his surprise visit has thrown me for a loop. "What are you doing here?"

He glances over a broad shoulder as one of my neighbors passes with her young sons. The older of the two boys stares up at Gavin, his eyes going wide.

"Are you The Wall?" The awe in his voice is kinda cute, but I still roll my eyes because it's freaking Gavin he's all slack-jawed over. If the kid knew what I know, he wouldn't be half as impressed.

Sure, Gavin is an awesome rugby player, but he's goofy as hell and can't carry a tune to save his life. He almost failed home ec. because he set the school kitchen on fire and accidentally farted during my mom's birthday dinner when I was sixteen.

Oh, and he's a dirty dress ruiner.

Turning away from me, Gavin crouches down, getting on the little kid's level. "I am. You watch rugby?"

The mesmerized boy nods, moving his head up and down at a breakneck speed.

Gavin lowers his voice, leaning a little closer. "You want to know a secret?"

The boy continues his bobbing nod.

Gavin tips his head my way. "Her brother is Catapult."

My pint-sized neighbor's adoring gaze comes to me. "Really?"

I force on a smile, even though I want to drop kick the giant man in front of me. I'm going to kill Gavin if that kid starts showing up at my door wanting to talk about my dumbass brother.

Gavin slowly straightens, coming to his feet, looking even bigger than normal next to the kids. "Really."

"Come on, boys." Their mother hooks an arm around each small set of shoulders, urging them to keep moving. "We're running late for dinner at Nana's, and I'm sure Miss Alexis and..." She pauses, brows pinching together for a second before she finishes, "*Mr. Wall*, want to get on with their evening plans."

I press my lips together to stifle a laugh, offering a wave as they make their way to the elevator. Once they're loaded on, and well out of earshot, I'm forced to return my attention to the unexpected visitor who I'm guessing isn't here to collect cookies or offer Christmas well wishes.

Lifting my chin, I meet his eyes, repeating my earlier question, but with a twist. "Why are you here, Mr. Wall?"

Gavin shifts on his feet, eyes moving to one side then the other before coming back to me. "Can I come in?"

I hear another door open down the hall, and don't particularly want to deal with any more of my neighbors discovering I know the most popular rugby player in the country, so I step back and wave him in, quickly closing the door.

It's so odd to see Gavin in my space. He was here once before—helping my dad and Leo carry in the heaviest of my furniture when I first moved in—but that was different. All my shit was in boxes and the place was nothing more than bare walls and uncovered laminate floors.

Now it's my home. A space I've spent countless hours making into mine.

And he's looking over every inch of the one-bedroom corner unit I snapped up the second it was available, his amber eyes taking in each nook and cranny like it's the most interesting place he's ever seen.

"So?" I try redirecting him, because I'm starting to accidentally notice a lot of nooks and crannies myself. Like the ones sculpted into his arms. The shadowed divot cutting down the center of his T-shirt, hinting at the definition of his pecs. The thick bands of thigh muscle fighting the denim of his jeans.

He pulls a familiar box from behind his back, redirecting my attention. "You forgot your scarf the other night." Gavin takes a deep breath, the broad line of his shoulders lifting with the action. "And I want to apologize." His gaze darkens and his voice lowers. "For what happened at the party."

Oh.

I didn't know how smug I felt over our little rendezvous until he ripped the rug out from under me. Thinking maybe he'd been unable to control himself around me boosted my ego and vindicated the inner dejected teenager still holding onto the past with both hands.

Lifting my chin, I try to look unbothered. "It's fine. I figured you regretted it, so—"

"I didn't say I regretted it." Gavin steps closer. His voice is lower, rougher, when he says, "The only thing I regret is that you left before I could return the favor."

I stare at him for a few seconds, trying to process exactly what's going on here. "So, you didn't come to apologize and tell me it was a mistake?"

"It *was* a mistake, Al." His eyes drop to my lips. "I just don't regret it." Gavin continues coming my way,

71

each step slow and methodical as his bulky body towers over me. "I came here to figure out a way to make things right between us."

I almost always wear heels. People love to make stupid comments when you're short, and adding on a few inches usually keeps that shit to a minimum. It also keeps me from feeling like I'm staring at everybody's belly button. Which is exactly how I feel right now. While it's annoying, it also has me wondering what Gavin's belly button looks like. I should have taken a closer look when he whipped his shirt off the other night, instead of nearly breaking my neck running away.

Tipping my head back, I force my thoughts back in line. "Does that mean you think things are wrong between us?"

He gives me a slow nod. "It does."

I wait for a few seconds, expecting him to elaborate. Gavin is normally very talkative. He's the kind of guy who charms his way through every interaction with smooth words and a smile. I could use a few more of those words in this moment, because his closeness and the intensity of his gaze is making me want to think all sorts of things that I'm sure aren't actually true. The same things I've been working hard not to wonder about since racing from the treehouse in his T-shirt. I've read too much into his actions before and felt like a freaking idiot. I'm not doing that again.

"Okay." I swallow hard as he moves in a little more,

continuing to close the tiny space that remains between us. "How do you plan to make things right?"

His body is almost brushing mine now, and every cell in my front is on edge. Bracing for contact.

"I want a do-over." Gavin leans down, bringing his face closer to mine so our eyes align. "I'm better than what happened at the party, and I want you to know it."

Is he offering to... Does he mean...

No. Definitely not. I'm just still that stupid girl who...

"I want to touch you again, Al." Gavin leans closer, but this time I step back, overwhelmed at what he's put on the table. The way it's left no room for misunderstanding.

A second ago, his body touching mine was something that *might* happen. Would have been nothing more than the result of an accidental shift or single step too far.

What he's offering now *guarantees* physical contact, and all those cells have gone from being on edge to fully engulfed in flames.

But that doesn't seem to be enough for him. Like he doesn't care I'm about to pass out, Gavin keeps going, laying out a plan of action I assumed would only happen in my dreams.

"I want to taste you." Another step for him, and another step for me. "I want to feel you come on my tongue and around my fingers."

This time when he steps forward, I run out of space.

The backs of my legs hit the sofa, and I'm so distracted, I drop right down to my butt, bouncing against the cushions.

And Gavin just keeps coming. Leaning down, hands bracing against the back of the sofa on one side and the arm of it on the other, blocking me in. "What do you think, Al? Wanna give me a do-over?"

Do I? Hell yes, I do.

Is it a good idea? Probably not.

However...

"I'm going to be pissed if you make a mess on my couch the way you did on my dress." It's sort of a lie, because imagining Gavin being so hot for me he loses control again practically has me panting like a dog. "I'll make you clean it up yourself."

His lips slowly lift, like a predator who knows their prey is close enough to catch. "Deal."

My fingers sink into the cushion under my ass as he leans closer. I'm starting to panic over what I might have just accidentally agreed to.

"But we can't have sex." Drawing a clear line makes me feel a little better about a situation I should be way more prepared to handle considering how many times I've thought about it the past few days. But again, I can't let myself think whatever happens will be more than it is. This is only about evening out the universe. Leveling the field so the awkwardness between us is balanced enough to cancel itself out. "Just other stuff."

One of Gavin's thick brows lifts. "Sex is a really broad term, Al."

"No putting your dick inside me." I pause, accidentally licking my lips before I amend. "Inside my vagina."

His nostrils flare. "But I can put it other places?"

"Not my ass." The second qualifier pops out, and for some reason embarrasses me, sending the prickle of a blush racing across my skin.

Gavin is so close now I can feel the warmth of his breath fanning over my already hot face as he asks, "Can I put other things in your ass?"

Maybe this is a mistake. "Like what?" That wasn't a no. *Why the fuck didn't I say no?*

Gavin makes a low humming noise. "I think maybe we should table that discussion." He pauses. "For now."

It's a whole discussion? How many options could there possibly be?

"Are those your only conditions?" Gavin's lips brush along the edge of my jaw and I nearly melt into the cushions.

"I think so." My breath stutters to a stop as his mouth teases down the side of my neck.

"If you come up with any more, all you have to do is tell me." His lips move against my skin as he speaks in a low voice. "If you say stop, we stop."

I've never had anyone lay things out quite so clearly before, and I have to admit I like it. I like knowing that, even though I'm about to become a puddle of quivering anticipation, I'm still the one in charge of this...

Interaction.

That's all what's happening will ever be, and I'm okay with that. As long as things don't go all the way, it's just us balancing the scales and scratching some itches.

And boy do I need scratching.

"Okay." I tip my head so I can meet his eyes. "Do you have any conditions?"

Gavin holds my gaze, lids heavy over his toffee-colored eyes. Slowly he shakes his head. "No."

8

Mistakes Have Been Made

Gavin

I SHOULDN'T HAVE come here.

I just wanted to apologize. To fix what happened so things can go back to the way they were. Then I saw her and it all went sideways. Now my train of bad decisions is barreling down the tracks so fast, I don't know if I can stop it.

Or if I want to.

My fingers flex against the couch as I ease down to my knees, bringing us almost eye level. "Can I touch you now?"

Alexis gives me a jerky nod, her chest rising and falling on quick breaths. Her expression doesn't give anything away though, so I can't tell if she's breathing heavily because she's nervous or excited.

God I hope it's the second one.

Her eyes snap from my hands to my face. "I thought you were going to touch me."

A slow smile works across my mouth. "I like how impatient you are, Al."

"I'm not impatient." She chews her lower lip, trying to hide a smile. "I'm just worried this is a time-sensitive opportunity."

A sharp laugh slips out. "Was that a premature ejaculation joke?" I work my hands toward her hips. "At my expense?"

She nods, that full lip going back between her teeth. "It was."

"Funny girl." I hook my fingers into the waistband of her pants, stretching the elastic a little as I work the soft knit over the curve of her hips. "Lift."

She doesn't hesitate to raise her ass off the couch, watching me with those pretty blue eyes as I reveal more and more of her body. The softness of her skin brushes my knuckles as I skim them down, my cock so hard it aches even before I get my first peek at the perfectly shaped triangle of light brown hair covering her pussy. I don't know how much work it takes to get it to look like that, but I plan to show my appreciation for her effort.

It's nearly impossible not to get distracted by what's in front of me, but I've made an ass of myself once with her, and I won't do it again. So, even though all I want is to bury my face between her soft thighs, I force myself to continue peeling away the layers hiding the rest of her beautiful body.

Since I showed complete disregard for her clothing

the last time we were together, I carefully drape her pants over the chair next to me before moving on to her T-shirt. I gather the front of it in one hand and use it to bring her closer, lifting Alexis up so I can more easily drag it over her head. Like last time, her bra and panties match. As I work the back hooks open, I lift my eyes from the satiny, pale pink cups to her face. "Do you always wear matching sets?"

Seeing Al wearing coordinating red lace the night of the party had me reacting in an unexpected way, rearing the ugly head of an emotion I've spent my adult life avoiding. But tonight, seeing her again wearing what would normally indicate preplanning when she was clearly spending her evening alone, makes me kick myself a little bit. I should have known better. Should have known Alexis would consider every aspect of what she's wearing—including the parts no one else would see—regardless of the situation.

But *I* get to see them, and it makes me a little smug. A little less jealous than I was.

But only a little, because now I want to know—

"How many people have touched you besides me, Al?" I slide away her bra, stifling a groan as the weight of her tits brings them closer to me.

"That's none of your business." Her retort is almost indignant sounding.

She's always been a temperamental little thing. If she felt it, she said it, and Al doesn't pull any punches or mince any words. She's a whole pile of attitude packed into a tiny package, and I love it. The attitude, and the package.

And I want to know who else has loved it.

Hooking my hands behind her knees, I lever them higher until she tips back against the sofa. "Tell me anyway."

I turn my head as I wait for her answer, running my lips along the inside of her thigh. Last time I was lucky enough to get my hands on her, I wasn't in any way prepared for how good it would feel. Hopefully, having some time to wrap my head around what it's like to touch her has given me the edge I need. The ability to make sure the tables stay turned in my favor.

I've almost reached the apex of her thighs when Alexis whispers a single word. A word I wasn't expecting to hear.

"One."

I lift my eyes to her face, sure I didn't hear her right. "Did you say, *one*?"

The tip of her tongue slides across her lower lip, teasing me with a peek at a part of her I've thought about way more than I should have this past week. She gives me a slow nod.

One.

Fucking *one*?

"You've only been with one person?" There's no hiding the strain in my voice as a pressure unlike any I've ever known sinks into my skin.

Her eyes narrow, her brows lowering as she gives me

a glare. "Not all of us have groupies ready to drop their pants at any moment."

That stops me for a second. "Do you wish you did?" The thought of men whipping their dicks out right and left for Al has my fingers tightening where they grip the soft flesh of her thighs. And that possessive jealousy I hate so much is rearing its ugly head yet again.

"Women have needs too, ass." She practically spits the words at me. Like she can't believe I have the audacity to judge her for something I've done.

I honestly can't believe I have it either. I've never given a single shit about who else a woman has been with. It wasn't my business.

But Alexis? I want to hunt down that dick she dated in college—since he has to be the one—and rip his hands off. Maybe his lips too.

My eyes drop to the gleaming pussy begging for my attention. "And did Huge-nose satisfy those needs?"

Alexis scoffs. "His name was Hugo."

"I know his fucking name, Al." I pull her closer, eliciting a yelp as I drag her farther down the cushion. "Now answer my question."

I'm not normally like this, and, once again, my whole game is thrown completely off by my reaction to the woman in front of me. Thank God I had the foresight to keep my pants on, because I'm not sure where I'd have my dick right now. Probably sliding against her skin, painting it with my cum like a fucking caveman trying to mark his territory.

"Again, that's none of your business." She shuts me down sharper this time. Hard enough I know she won't be making any more admissions.

That's fine. I don't need her to tell me he didn't get her off. I can tell by the emotions fixed across her pretty face. There's only anger and outrage. No embarrassment. No flush of her skin at the memory of a job well done.

Knowing Huge-nose didn't leave her with fond memories eases a little of the jealousy coursing through my veins.

But only a little.

"You stayed with Huge-nose an awfully long time considering he didn't get you off." There's smugness in my tone and I don't care. I always hated that dick. He was never good enough for her. Acted like she should be grateful he was with her. Talked down to her in a way that he tried to pass off as teasing, but I could see the truth.

Hearing he's just as big of a dud in bed as he is outside of it, has me smiling as I lean closer, ready to put my entire focus on the task in front of me. To set a new standard so Alexis never settles like that again.

Except, the thought of someone else touching her like this sends a feral sounding growl rumbling through my chest. I'm no stranger to making threatening sounds. It's a big part of my career. But it's never been a big part of my bedroom lineup.

Al's hand fists in the front of my hair, gripping tight

so she can shove my head back until our eyes meet. There's an incredulous expression on her face. "Did you just growl at me?"

"No." That growl wasn't for her, and I don't want to think about who it was actually directed at. So before she can dig any deeper, I bring my mouth to her skin, fighting the grip of her fingers as I drag my flattened tongue up her slick slit.

Alexis doesn't move—doesn't even breathe—until I reach the hardened nub of her clit and flick it. That's when all the air rushes from her lungs and her body jerks against the hold I still have on her.

A smile curves my lips and that low rumbling sound works free again, but this time it's from satisfaction.

Seems like Huge-nose couldn't find her clit even when it was right in front of his face. I flick it again, just so she knows I did it on purpose, lifting my eyes to her face as I continue teasing the little bundle of nerves at a steady pace.

Her hand is still in my hair, but she's no longer trying to push me away. Now she's holding me in place. Like she's afraid I'm going to stop and leave her hanging.

It's a fair concern given what I just learned, but I want to make sure she knows I'd never do that to her. Not on purpose anyway. If she tries to run away again, that's on her.

I'm just settling in, hooking her thick thighs over my shoulders, when her muscles tense, hips flexing as an orgasm seems to hit her out of nowhere. I drink in the soft sound she makes and the way her body shakes, trying to soak up as much of the moment as I can. Because that was quick. I'd be proud if I wasn't so fucking let down.

I came here tonight only to apologize, but the second I had the opportunity to get my hands all over her, I jumped right on. Unfortunately, that opportunity turned out to be very short-lived. And now I'm kicking myself, because the only excuse I had to justify touching her— flimsy as it was—is gone. I owed her one. Now we're even.

And I've never been more disappointed in my life.

When I look up, Al's eyes are wide on mine, her mouth dropped open, like she can't believe what just happened.

I scan her features for any hint of regret, but I don't think it's there. I hope not anyway, since after this we're supposed to go back to how we were. Act like nothing ever happened.

Her tongue flicks against that lower lip again, eyes dropping down my body to fix on where my dick is straining against the front of my jeans. "What about you?"

"What about me?" I should stop touching her now, but I can't seem to pull my hands from the smooth soft-ness of her skin.

"Aren't you…" Another flick of that sweet, tempting tongue. "I mean, don't you want to…"

The flush she didn't display earlier flares across her skin, proving my assumptions right. This is how Al would have looked if Huge-nose had given her anything fond to remember.

"Are you offering to get me off?" I should be strong enough—smart enough—to turn an opportunity like that down, but I already know I'm not.

She pinches her lower lip between her teeth once more before the fullness of her mouth lifts into a teasing smile. "I was thinking since you got me off on purpose, it's only fair I get you off on purpose." Al's hungry gaze moves over my body. "But we should probably get any possible casualties out of the way. You know, since you have a little bit of a hair trigger."

9

We've Met Before

MY RUSE TO get Gavin naked is pretty obvious, but I don't really care. I've wanted to see this man's body up close for years, and I would be an absolute fool to waste the chance.

I watch with eager eyes as he slowly reaches behind his head to grip the back of his T-shirt, tugging it up and forward, gaze fixed on my face until the cotton fabric blocks his view. I take the opportunity to soak up every inch of bronzed skin he reveals. I swear there's muscles on his muscles, each one moving and flexing as he rids himself of the garment and tosses it to the floor.

He moves on to the waistband of his faded jeans, and I swallow hard. Technically, I've met his dick before, but I didn't have the time to really get acquainted with it. I know it's as big and thick as he is, but I still have to stifle a gasp as the heavy weight of it breaks free from the confines of denim and brief.

The thing is a monster. Without clothing around to somewhat camouflage its size, the full scope of what's looking me right in the eye is more than intimidating. I know vaginas are made to accommodate entire humans, but that beast looks like it would split me in half.

And I might like it.

Imagining Gavin gripping my hips, his powerful body thrusting all that girth into me, has my thighs trying to clench. But since he's still positioned between them, all they do is flex against the newly bared skin of his waist.

Gavin shifts around, leaning closer while kicking away the remainder of his clothing, shoes and socks tangled into the same pile. I'm so busy gawking at his dick, the heat of his mouth closing over one of my nipples catches me by surprise. The deep draw against the sensitive peak has my thighs flexing again, arousal flaring like I didn't just get off.

His skin is warm as the weight of his body presses into me, wide palms sliding up the outside of my thighs and over my hips as he continues teasing my nipple with the same tongue that changed my opinion on oral sex. I didn't really see why everyone made such a fuss over it.

Now I get it.

"I fucking love your tits, Al." He palms the weight of one, lifting it to his lips as he switches sides. His other hand is there to catch the one he abandoned, fingers nimbly plucking the wet pucker as his teeth tease against its twin. "I could play with them all night."

I'm struggling to breathe, but again, I don't want to pass up an opportunity. "Is that an offer?"

Gavin goes still, his eyes lifting to mine. Seeing him staring at me, mouth full of my breast, body wedged between my thighs, might be almost enough to make me reconsider my 'no penis in the vagina' rule. There's something about the way he's looking at me that has my stomach twisting in the best possible way. An intensity that makes it seem like I'm all he sees.

"That depends." The words are even and measured as he turns the question around. "Is that an invitation?"

He doesn't sound put off by the possibility, but I'm still not quite ballsy enough to say yes, so I counter. "Do you have other plans?"

"Do you?" He comes back at me quickly, putting the ball, once again, in my court. One of us is going to have to nut up, and I guess it's going to be me.

"No." I let one hand creep onto his forearm, fingers tracing the line of a bulging vein. "I don't have any plans."

Gavin's eyes slide to my abandoned popcorn on the coffee table before lifting to the television I forgot was playing in the background. "You mean besides watching *It's a Wonderful Life*?"

There's a hint of judgment in his tone and it has me scoffing.

"*It's a Wonderful Life* is the best Christmas movie,

and anyone who doesn't watch it is a miserable Scrooge."

He angles a brow, lips twitching on a hint of a smile. "Then I guess I shouldn't tell you my plans for the evening were drinking beer and watching the *actual* best Christmas movie, *Elf*."

I let my jaw go slack in mock outrage. "*Elf*? Tonight?" I've never had a conversation like this naked, and definitely not while a guy's hands were still on both my boobs. But it doesn't feel awkward, which is especially strange since it's Gavin's hands on my boobs. "Everyone knows *Elf* is a Christmas Day movie." I keep my expression firm because this shit is serious business. "Christmas Eve you watch *It's a Wonderful Life* and *White Christmas*. Christmas *Day*, you watch *Elf* and *A Christmas story*."

The last two aren't high on my list of best movies ever, but they remind me of Christmas as a kid, so it's a tradition I carried over even into my adult life. Once breakfast is over at my parents' house, I come back to my apartment and put them on. Even though I'm the only one here to watch them.

Gavin hums, the sound somewhat like the growling he did earlier, but a little more playful. "I guess I could stick around and try your way. See if I like it."

"You just want to watch movies?" The question jumps right out, rushing from my lips fast enough to give me away.

Gavin's slow smirk is devastatingly sexy. "I didn't say

that was *all* we were gonna do, Al." His head dips, mouth closing around my nipple again as his tongue gives it a quick flick. Before I can even fully enjoy the sensation, he's pulling off, fingers staying behind to tease the wet bud as he leans closer. "I can multitask if you can."

There's a cockiness in his tone. The ass is smug as hell over my worry we'd just watch movies, and I want to take him down a notch.

Luckily, I think I know how to do that.

Using one hand for leverage, I push upright, bringing my face closer to his as my other hand grips his dick. "If I remember correctly, my multitasking skills are way better than yours."

Gavin's jaw clenches and his lids droop as I work my fist down his length, giving it a little squeeze at the base. Part of me expects him to pull away. Instead his hands stay on my tits, and he lets out a deep groan as he pushes them together and thrusts into my palm.

"I don't know what sort of magic you've got in that hand of yours, Al, but I've never gotten off from a handjob until you."

I've always felt a little behind when it comes to sexual experience. Yes, I've done it, but it was never much more than a couple minutes of lackluster thrusting that did less than nothing for me. As a result, just like oral, I didn't really get what all the excitement was about.

But the way Gavin's lips part and his eyes glaze as he

watches my hand move over him makes me realize I formed an opinion using incomplete information. Because this? This is freaking hot as hell.

One of his big hands moves to grip my hip, holding me in place as his body crowds mine. The position we're in is almost exactly how we'd be if we were fucking. Even the movement of his body is similar as he flexes his thighs, tunneling into my grip.

Again, I'm regretting the parameters I put out, because I'm clenching at the thought of those strokes filling me, and it has my need building at record speed.

Gavin's fingers sink into the softness of my hip as he groans, spearing into my hand one more time as heat splashes across my belly.

Last time this happened it was a surprise. I was more shocked than anything. But tonight, I knew exactly what I was in for. I still don't know that I love being covered in jizz, but at least none of my clothes were in the line of fire.

Now that he's done, I'm a little uncertain what to do next. I lie very still because I don't want anything sliding off my body and onto my couch. The only sex I've had was always a quick missionary ride with a condom. Definitely nothing that involved cleanup of this caliber.

Gavin's hooded gaze skims over my belly and the glistening lines across it. I could almost swear I hear a hint of that earlier rumble, but it disappears before I'm fully able to identify the sound. Gavin blinks a couple times before finally tearing his gaze from my body. He leans to retrieve his T-shirt, then uses the soft cotton to clean me up.

The tenderness in his movements would be easy to read into, and it has me reminding myself what this is. "I guess now we're even. We both had clothing get victimized." I'm trying to tease him, but teasing isn't my strong suit, so it comes out a little dry. A little sarcastic.

Gavin's gaze lifts to mine and it doesn't carry an ounce of amusement. Guess I should leave the teasing up to him.

He leans closer, tossing his soiled shirt away as the weight of his body presses me into the sofa. When his lips are less than an inch from mine and our noses are nearly touching, he stops and looks me straight in the eye. "Actually, I don't think we're even at all." His hands slide up my thighs, lifting them higher on his hips. "The score is two to one now, Al. I'm still behind."

I rub my lips together, because with his face so close, I'm struggling to think of anything besides the fact that we haven't actually kissed. "That is true."

"What if," he leans to one side, the warmth of his lips brushing along the line of my jaw, "we take a little break and watch one of those movies you like? See where we end up?"

I offer a breathy, "Okay." It's an easy agreement to make. He did say he owed me one, right? I might as well let him stick around until I get it.

The hard lines of Gavin's big body seem to relax a little, and when he leans back, there's a hint of a smile teasing his lips as he reaches to collect my clothes. Grabbing my T-shirt, he gathers it up around the neckline. "Sit up."

My eyes jump to where my bra is sitting, ignored. "I think you're forgetting something."

Gavin's eyes drop down my chest, resting squarely on my boobs. "I'll put it on if you really want, but I'm going to be trying to take it back off in under five minutes, so I figured I'd save us both a little time."

I frown, even though his plan sounds pretty appealing. "It's uncomfortable when they're not supported."

I like my boobs. Love them, even. But the bitches are high maintenance. They eliminate lots of shirt options, need special bras, and make it impossible to sleep on my stomach. I still wouldn't change them for the world, but sitting on the couch with them going every which way doesn't sound like a fun night.

"I didn't say they were going to be unsupported." Gavin doesn't wait for a response, just tugs my shirt over my head and starts pulling it into place. "I promise I'll take good care of them."

I roll my eyes even though I kind of believe him. And I can't say I hate the thought of Gavin's hands on my tits all night. But the main reason I stop arguing, is because Gavin is taking care of more than just his mess and my boobs.

His touch is careful as he settles my shirt over my upper half then retrieves my panties and pants, carefully skimming them back into place before pulling on his own underwear. He ignores his jeans, leaving them where they lie before turning to head for my kitchen. "You want something to drink?"

"Sure?" I'm back to being thrown off again. My parents have a great marriage. One I've always based my hopes for the future on. But their relationship leans a little to the traditional side, so my mom is always the one collecting drinks while my dad sits on the couch.

I watch—still a little shocked—as Gavin opens my fridge and scans the contents. "Water or Coke Zero?"

Normally I'm just as protective of my private space as I am my personal space, but seeing Gavin's hulking form in my kitchen is so bizarre, I struggle to come up with a coherent answer. "Coke, I guess?"

He grabs a can and a bottle of water, holding the latter up. "I'm taking one of these too."

"Good idea." I swallow hard as he twists the cap free and tips it back, guzzling down half in one go. "You should probably hydrate."

He flashes me a grin, lips still wet and glistening. "That sounds promising, Al."

Was that how I meant it? A suggestion of what was to come? Sadly, no.

In addition to having an incurable case of resting bitch face, I'm also terrible at flirting. So bad, that I actually admit the truth of what was behind my suggestion. "I figured you probably sweat a lot at practice."

Gavin comes back my way, opening my can of soda before setting it on the table. "Actually, we're still in the off-season, so I'm just in the gym a few days a week. Official practice doesn't start until after the first of the year."

Even though my brother also plays professional rugby, I'm not super up on their schedule. I go to his matches, but, generally speaking, sports aren't my thing, so my attendance is strictly to be supportive. "I assumed you guys practiced year-round."

Gavin settles onto the couch beside me, angling his body into the corner by the arm. "We follow a pretty strict schedule. Playing Rugby is intense, and without a break for our bodies to recover, the risk of injuries would be astronomical."

Leaning back, he swings one leg over my head, displaying a flexibility I wouldn't have thought possible for someone of his size. "Come here." Gavin doesn't wait for me to comply, but reaches out and grabs me, hauling my body back until I rest between his thick thighs, my back to his chest. His arms band around my middle, forearms crossing at the center of my chest so one big hand can cup each breast, supporting their weight better than any bra ever could.

His head tips forward so his face is in my line of sight. "See?" Gavin smirks. "I told you it would be fine."

10

Behaving's No Fun

IT TAKES ME a few seconds to get my bearings when I open my eyes, but the second the daylight peeking in from the wrong angle registers, I jerk upright.

Fuck me.

I accidentally spent the whole night at Al's. And not just at her apartment.

In her fucking bed.

Last night, after we watched the first movie on her couch, she started looking sleepy. I figured it wouldn't hurt to move to her bed so she could be more comfortable and doze through *White Christmas* if she wanted to. I never expected to fall asleep myself.

Not once have I spent the night with a woman. Never so much as drifted off. I didn't run out the door the second the deed was done, but I always went home.

Only last night, there were technically no deeds

done. No reason to rush myself from the comfort of Al's bed. So is it really so bad that I stayed?

Yes. Yes, it is.

Alexis stirs beside me, pulling in a deep breath before letting it out on a yawn as she rolls my way. Her eyes go wide, like she forgot I was here.

That makes two of us.

"Morning." I reach out to smooth back her hair, letting my fingers linger over the pillow-creased skin of her cheek. "Sleep well?"

Alexis gives me a sheepish nod, lower lip pinching between her teeth as her eyes drift down my naked upper half. I don't have to look hard to see the heat flare in her gaze, but we're supposed to be at her parents' house in under an hour, and, after fucking up in every way possible, the least I can do is show up on time.

"I need to go home and shower and get changed for Christmas breakfast."

Alexis drapes one arm across her eyes. "Shit. What time is it?" She sits up, grabbing her cell phone beside the bed. Her brows pinch together as she holds it up, scanning the attached cord. "Did you plug my phone in?"

I force my feet to the floor, knowing if I linger too long, I might try to convince myself I don't need to leave. "You left it out on the coffee table, so I brought it in after you fell asleep."

Alexis unplugs it as she slides off the mattress, giving me an odd look. "Thank you."

I shrug, because it's genuinely not a big deal. "Not a problem." I give her a little smile. "I wish I'd thought to put my T-shirt in the washer. You think your neighbors will notice me sneaking out shirtless?"

Again, her eyes drag down my body. "You're hard to miss." Her eyes widen, jumping to mine as she lifts a finger. "Hang on." She disappears into the closet, coming back with the green shirt I wore to the Christmas party. "Here."

She passes it off and I tug it over my head, offering a grateful smile. "Perfect."

Alexis glances at her phone again, frowning at the time flashed across the screen. "We have to be at my parents' house in forty-five minutes."

I jerk my chin toward her bathroom. "You start getting ready. I'll let myself out." I know Alexis likes to look nice, and while she's gorgeous bare faced in sweatpants and a T-shirt, I know she wouldn't want to show up anywhere looking like this.

"I'm going to take you up on that, because it's going to be cutting it real freaking close." She shifts on her feet a little bit, looking uncertain. "I guess I'll see you soon."

Before I know what I'm doing, I snag her by the front of the shirt, pulling her close. The second my mouth meets the plush softness of hers, I realize what a terrible mistake I've made.

Up to this point, we haven't kissed. And maybe that was by design. Maybe I knew what would happen if we did.

My intended quick peck goodbye, quickly turns into something else. Something more. Something undeniable and unavoidable. For years, I refused to let myself see Alexis as anything besides Leo's little sister. Refused to admit the anticipation I always felt at seeing her. But with her soft body pressed tight to mine, I can't ignore the truth anymore.

There's something there between us.

I palm the curve of her ass with one hand, tangling the other in her hair as I pull Al as close as I can get her, tilting my head so I can fully claim her mouth. Fuck morning breath. Fuck bad decisions.

Fuck the fallout.

I'm nowhere near ready to let her go when she pulls away, hands pressed to the center of my chest, breathing heavy. "I need to get ready."

I should be grateful she did what I couldn't, but all I want is for her to be against me again. Under me. To feel those lush thighs wrapped at my waist as I plunge into her body.

Alexis shoves at my chest, giving me a stern look. "And you need to go home and shower, because if you show up in jeans and a T-shirt, my mom's going to be pissed."

The mention of Babs sobers me, knocking the need and want coursing through my veins down a few notches.

Fuck. I keep making the same goddamn mistake.

Keep pretending like what I'm doing won't lead to losing so much of what matters to me.

The worst part is, I don't see that changing. Not when that mistake is Alexis.

She pushes at me again, harder this time. "Go."

I don't think I've ever been shoved out of a woman's house before, but it doesn't surprise me that Alexis would be the first.

Giving her one last look as she disappears into the bathroom, I collect my clothes from the living room floor. After pulling on the discarded jeans and tying my shoes, I grab my keys and head for the door. Jerking it open, I come face-to-face with another guy. He's carrying a bouquet of red roses with some sort of green ball things dispersed throughout. Deep green paper inlaid with gold plaid wraps around the stems, reminding me of the packaging on the scarf I gave Alexis.

It doesn't take a genius to know who the flowers are for, and it has my teeth grinding together.

Al's unexpected visitor doesn't seem any happier to see me. His brows shoot up, lips flattening out as he looks me over.

Leaning against the doorframe, I tuck my keys into the back pocket of my jeans so he can't see them and won't deduce I was on my way out. "Can I help you?"

The guy is the polar opposite of me. He's clean-shaven, with perfectly styled blonde hair. Where I prefer jeans and T-shirts, this guy is fully decked out in tailored slacks and a well-cut button up layered under a jacket. He's not short, but he's nowhere near as tall as I am. And while he looks like he works out, he sure as shit wouldn't win a fight between us.

Not that there's anything to fight about, because I was in Al's bed last night and he wasn't.

I tip my head at the flowers. "Those for Alexis?"

The guy doesn't answer me, but his scowl tells me they are. "Who the fuck are you?"

"None of your business." I grab the bouquet, yanking it from his grip. "Merry Christmas." I slam the door in his face.

Then I stand there for a second, because what in the hell do I do now?

And what the fuck would've happened if I wasn't here when that prick showed up? Would Alexis have jumped out of the shower and answered the door in her robe?

Worse, would she have let him in?

"You're still here?"

I spin at the surprised sound of her voice. The sight of Al in her robe comes too close to confirming my worst fears. "You shower fast."

"Not usually." She huffs out a little laugh. "I skipped a few steps." Her eyes drop to the flowers in my hand. "Where did you get those?"

I don't want to tell her about the twat at her door,

but I do want to gauge her reaction to the news. See if he's anything to worry about. "Some guy dropped them off a minute ago."

Her brows pinch together as she comes my way. "Some guy?" Her full lips press into a frown. "Who?"

I shrug. "Some preppy looking asshole." I sound aggravated. I am. I don't like knowing men who look like that are trying to bring Al flowers.

"Ugh." She grabs the bouquet from my hand. "Did he have highlights?"

"I didn't look that close." I was too busy glaring. "He had a stick up his ass though."

Al's nose wrinkles as she plucks the card from the roses. "Dillon." She pulls the square out of the envelope and gives it a quick scan before rolling her eyes and dropping both onto the counter. "We work together."

Fucking great. Not only does this ass know where she lives, he also gets to spend five days a week with her. "He came to your doorstep on Christmas morning with flowers, Al. I think that's more than a coworker situation."

Her brows lift at my accusing tone. "Why are you being weird?"

"I'm not being weird." I shift on my feet. "I'm just pointing out the obvious."

She crosses her arms. "*You* spent the night in my bed." Her chin lifts. "And *we're* not more than a *situation*."

I work my jaw from side to side because I don't know what to say to that. She's not technically wrong.

But she might not be right either.

So I do the same thing she did to me when shit got complicated at the party. "I gotta go."

I turn and stalk out into the hall, digging the keys from my back pocket as I take the elevator to the main floor.

My scowl holds the whole drive home. It's still there as I let myself into my condo, stripping away my clothes on the way to the shower.

We're not more than a situation.

I don't like the way she said it. So easily. As if it never crossed her mind to want more. It's not like I want her to want more, but she could've at least considered it.

Jumping under the hot spray, I scrub down, rushing through the process before toweling off. I run a quick comb through my hair, pausing a little too long to question if I should be spending more time on my grooming.

Was that dick on Al's doorstep the kind of guy she wants? Someone with a line of hair products on his counter and an expensive wardrobe in his closet? It would make sense. I used her bathroom. I saw how much stuff she smears on her face and hair every day. Why wouldn't she want a man who does the same?

I glance down at the items next to my sink. I've got a bottle of Jergens I've had for a year, deodorant, and cologne. That's the fucking extent of it.

My wardrobe is even worse.

After brushing my teeth and tucking a towel around my hips, I fish through the racks of jeans and T-shirts— glaring at the limited options like I'm not entirely responsible for the lack of selection—to find the reindeer pajamas I bought to wear this morning. I dress, spray on my cologne, collect the gifts I got for Babs and Dan, and I'm back out in the hallway in under fifteen minutes.

The drive to Al's parents' house isn't long, but I'm still late. And I'm not the only one who's late.

Alexis is just getting out of her car as I pull up, and fuck if she doesn't look as amazing as always. I can tell she cut some corners getting ready, but only because I know she was short on time. The curls that are usually cascading over her shoulders have been replaced by smooth straight strands. Her makeup is minimal, giving her a softer sort of expression than her normal sexy smirk. The silky pajamas she's chosen to wear accent every curve of her body, but the accessories she usually adds are missing.

Only one single item accompanies the satiny pants and top, and it pleases me to no fucking end.

"That scarf looks good on you, Al." I reach out to run my hand down the cashmere, tracing the tips of my fingers across one nipple in the process.

Alexis shifts the gifts she's carrying to hide where I'm touching her, eyes darting to the front porch before bouncing back to me. "Behave."

"That doesn't sound like any fun." I stall, because the minute we step in there I've got to pretend like I don't know how she smells. How she tastes. The expression she makes when she comes. "Or possible with you wearing something so fucking sexy."

Her brows pinch together as she glances down. "I don't know what it says about you that you think these pajamas are sexy."

It probably says a lot more than I want to think about. Luckily, I'm saved from myself when Babs opens the door. Instead of greeting us with a boisterous '*Merry Christmas*' like usual, her lips are pressed into a deep frown. Her eyes barely find where her daughter and I stand close together before she turns away, leaving the door open.

Alexis turns to me, brows lifted in surprise. "What was that about?"

"I don't know." I'm afraid I do know though. Someone at the party must have seen Al and I sneak off to the treehouse and Babs is ready to lay into me for not only taking advantage of her daughter, but also ruining her sanctuary.

Al's frown matches her mother's as she takes a tentative step inside.

Like it or not, I've got to face the music, so I follow her, stomach clenched with dread. I'm barely two steps in when I hear yelling in the kitchen.

Alexis turns to me as her father bellows something

about stupid decisions. Her eyes are wide as she mouths, *What the fuck is going on?*

I shrug, but again, I'm afraid I do know.

And I hate how relieved I am that it's not my ass getting chewed out.

11

In His Defense

Alexis

I DON'T KNOW what Leo did, but I've never heard my dad this mad before, and it has me considering turning around and walking out.

I actually make it halfway through the process, but Gavin's big body blocks my escape. He must know what I'm thinking because he shakes his head at me, expression serious.

I sigh. He's right. I have to stay. My brother wouldn't leave me on my own in a situation like this, so I can't leave him. Leo's a pain in the ass, but he's loyal as fuck.

Letting my head fall back on a quiet groan, I turn toward the kitchen, blowing out a breath before sliding my gifts onto the entry table and going to my brother's defense.

I hope he deserves it.

With Gavin still right behind me, I march into the kitchen, not giving anyone time to react to my appearance before crossing my arms and barking out, "What's going on?"

My mother is giving Leo a look that might kill him and my dad's face is so red I'm worried he might die right after my brother. No one says anything for a few seconds. They all just keep scowling at each other. I raise one brow, focusing on my brother since he's the most likely to cave.

And he does.

"They're acting like two consenting adults can't do what they want." Leo's jaw is set so tight I can see it twitching as he talks through clenched teeth.

"You don't have any fucking clue what you're talking about." My dad points at the living room, but I'm not sure why because no one's in there. "The last thing that girl needs is you butting your nose into her shit."

Leo scoffs, stretching his arms wide. "You just wanted me to stand there like nothing was happening?" He shakes his head. "No fucking way."

I take a step toward my brother, zeroing in on his knuckles. "What happened to your hands?" Gavin told me they're not practicing right now, just hitting the gym, so the scabs and redness across his skin wouldn't be from rugby.

My mother's nostrils flare, her teeth barely separating as she says, "He beat the shit out of Maddie Miller's husband."

"Ex-fucking-husband." Leo turns to me and Gavin.

114

"She filed for divorce three months ago when *he* beat the shit out of *her*." His chin lifts in defiance. "So as far as I'm concerned, he got what he had coming."

I think I might have to agree with him, and to be honest, I'm shocked my parents don't. My confusion over the situation clears up when my dad says, "He's fucking dangerous, Leo. He's already threatened to kill her, and he did it at the fucking courthouse in front of both their attorneys. You didn't help her. You kicked the fucking hornet's nest."

I've never heard my dad say the word fuck so many times in a row, and it sends me stepping back into the hard line of Gavin's chest. I should move away, but the stability of his strong body helps me feel less overwhelmed by what's going on. Gavin's hand comes to my shoulder, giving it a squeeze, offering support I desperately need.

"Isn't it a good thing her ex knows what will happen if he tries to fuck with her again?" Gavin sounds genuinely confused. Like he doesn't understand the reality of what women have to deal with on a regular basis.

Most men don't.

I shake my head, a pit growing in my stomach. "That's not how it works with men like that. He'll be even more dangerous now." I swallow hard as fear for a woman I barely know creeps across my skin. "Where is she today?"

A guilty expression flashes across my brother's face

and my mother tosses both hands up in the air. "For fuck's sake." She laughs, but it's not an amused sound so much as an unhinged one. "She's at your house, isn't she, Leo?"

"I can't just leave her at her apartment now that he's found her." Leo's jaw takes on a murderous set. "You should be fucking happy I was there when he showed up. Otherwise, who knows what would have happened."

"She would have called the police and let them handle it." My mother's voice shakes as she continues. "He would have been arrested for violating a protection order and been booked in jail." She advances on Leo, looking more than capable of taking my fully-grown brother down. "Now he's plotting how to punish both of you for making him look weak."

My dad rakes one hand through his hair. "I need to call Matt Miller. See if there's anything we can do since it's your fault his daughter's problems just got bigger." He shoots Leo a glare. "If you're smart, you'll leave that girl alone before you make things even worse for her." He storms off in the direction of his office.

My mother wipes at her eyes, giving my brother a final look that would melt the skin off most people, before turning away. Her watery gaze barely pauses on me as she passes. "I'm sorry. I don't feel much like celebrating this morning." She walks out in the opposite direction my dad went, leaving us alone with Leo.

He lifts his brows at us. "You two want to take a shot? Everyone else fucking does."

I shake my head. For the first time in my life, I feel bad for my brother. He's always made friends easily. Did well in school without trying. Managed to score a spot on one of the best rugby teams in the country.

Now he's in the middle of a mess he's not equipped to handle, and the guy who's always cool, calm, and confident, looks like a cornered animal, ready to bite anyone who comes close. There won't be any reasoning with him this morning, and I'm not going to try.

Leo turns his gaze to Gavin. "You?"

Like me, Gavin shakes his head, probably because he knows Leo just as well as I do.

"Good." Leo stalks past, storming out the front door. The engine of his Charger revs as he races away, then everything gets quiet.

That's when I notice Gavin's hand moved to my hip at some point, holding me close. His fingers flex against the extra padding there as he slides the gifts in his free hand onto the counter. "What do we do now?"

I've never been faced with a situation like this. Sure, both Leo and I clashed with my parents when we were teenagers, but never like this. I have no clue how long the fallout will last or how bad it will get.

I *do* know I don't necessarily want to be around to find out. "I guess we leave?"

"Thank God." Gavin lets out a sigh so deep it ruffles

my hair. "I was afraid you were going to say we needed to stick around and try to help them work their shit out."

I turn, hating that the movement sends Gavin's hand sliding from my body. "Am I a bad sister and daughter if I say I have zero interest in that?"

Gavin gives me a small smile as he reaches out to tuck back a strand of my straightened hair. "If it does, then I'm a bad friend, because I don't want to deal with it either." His eyes leave mine to roam around the kitchen. "It sucks because it looks like your mom worked really hard on everything."

It does. Two pans of homemade cinnamon rolls are on the counter next to a giant tray of fruit. Two bottles of champagne and two bottles of orange juice sit next to a line of glass flutes. "It seems like a waste to just leave it all here." I know I should feel bad about taking advantage of a situation like this but...

Gavin grabs one tray of rolls and a bottle of champagne. He tips his head at the juice. "Grab it."

The guilt I was wrestling abates at his decision-making skills and I snag the bottle from the counter, following him out the door. He leads me to my car, opening the door and waiting while I get behind the wheel. Then he leans down, one hand braced against the top of the opening as he says, "I'm coming to your place and we're watching *Elf* and *A Christmas Story*."

I agree easily. "Okay."

Gavin's hand slides from the opening, his fingertips tracing a line along my jaw as his eyes roam my face. For a second I think he's going to lean in and kiss me like he did this morning, but then he straightens, stepping back. "I'll follow you."

12

The Inevitable

I WAS ALL prepared to act like shit was normal at Christmas breakfast. To do whatever it took to hide what's going on between me and Alexis.

Then Leo threw the shit at the fan and no one even glanced at me or Al. Certainly not long enough to notice I had my hand on her hip and her body pressed to mine as the situation got more and more tense. Holding her was a complete accident, but one I didn't rectify when I should have.

Now I'm pulling into the parking lot of her apartment building, planning to spend the holiday at her side, wondering how in the hell Babs and Dan would react if they knew. Surely not the same way they reacted to Leo and Maddie Miller.

Right?

"Hey." Alexis gives me a soft smile as she gets out of

her car, carrying the orange juice we poached from her parents.

I look her over. "You okay?" I grew up with parents who yelled all the fucking time, but she didn't, and I can't imagine what's going through her head.

She lifts one shoulder and lets it fall. "I don't know." Al shifts the bottle around in her arms so she can punch in the keycode to open the door to her building. Her brows pinch together as the dead-bolt clicks open. "How did you get in here last night?"

I stay silent because Al's one of the few people who's never been impressed with my fame. If anything, it seems to annoy her.

Her focus comes to my face when I don't reply, and it takes her about two seconds to register what happened. Then she's rolling her eyes. "I should have known."

I open the door, holding it as she goes in. "There are some perks to being Mr. The Wall."

"I guess it saves you the effort of breaking and entering." She presses the button to bring the elevator to us then turns to me, expression thoughtful. "Doesn't it get old though? Dealing with people coming up to you everywhere you go?"

"I mean, it's not *everywhere* I go." There are still some places where no one gives me a second look. Not many, but some.

I can't think of any, but I know they exist.

"*Sure.*" The elevator arrives and Al gets in. "I don't believe that for a second."

I get in behind her then press the button to close the doors. "I guess I just go with it." I was never the kind of guy who flew under the radar anyway. I'm six and a half feet tall, for God's sake. People can't really miss me. "And it's kinda cool when it's kids like your neighbor. I like seeing how excited they are."

Alexis gives me a dirty look as we get out of the elevator, but the twitch of her lips hints at a smile. "You mean like the one who's going to start showing up on my doorstep every day hoping for a chance to see *The Wall*?" She widens her eyes when she says my nickname, like it's the goofiest thing she's ever heard.

"I'll bring you some signed shit to give him so he'll go away." I grin at the image of Al having to deal with random kids showing up wanting to discuss rugby with her. "But maybe you should talk to him a little first. Actually learn something about rugby."

Her jaw goes slack and she pauses midway through opening her door. "I know stuff about rugby."

I lift a brow. "Name one thing."

Al comes to all our home matches, but most of her attention stays on her phone. Occasionally her eyes will drift to the pitch, but it doesn't take a genius to know her interest in what I do for a living is slim to none.

"I know your dumb asses don't wear padding." She lifts her chin as she walks inside, smirking like she's just proved herself an expert on the sport.

"That it?" I won't be shocked if she's got nothing to follow it up with. Or offended. Al's disinterest in the thing most people know me for has always been appealing.

It's one of the many reasons she's never been in the same category as the rest of the women I know. Nothing against the rest of the female population, Al's just always been...

Different.

Proving my point, she shoots me a scowl. "And I'm sure you know *all kinds* of shit about my job."

That has me scowling back at her. "I know you work with a dillhole who brings flowers to your apartment on Christmas morning."

Fucking Dillon. I'd almost managed to forget about him with the shit that happened at her parents' house, but now that he's come back up, that asshat's appearance has my jaw clenched so tight my back teeth might crack. The more I think about it, the more I can't believe he just showed up here out of nowhere. "It's kinda weird he would do that unless he had a reason to think you'd be excited to see him."

Al's brows slowly climb up her forehead. "What's that supposed to mean?"

Jealousy's not a good look for me. It's one of the reasons I've been so careful to avoid putting myself in a position where I'd end up wearing it. Because once I've got it on, it fits like a second skin.

"I don't know, Al. What are the reasons you think a

guy would show up at a woman's house Christmas morning? Because I can tell you the only reason I'd do it is because she made me think I had a shot with her."

"*You* showed up on my doorstep Christmas Eve." She thinks she's proving a point, and she is.

Mine.

"And I had you naked in under ten minutes, so it seems like I was right."

Al's jaw drops open and I know I've fucked up. Know I've shown the ass I inherited from my old man. And that's probably a good thing. Better it happens now. Before I ruin more than just my relationship with Alexis.

Al stabs a pointed finger at her door. "Get out."

"Fine." I shove the rolls and champagne onto the counter then stalk out into the hall for the second time today.

I'm not even in my car before the regret hits. The frustration. The humiliation. I slam both hands against the wheel, snarling at my inability to be better than I was taught to be.

I don't want to be like my dad, but maybe I can't fight it. Maybe he's drilled too much bullshit into my head for me to ever shove it all back out.

And if that's the case, I can't be around Al. Not anymore.

I'm too weak to keep my hands off her and too fucking dumb to deserve her.

13

No One Likes a Hostage Situation

I'M JUST FINISHING wiping down the office coffee station when my boss strides through the door. Grant flashes me a grin as he crosses the small main lobby. "Good morning, Alexis."

I return his smile as I chuck the paper towel I'm holding into the trash can beneath the counter. "Morning." After settling his favorite mug onto the platform of the single-serve maker, I rattle off his morning agenda. "Mr. Rivera's your ten o'clock. His company's file is on your desk." I load in a coffee pod and set it to brew. "Since he usually runs over his allotted time, I placed a lunch order so you wouldn't be rushed for your one o'clock with Miss Burton."

"Shit. I forgot about that." Grant pauses beside my desk. "I told Jules I would take her to lunch today."

"I can call and add another meal to the order." The coffee finishes brewing and I tip in a tiny bit of half and half from the hidden mini fridge before passing it off to him. "Do you want to choose it or should I pick?"

Grant snorts. "You already know the answer to that." He turns toward his corner office then stops, twisting back to face me. "And I forgot to tell you how much she loved her Christmas gift. She says you have amazing taste."

My eyes widen. "You told her I'm the one who ordered it?"

My boss is a great guy. He's kind and smart and pays really fucking well, but he has terrible taste when it comes to women's clothes. Luckily, he knows it, which is why Grant always enlists my help when it comes to birthday and Christmas gifts for his wife, mother, and grandmother.

"Oh, no. I tried to take full credit." Grant sips his coffee before continuing. "She knew damn well I didn't pick out those pajamas."

Technically I didn't pick them out either. I had them specially made. When my boss told me his wife's favorite pair of pajama pants were falling apart at the seams and he wanted to replace them, I discovered a complete lack of banana-printed loungewear. Lucky for him, I don't mind putting in a little leg work when it comes to fashion, so I spent an afternoon tracking down every cotton stretch banana fabric I could find, ordering two yards of each. Then I took the fabric to the seam-stress who does all my altering. She used Julia's old pants to make a pattern and stitched up ten pairs of sleep pants.

Plus a couple pairs for me from the extra fabric. Sometimes it pays to be pint-sized.

"I would have backed you up." After trashing the spent coffee pod, I wipe the counter again, removing any trace of oversplash.

"Then she would have called us both dirty liars." Grant lifts his coffee cup. "Thanks for this."

"Anytime." I finish with the coffee bar as he goes into his office and gets to work. After that, I check the bathroom, replacing the vial of scented oil in the warmer plugged into the corner outlet. Then, using a Clorox wipe from the cabinet below the sink, I give the counter a quick wipe down.

Technically none of this is in my job description, but I like the office to look as put together as possible. It's the same as adding accessories to a really great outfit. Without them, the clothes look fine. But once they're layered on?

Impeccable.

I'm just getting back to my desk when Helen, Grant's former assistant, walks through the door. After she graduated with her accounting degree, he promoted her to help him juggle his constantly growing client list and hired me to take her former position.

At first I was a little worried she'd judge everything I did and compare it to the way she'd handled things.

Nope. Helen is awesome. She's cool and calm and kind and happy to let me do things my own way.

She's also freaking gorgeous. Tall and slender, with rich brown skin and long shiny braids, she's exceedingly glamorous, and I look forward to seeing what she's wearing every morning. Today, the former beauty queen has on a pair of wide-leg, camel-colored pants, paired with a white knit top. Chunky gold jewelry is draped around her neck and wrist, and a pair of large diamond studs dot her earlobes, completing the ensemble.

As always, she looks insanely good. And, as always, it's an outfit that would look way less fantastic on my five-foot-one curvy frame.

But maybe I could pair a shirt like that with a nice pencil skirt—

"Good morning, Alexis." Helen's brisk tone doesn't bother me. Probably because it's a whole hell of a lot like mine. As is her temperament. And her love of quiet.

"Good morning," I greet her. "I'm placing a lunch order for Grant. Would you like me to order something for you?"

She pauses at my desk to collect her mail, quietly contemplating for a second. "I don't think so. I'll probably work through lunch."

Dillon, Helen's assistant and my biggest recent mistake, strides into the office, the remnants of his morning protein shake sloshing around the shaker cup in his hand. "We're working through lunch today?"

Up until a few months ago, I was juggling both

Grant and Helen's needs. It wasn't easy, but I was managing. When Grant discovered I was taking work home with me—as well as coming in early and staying late—he hired Dillon, bumping me up to the title of office manager. I didn't complain because it came with less work and more pay.

It also came with Dillon, which I thought was a good thing at first...

"*I'm* working through lunch." Helen sorts through her mail as she passes Dillon on her way to her office, eyes never going his way. "*You* can do whatever you want."

Dillon watches her go. Once she's safely closed in her space he turns to me with a scoff. "What does that mean?"

"It means you can do whatever you want." I don't look at him either, focusing on the emails I need to respond to as he continues loitering in the main lobby instead of finding his way to his own desk.

The footprint of Grant's accounting firm was originally two separate businesses. When we moved from his old office—in a strip mall a few blocks down—to this much larger and much nicer building a year ago, a couple walls were torn out to create the open area where I work. But the small waiting room connected to Helen's office was left intact because it was oddly positioned and wouldn't add any useful space to the lobby.

But it's perfect for Dillon. When he freaking uses it.

"If I can do whatever I want, then maybe I'll take

you to lunch." Dillon comes my way, one hand tucked in the pocket of his slacks. "Now that the holidays are over, it seems like things have finally calmed down in your life, so we can have that second date you promised me."

Ugh. I knew this was coming.

Dillon had barely waited until I'd finished my coffee on our first day back after Christmas before he was sniffing around, trying to figure out how I knew Gavin and what he was to me. As much as I wanted to lie, Gavin's too well-known for me to be able to pull it off, so I was forced to tell him the truth.

Gavin is nothing more than my brother's best friend.

He's also an asshole, but I left that part out.

In light of that information, I was expecting Dillon to ask me out then and there. Instead, he's made it all the way into the second Friday of the new year before making me hurt his feelings.

Because there's no way we were ever having a second date, and I sure as hell didn't promise him we would. He's not what I'm looking for. At all.

I take a deep breath before spinning in my office chair so we're face-to-face. As if he has no idea what's coming, Dillon perches one ass cheek on the corner of my desk, giving me a smirk. "Unless you'd rather I make *you* my dinner."

My stomach turns at the thought. Once upon a time, I tried to talk myself into liking this guy. Actually thought it would be relatively easy to accomplish. He's technically good looking, with blond hair, blue eyes, and a dimple in one cheek. He's also got a nice body and great teeth.

The only thing that's lacking is his personality. And boy does it leave a lot to be desired. I might not be a huge talker, but I want to be with a man who listens to what I say when I do. A guy who pays attention to more than just himself.

A flash of a red and white cashmere scarf skips across my brain, the reminder of how soft it felt under my fingers making them twitch. I can't believe Gavin even noticed I owned a scarf, much less the colors and patterns on it.

I mentally kick myself.

Because Gavin—and his attention to detail—is irrelevant to this conversation. And my life.

Shoving all thoughts of dark hair and broad shoulders aside, I return my attention to the man in front of me. "I'm going to have to pass." I say it slowly, hoping it will sink into Dillon's self-centered brain.

Proving he only listens to himself talk, the man continues on like I didn't just try to let him down easy. "We could go to The Pearl for a nice meal, and then I can eat dessert at my place." His hungry gaze drops to my lap like I wasn't already picking up what he was putting down.

It's probably an offer most women would jump on, but the mention of that act only drags my brain right back to the jerkface of a man I've been working hard to forget.

Freaking Gavin. Why'd he have to go and be a dick? We could have had fun together.

Plus, he owes me one.

"Still going to pass." I say it with a little more force. If this was some guy I met at a bar or on a dating app, it would be easy to cut him loose. But I have to work with Dillon every day, so I don't feel the least bit bad when I start stretching the truth. "I've got some family issues going on and it's been a really hard time for us."

The claim isn't entirely false. My family *is* having issues. Thankfully I've managed to keep myself out of the line of fire, but Leo's relationship with Maddie Miller is really driving a wedge between him and my parents, and it's making shit weird.

Dillon's jaw clenches and, for a second, I think he's going to keep pushing, but then he reaches out to take my hand with his. "You still need to take time for yourself."

"I'll keep that in mind." I try to pull my hand away, but Dillon grips it tighter, forcing me to use more and more strength until it finally flies free.

"Did you want me to make Helen her tea?" I redirect the conversation, hoping he gets both hints I'm not so subtly throwing at him. I'm done with this conversation and he needs to start doing his job.

Dillon stares at me a second longer before offering a tight smile as he slides to his feet. "Of course not." His expression hardens just enough that I know he suspects I'm lying. "Wouldn't want to put anything else on your already full plate."

He's being sarcastic, and it takes every bit of self-control I have not to match his tone. "Thanks. I appreciate it." Turning to my computer, I go back to the list of emails filling my inbox.

As the office manager, it's my job to field the inquiries that come through our website, and today there's a ton. It's always like this after the new year. Business owners wake up January first deciding they need to get their shit together, and Grant has built a reputation as the go-to guy to help make that happen.

But even with Helen now handling some of the workload, there are more potential clients than we can juggle. I spend the rest of the morning writing up preliminary reports on each one so Grant can start narrowing them down to the ones that might be a good fit. Between that, answering the phone, and checking in appointments, the time flies by.

Before I know it, Grant's wife Julia is coming in, all decked out in her army green pants and matching T-shirt printed with the logo of the botanical garden where she works. As usual, she's a little dirty and sweaty, but sporting a wide smile when she sees me.

"Hey, Alexis." She stops at my desk, looking over my pleated midi-skirt and the emerald green blazer I buttoned over a tweed bustier. "You look cute as shit today."

"Thanks." I smooth down the front of the white, light as air fabric covering my lower half. "I love after Christmas sales."

Julia purses her lips. "I need to take you shopping with me the next time I go." Her mouth twists into a wicked little smile. "I used to drag Grant's grandma along, but her taste is a little scandalous."

"Not shocked." Sylvia comes into the office pretty regularly, usually to steal coffee and snacks while she's out and about town. "She once told me if her books looked like mine she'd go topless everywhere she went."

"I feel pretty confident saying that's probably true." Julia glances up as Grant steps out of his office. "Hey, nerd."

He flashes her a panty melting smile. "You're early."

I try to look away, really I do, but the way my boss's gaze devours his wife holds my attention. And brews up a little envy.

Not jealousy. I'm happy Julia has someone who looks ready to eat her up, even when she's sticky and muddy. She's sweet and funny and kind and deserves the adoration Grant has for her.

I just feel like that's never going to happen for me. I'm not like Julia. I'm not sweet or funny or particularly kind. I'm standoffish, and dry, and serious. So far the only men I seem to attract are the ones who only care about themselves. At least I've gotten better at identifying them.

At one point in my life, I would have convinced

myself Dillon was the cat's tits instead of figuring out what a turd he is on the first date. Too bad I didn't notice it earlier. Then I wouldn't be stuck trying to come up with a way to avoid his advances without making shit awkward and tense at work.

"I'm early because you said Alexis was ordering me lunch and I didn't want to miss it." She moves in close, grabbing the front of Grant's button-up and pulling him in for a kiss before snapping one of his suspenders. "And because I wanted to come stare at you."

Ugh. Puke. I hate the way they interact as much as I love it, so I'm relieved when they disappear into Grant's office. A few minutes later, their lunches—and mine— arrive. After delivering theirs, I settle in at my desk, enjoying my egg salad on a croissant as I scroll on my phone, pausing to watch a few of my favorite creators put outfits together. I'm so focused on a cute and casual combo of cropped jeans and a chunky cardigan layered over a fitted tank, that when my phone vibrates to let me know I have a new message, I drop it right into a pool of the creamy, eggy goodness that leaked out of its vessel.

"Shit nuggets." I set down the sandwich and pull my phone free of the mayonnaisey muck. "Gross." I love egg salad in my stomach. Not so much on my electronics.

As I go to work wiping it down, first with a napkin, then with one of the Clorox wipes I keep handy, the vibrations continue. By the time I finally have it cleaned off, I'm already over whoever's messaging me—especially since it's probably a freaking group text.

Aka, a hostage situation.

To my extreme disappointment. I'm right. After opening the message app, I find an already lengthy stream of texts from my friends reminding me we're going out tonight to celebrate Lola's birthday. The final message—from Isla—dashes any hope I had of a nice, quiet evening at home.

> And don't try to get out of it, Alexis. You're coming out and you're going to have fun. We might even find you a date. God knows you could stand to get laid.

14

The One-Eyed Monster

Gavin

"DID YOU GET fucking faster?" Leo swipes one forearm across his brow, wiping away the sweat trickling toward his eyes. "I swear you got faster."

"Maybe you just got slower." I look him over as he pants, trying to catch his breath during our break from drills. "You've been expending all your energy elsewhere."

Leo doesn't even have the decency to look ashamed. "You're just jealous."

I rock my head from side to side, trying to hide my reaction to his comment. My friend isn't wrong. I *am* jealous.

Just not in the way he thinks.

Leo tips back a water bottle, squeezing a steady stream into his open mouth before swallowing it down. "And for the record, Miss Miller and I are taking it slow."

Sure they are. So slow she's already practically living with him.

"Line up," the conditioning coach barks at us from where he stands on the edge of the pitch, ready to push us to our limits. Power and speed are two of the most important skills a player can have, so developing them is a large part of our pre-season training.

I take my spot and narrow my focus, putting everything I have into the drills he puts us through. By the time we're done, I'm dripping with sweat and every inch of me is protesting, but it's clear Leo is right. I am faster than last season.

At least something's going right.

When our field speed session is done, we separate out into forwards and backs for unit skills. Leo's with the forwards and I join the backs, slapping hands with Owen, the other winger. Together, we bring the best of both worlds to the team. I'm big enough to power my way through just about anyone and fast enough to dodge the rest, and he's a fucking speed demon with an amount of agility that makes him a nightmare to catch.

After another hour of grueling exercises, we finally head in to prep for the weight room where we'll wind down our day with lower body strength training. Tomorrow's a rest day, so everyone is in a great mood and there's a good amount of laughing and conversation happening alongside the heavy, metal clang of weights meeting, and the accompanying grunts.

I push myself, wanting to be bigger, stronger, better

—worth what they pay me to be here. When I'm done, my thighs are on fire and I can barely walk, but I feel fucking fantastic. One step closer to the best season yet.

That's what I need this to be. I learned a lot from my short time with Al, but the biggest thing is that my career will have to be enough. I'm not capable of handling anything more, so I'm going to do everything I can to find some sort of fulfillment in my life.

After taking a quick shower, I'm getting dressed when Leo props a shoulder against the wall next to me. I lift one brow as I button the fly of my jeans. "Can I help you with something?"

"Me and a few of the guys are taking you out tonight." Leo looks over my upper half. "You need to find another outlet for your energy. You're making us all look bad out there."

I tug a shirt over my head and pull it into place. "I don't want to go out."

"Didn't ask." Leo shoots me a grin. "I'll pick you up at eight."

I scowl as he strides away, looking un-fucking-bothered that he's being a dick. If he'd pop his head out of Maddie Miller's ass for ten seconds, he might have noticed I'm a fucking mess. That I'm miserable and fucking disgusted with myself.

But maybe it's better he's distracted. I can only imagine what he'd do if he found out the shit I said to Al. Probably kick my ass. And I'd likely let him. Might make me feel better to get some of what I deserve.

I finish getting dressed, grab my bag, and head out into the afternoon. After loading my bag into the back seat, I climb behind the wheel and start the engine.

The drive home gives me time to reconsider my aversion to going out. Maybe an evening of hanging out with a few friends is exactly what I need. A break from the nights of lonely self-loathing I've been attending.

And maybe it will be the start of finding my way back to where I need to be. I've proven I'm not capable of handling anything more than a casual hook-up, so—like it or not—that's where I have to stay.

Even though the thought of touching someone besides Alexis turns my stomach.

After parking in the underground garage beneath my condo, I ride the elevator up to my floor. I've barely got one foot out when Val yells my name.

"*Gavin*. There you are." Valerie lets out a sigh of relief as she turns from my door, where she's probably been banging at the steel for ten minutes instead of calling me like a normal person. "I have a problem and Fynn is taking his mother to a doctor's appointment so I don't want to interrupt him."

I like Val. A lot, actually. She's sweet and smart and makes Fynn the happiest I've ever seen him. She showed up in his life when he needed someone most, and I'll always be grateful. My friend was in a real bad way before she came along. Now he's a husband, and in a few months he'll also be a father. And he's loving every fucking minute of it.

"What's going on?" I drop my bag by the door to my condo, unworried about abandoning it since it's only their place and mine on this floor.

Valerie's steps are quick as she rushes back to her own front door, cautiously opening it to peer through the widening gap. Suddenly, she yelps, jumping back as she slams the door closed. Turning to me with wide eyes, Val lowers her voice to a whisper. "There's a lizard."

My brows lift in surprise. "In your condo?"

She nods, lower lip pinching between her teeth. "It was so nice outside and I wanted some fresh air, so I left the door to the balcony open. I've done it a million times and it's always been fine, but I went to the bathroom because I constantly have to pee now, and when I came back, it was right there." She widens her eyes. "Staring at me."

I scrub one hand down my face. How in the hell am I going to catch a tiny little lizard as it runs around all of Fynn's expensive shit? "Do you have a net or anything?"

Val shakes her head. "Can't you just grab it?"

She wants me to pluck a minuscule, scrambling anole off the wall as it whizzes past me? I'm fast, but I'm not that fucking fast. "Let me see what we're dealing with here." I grab her by the shoulders and gently shift her to one side.

Maybe I can use a pillowcase or something. Possibly an old takeout cont—

I open the door, but instead of the cute little reptile

I've imagined, I come face to face with a fucking dinosaur. It's huge. At least five feet long from nose to tail, with lethal looking claws. Spikes run down its spine and it's missing an eye. Scars mar the muted green skin of its body and a flap of skin hangs from the underside of its powerful looking jaw. The one-eyed glare it shoots my way sends me taking a step back. And thank God I do, because it starts to charge me, nails scratching the floor, maw gaping like it wants to swallow me whole.

I quickly pull the door closed and turn to my neighbor, waiting for her to meet my gaze. "Val."

She scrunches her face in a way that wrinkles her nose and squints her eyes. "Yes?"

"That's not a lizard. That's a fucking monster." I risk another peek, cracking the door a tiny bit to confirm the thing is as big as I thought it was. "You wanted me to pick that behemoth up?"

"Well *I'm* not going to pick it up." Val sounds shocked I'm not willing to grab the intruder and chuck him off the balcony. "It's as big as I am."

I look through the crack, then at my buddy's wife. She's actually not far off. Which makes me even less interested in trying to catch it with my bare hands. "Have you tried calling someone to come get it?"

Her lips press into a thin line. "They said it's an invasive species and that they would kill it."

I'm not seeing the problem here. "Okay…"

Her light brown eyes widen. "He isn't hurting anything. I just don't want him in my house." Her chin wobbles a little and I know I'm done for. "You can tell he's already had a hard life and I didn't want—" Her voice breaks.

"Fucking hell, Val." I take a deep breath, bracing for what's to come. "Next time just tell me to shut up and get my ass in there and do what you asked. You don't have to attack me with emotional warfare." Whatever's on the other side of that door has become the lesser of two evils, because I'd rather face it than the way she's looking at me now.

I open the door and duck inside, closing it behind me so the beast won't get out into the hall where Valerie is. I nearly shit myself when the lizard charges me for a second time. But instead of attacking me like I'm expecting, it stops at my feet, blinking up at me with that one eyeball. I slowly bend at the waist, lowering my hand toward it, ready to yank my fingers back at the first sign of aggression. When I brush them across the top of his head, I'm surprised to see the things sticking up down his back aren't spikes at all, but some sort of scaly protrusions. As I stroke along its dry skin, the animal's one eye closes, almost like he's enjoying the attention.

An awful thought occurs to me. "You were somebody's pet, weren't you?"

Thanks to the temperate climate, Florida is the kind of place where all sorts of things can survive. So if an exotic animal outgrows its cage, and their owner throws them outside instead of taking them to a wildlife center, they don't die. Instead, they stick around and fuck up the ecosystem.

Or break into million-dollar condos.

"What in the hell am I going to do with you?" I carefully hook my hands under its middle and slowly lift the lizard up. Solidifying my suspicions that it was once a pet, the animal doesn't seem to mind. Actually, it kind of looks like it might be smiling as I carry it to the door.

I'm almost there when it opens and Fynn stares in at me, his wife peeking out from where he has her pinned behind his back. His eyes widen, expression incredulous. "What the bloody hell is that?"

"Do I look like a fucking zoologist?" I adjust my hold on the unexpected visitor. "It's pretty calm though. Seems used to people. I bet it was someone's pet and they set it loose when it got too big."

"Oh no." Valerie darts out from behind Fynn. "Poor thing."

Fynn snags her by the arm, stopping her from reaching my side. "Darling, that could have a disease."

Val pushes her lower lip out, brows pinched together in concern. "You think it's sick?"

I look over the animal, who seems perfectly happy being handled. "It doesn't look sick. Just old." I notice it appears a little thin in the middle. "Probably hungry." Continuing out the door, I carry it past Fynn and Val.

My friend sidesteps, getting his body back between the lizard and his pregnant wife. "Are you taking it with you?"

"Unless you want me to put it back where I found it." I make like I'm going to go back inside his posh home.

"*No.*" Fynn's rejection of my bluff is sharp and immediate. "No. I think it's best if you take it with you."

"Thank you so much, Gavin." Val gives me a smile. "You're a sweetheart."

"There's a whole lot of women who would beg to differ." One in particular. "It's a good thing I didn't cross your path first, or you'd be one of them."

"Bugger off, prick." Fynn flashes me a smile. "Before you give her ideas."

I'm still laughing as I let myself into my condo, but as I kick my discarded bag through the open door and look down at the lizard in my arms, my laughter turns to a groan. "What the fuck am I going to do with you now?" I have no clue how to care for this thing. I don't even know what it eats. Movement catches my attention and I glance up, finding my cat Cilantro meandering our way.

Looking back at the lizard, I tell him, "Hopefully you don't eat cats, because if you try, she'll tear you apart."

That's how I ended up with the temperamental tabby. A few months ago, I discovered celibacy is lonely, so I made a trip to the local shelter. When I stuck my fingers into Cilantro's cage, the woman with me gasped because so far no one had been able to get close to the stray. But instead of peeling the skin from my bones, she started to rub against me, her purr loud and insistent. She's an acquired taste—one some people will never get —but I love the shit out of her.

Blowing out a breath, I dig my cell from my pocket and call Leo up, planning to tell him I won't be coming out tonight.

"Don't try to get out of it, dick." He doesn't even say hello. "You're going with us even if I have to drag your ass there kicking and screaming."

"But—"

"Don't care if the world is ending. I'll be there at eight to pick you up." Leo hangs up on me.

Cilantro weaves between my legs, meowing because she expects to be fed, and the lizard starts to sag, single eyeball closed.

Is it asleep?

I made it well into adulthood only having myself to take care of, and now, in the span of a few months, I've acquired two more mouths to feed.

One of them being a squatter.

I'm back to thinking going out is a good idea. I could use a fucking drink.

15

How Not to Diffuse a Situation

I DO A spin as I look myself over in the full-length mirror propped up in the corner of my bedroom. After sifting through the contents of my closet, I decided to wear the flowy black and gold romper I picked up at an after Christmas sale. Is it a little light for January? Possibly. But I'm willing to suffer so I can use it as an excuse to go the heck home when my social battery flatlines.

I'm usually the first to dip out, but I try to have a reason. It might not always be a *good* reason, but it makes me feel less bad about not being able to last as long as everyone else in a loud, crowded bar.

I peer over one shoulder and frown, scowling at the pantylines peeking through the delicate fabric. I could wrestle on some shapewear, but fighting a romper when I have to pee is bad enough. I don't want to add the evils of spandex into the equation.

"Welp. Guess you've got to go." I strip down, dropping the garment to the floor before kicking away my panties and pulling the fluttering fabric back into place. Then I do another spin, making sure all my bits and pieces will remain under wraps if I bend over. Thankfully, it appears—barring any high-kicks—no one will get a glimpse of my nethers.

After smoothing down my hair and double checking my lip gloss, I grab my bag and shoes and make for the door, hustling through the high-ceilinged space because —shocker—I'm running late.

After pausing at the door to slip on a pair of strappy, thick-heeled, black pumps, I duck out into the hall and book it to the elevator. It's on the floor under mine, so soon I'm outside, rushing to my car.

We're meeting at a tiny spot in downtown Sweet Side not far from the office building where I work, so it's a short drive. Just long enough to give me time to wish I was in my sweatpants on my couch, eating pasta while watching Netflix. Which is still not as much fun as other things I've done on my couch, but stupid Gavin had to go and be an idiot and screw all that up for me.

When I reach the bar, I nearly groan at how full the lot behind it is. Again, I consider turning around and going home, but my friends would kill me. And I don't necessarily want to do all the work it would take to find new ones. After circling the lot, I finally get lucky and someone leaves. I tuck my small, white crossover into the spot, then get out, adjust my romper, and head for the door.

The noise of the bar hits me like a wall as I walk inside. It's overwhelming and has me wishing I called an Uber so I could get drunk enough not to care about the way it grates on my nerves. But without my car, I'm at someone else's mercy, and that's not an enjoyable spot for me to be. I like knowing I can leave whenever I want. That my escape is close by. It helps take the edge off.

Isla waves at me from across the room, flagging me down with exaggerated movements–like I might miss the flaming redhead yelling my name. I flash her a smile and return her wave so she stops pulling every-one's attention to the group of single women circling the high-top. As much as I don't love being in a noisy bar, I love it even less when I'm sitting around while my friends get hit on by everything with a heartbeat.

And frequently an insane amount of audacity.

Hooking one foot onto the stool's rung, I hoist myself into the only vacant seat as everyone tells me how great I look and I return the favor. Even though we're all very different, my friend group is an attractive one. Besides Isla and her long, attention grabbing, wavy red hair, there's Wren who is tall and willowy with a sleek black bob. Lola is warm and sweet with lush curves and dark curls. And Hazel's blonde hair and thick-rimmed glasses make men trip over each other, hoping for a chance with the hot chemist.

Then there's me. I'm just as cute as my friends, but my facial expressions make me look either half-ready to stab anyone who gets close, or half-ready to walk out the door. They don't necessarily lie, but I wish they would a little so I could be the one getting hit on now and then.

"How was work?" Lola leans across the table, nose scrunching with distaste. "Has Dillon tried to get you to go out with him again?"

I blow out a breath, slumping back in my seat at the reminder of how stupid I can be when it comes to men. "Ugh." The waitress comes to bring everyone else their drinks and I place an order of my own, buying myself a little time before I have to tackle that conversation. "I don't know what possessed me to go out with him in the first place."

"He can be kind of charming when he wants to be." Wren lifts one shoulder and lets it fall. "And lots of happy couples meet at work."

That had been my very same reasoning. Since I don't go out unless I have to, and dating apps make me want to throw up in my mouth, my opportunities for meeting a man are slim to none. I decided to give Dillon a shot, assuming he'd be able to keep it professional if things didn't work out.

Wrong. Wrong, wrong, wrong, wrong, wrong.

My drink arrives and I check my watch before taking a long sip so I know exactly when I drank and exactly when I can leave. "What about you guys? How were your holidays?"

For the next half hour, my friends go around the

table, lamenting the good and bad of holidays as single women. Lola's mother lectured her about her desire for grandchildren. Isla got stuck managing her siblings' spawn while their parents partied it up. Wren faced a formal dinner where she was the only person without a plus one. And Hazel—an only child—suffered through a nearly silent frozen lasagna dinner with her researcher parents. Personally, that sounds like heaven. Well, outside of the shitty food.

We're just starting to discuss the state of our careers when the first suitor of the night sidles up to the table, wedging himself between me and Isla. He tries to claim more space, but I refuse to budge, glaring at him as he flashes a smile around the table. "Ladies."

The guy is decently good-looking and has a nice set of teeth, but his whole approach irks me. I always say I wish more men hit on me, but this is a perfect example of why they don't. While my friends' expressions are pleasant and friendly, I'm scowling. I know I should try to fix my face, but I'm annoyed, and trying to smile only makes my nostrils flare more.

Which is why I nearly fall out of my seat when he turns to me, zeroing in as he holds out one hand. "I'm Tanner."

"Uhh." I blink, shocked and a little concerned. What does it say about this guy that *I'm* the one he decided on? That out of all the smiling girls at the table, he picked the one who looks most likely to punch him in the throat?

"This is Alexis." Isla speaks for me since I'm still gaping at him like a fish. "And she really likes margaritas."

If Tanner was paying attention, he'd notice my whiskey sour is not a margarita, but he doesn't even check. Just lifts one hand and orders 'me' a margarita. He doesn't bother to ask if I want a drink—I don't—and then he makes another attempt to claim more space, this time using his elbow to shove mine off the table so he can creep into my personal bubble even more. "It's nice to meet you, Alexis."

Is it though? "Okay."

"Are you from Sweet Side?" he asks, watching me intently over the rim of his glass.

"Uh-huh." My eyes dart to my friends, bouncing around as they each motion for me to keep talking. "What about you?"

"I actually just moved here a month ago for my job." He then goes into a fifteen-minute monologue about himself. Anytime I—or one of my friends—tries to get a word in, he gets louder, talking over us. He's so focused on himself, the guy doesn't even notice that Isla snaps up the margarita when it arrives and starts chugging it down. Probably to take the edge off the torture of his presence.

Finally, I'm over it. When he pauses to take a breath, I hold up one hand. "I'm going to stop you right there, Tanner, and let you know I'm really not interested."

His eyes widen. Like he's never heard those words strung together before. "But I bought you a drink."

"And I listened to you talk about yourself for fifteen minutes." I lean forward, lowering my voice a little. Like I'm talking to a five-year-old. "I think we're even."

He scoffs, looking fully affronted. "You aren't even hot anyway."

Lola gasps and I can see Isla picking up her empty margarita glass out of the corner of my eye. My friends are really sweet women. To a point. We're all a little overprotective of each other, and I know Tanner's about two seconds away from getting a tumbler to his temple, so instead of giving him the tongue lashing he deserves, I try to diffuse the situation. "I'm hotter than your mom."

So maybe my diffusing technique could use some work.

Tanner's mommy must be a touchy subject, because his face starts to get red and his eyes bulge out a little. "Little bitch. My mother's a saint."

I'm about to tell Tanner I'm sure that's true since she puts up with an asshat like him, but before I get another word out, a huge hand clamps down on Tan-the-Man's shoulder, jerking him away from me.

All the air freezes in my lungs as I look up, eyes stopping on the long-haired rugby player giving Mr. Personality an easy smile. "You probably shouldn't tell women you're a little bitch right out of the gate. Let them figure it out themselves." Gavin pivots, his hold on

Tanner staying tight as he switches their positions, putting his giant body between me and the reason I no longer want to get hit on. "And, for the record, she *is* hotter than your mom." Gavin gives Tanner a shove, sending the smaller man stumbling back. Then he turns to the table, draping one muscled arm across the back of my chair as he greets my friends. "You guys having a good night?"

I swear Hazel sighs, a stupid smile on her face as she stares up at my brother's best friend. "It's way better now."

Isla beams at him. "You are like a big, bearded, knight in shining armor, aren't you?"

Good god. The man doesn't need anyone else trying to inflate his ego. There's enough people doing it already. It's actually a miracle Gavin isn't completely full of himself.

Even if it appears a few of my friends wouldn't mind being full of him...

"You guys remember Leo's friend Gavin." I say it loud, trying to pull their attention my way. "He was just leaving." I appreciate him dealing with Tanner the Twat, but I'm irritated at the way he seems to think I'll just forget what a buttface he was the last time we saw each other.

I'm also irritated at the way my friends are staring at him. Like he's some sort of deity they would love to worship.

"*No.*" Isla grabs one of his hands. "Stay."

My eyes snap to where she's touching him. "I'm sure Gavin is here with someone else and—"

"I can stay." Gavin carefully pulls his hand from Isla's, using it to snag a chair from behind us. He settles it in the spot Tanner just occupied. But while Gavin's hulking frame takes up way more space than the other man did, his presence feels so much less invasive, even if I'm considering kicking him under the table.

He settles into the seat, adjusting his big body in a way that brings him even closer to me. So close, the thickness of his thigh presses tight to mine, baking it with warmth through the fabric of his jeans.

I'm wiggling in my seat, caught between liking the feel of all that hard muscle and knowing I should not enjoy having any part of Gavin pressed against any part of me, when I notice his thigh isn't the only place we're touching. The arm he draped over the back of my chair is still there, heavy and solid across my back, resting in a way no amount of rearranging my position will rectify.

And then his thumb slowly starts to drag across the bare skin of my bicep, making lazy passes as he carries on a conversation with my friends.

As if this is a completely normal situation.

As if he doesn't realize I'm already plotting ways to get away from him before I do something stupid. Like forget what a jerk he was on Christmas.

16

What Kind of Fast are We Talking?

I TRY NOT to react when Alexis jumps up, declaring she has to go to the bathroom and leaving me without so much as a backward glance.

"Are you getting ready for the upcoming season?" The redhead sitting at my side tries to keep the conversation going, but I'm struggling to follow along.

"Yeah." I straighten in my seat, scanning the bar for any sign of Al's blonde head, but she's so fucking short —even in heels—I lose her in the crowd.

"I bet it's super fun to play rugby for a living." The glasses one has her chin propped on her hands. "All that physical activity."

I've met Al's friends before, but always in passing. I've never been around them long enough to retain any of their names, and I'm regretting it now. I don't want them to think I'm a complete ass.

Even though I probably am.

"You do seem to be in really good shape." The woman directly across from me smiles, a dimple cutting into the curve of her cheek. "That's probably why you're so fast."

My brows lift and I drag my gaze from its search for Alexis. "You watch rugby?"

She shakes her head, the dark curls of her hair swinging with the movement. "No. I'm not really into sports."

That stumps me a little. "Then how do you know I'm fast?"

She's still smiling, looking like she's thoroughly enjoying our conversation. "Because Alexis told us."

Well, isn't that interesting. I'm feeling a little cocky over Al telling them about my skill as a player, but then it occurs to me that might not be the sort of speed she's told these women about. We might actually be discussing the events of her parents' Christmas party, and my dumb ass is too stupid to know it.

I scan the faces circling the table, looking for any hint they might know what happened in Babs' she shed —or worse, my shitty comment Christmas morning. Thankfully, none of them looks ready to stab me with the toothpick from their drink's garnish, so even if they know part of the story, they don't know all of it.

But while their expressions are friendly, they're also assessing. I'd initially thought Al's friends were flirting with me, but now I'm worried this is more of an interview. An analysis to see if I'm good enough for their friend.

And that has me standing just as fast as Alexis did earlier. "I should probably go find the guys I came with."

I back away from the high-top, needing to get away from their scrutiny before they see the truth. Because I know for a fact I'm not good enough for Alexis. I also know it doesn't matter. I fucked everything up and I need to let it stay that way. Be grateful I didn't completely destroy shit and can still hang around, soaking up the kind of family life I never had.

Once the mess Leo made blows over.

"It was nice seeing you guys." I keep moving. "Enjoy your night." Turning, I weave through the packed bar, making my way to the table where Leo and the rest of the guys are drinking their second round.

I'd been on my way back from the bathroom when I caught sight of that dick hovering over Alexis. The second I saw the expression on her face, I knew it wasn't a happy exchange and couldn't stop myself from stepping in. I didn't like how he was looking at her. How close he was standing.

What he was trying to accomplish.

It sent me straight to a place I don't want to go again, making me want to break bones and mark territory like some kind of fucking neanderthal.

That's why I need to get away from her. Because I

make terrible fucking decisions when she's involved. I fall back into the shit I've worked hard to stay out of.

"There you are." Leo passes me two bottles of beer. "You're behind."

I sit in my seat, but don't reach for the offered drinks. "You guys came to play, didn't you?"

"We just spent five days sweating our balls off, so yeah. We're here to get fucked up." Owen downs what's left of his second beer before looking right at me. "And you better start drinking, because I'm going to get us another round."

I look around the table and notice everyone has two empty bottles in front of them except for Leo, who's drinking a coke. I didn't have time to think the situation over before, but now it's starting to register how odd it is that my best friend offered to be the designated driver. It's not normally his style to readily give up the opportunity to get shit faced. "Why aren't you drinking?"

Leo shrugs. "No reason."

"Bullshit." I start to pick up one of the bottles, but my interest in getting drunk is now slim to none thanks to the dick who fucked with Alexis. "What's the real reason?"

My friend won't look at me, making me even more sure something's up. "I've got plans in the morning."

"You have plans." I stretch the unbelievable words out, enunciating each one. "In the morning." I lean closer. "You hate mornings."

"I don't hate mornings." Leo lies to my face. "I just wish they came a little later in the day is all."

Owen comes back to the table, a tray of beers balanced on one hand. He starts passing them out, adding a third drink to my lineup. "Bottom's up, assholes."

There's no way I want to drink *one* of these beers, let alone three. Not when Alexis might need me to be clear headed enough to stop that prick from bothering her again.

Pushing my chair back, I get to my feet. "I'll be back. Gotta pee."

Leo looks me over, brows pinched. "You just went."

"Gotta go again." I walk away without elaborating, leaving my friends staring at me, their mouths hanging open.

I'm usually the guy buying drinks and passing them out. The one ready to get loud and let loose. I like being that guy. Like making new friends I'll forget before dawn.

But tonight I'm in a shit mood and it only gets worse when I see the fucker from earlier ducking into the back hallway where the bathrooms are located. A quick scan of the room tells me Alexis hasn't yet returned to her table, and it has my steps coming faster. I don't make a habit of knocking the shit out of people off the pitch, but if that bastard lays a hand on Alexis, I'll make an exception.

I round the corner, storming into the isolated hall

just as she comes out of the bathroom to find him waiting for her. Her blue eyes widen in surprise and her skin pales. She spins, planning to go right back into the bathroom. Like a dumbass, he grabs her, the tips of his fingers sinking into the bare skin of her arm as he attempts to yank her closer.

Proving what a fearless woman she is, Alexis swings at him. I'm proud—so fucking proud—when her small fist connects with his nose and he stumbles back.

She's winding up to sock him again when I reach them, grabbing the guy by the pomade infested hair at the top of his head. The product is sticky, but that only helps my grip as I wordlessly drag him down the hall and around the corner. He squeals and squirms, working desperately to keep both feet under him on our way to the back exit.

Rocking back onto one foot, I kick the other against the bar at the center of the metal door, knocking it open. Using my momentum, I propel dickwad out into the dark, sending him sprawling across the pavement. I brace the door with a hand, keeping it open as I turn to where Al is standing behind me, her mouth hanging open. "You wanna hit him again before I close this?"

Her lips clamp closed and she seems to consider it a second before shaking her head. "I think I'm good."

The prick is groaning and trying to get up as I slam the door and turn to where Alexis watches me with a wary gaze. She lifts her chin. "Thanks."

I rock my neck from side to side, trying to work out

the tension lingering from seeing that fucker put his hands on her. "Are you okay?" I move toward her, gently picking up the arm he grabbed. "Did he hurt you?"

She holds very still as I brush my fingers over the red marks marring her skin. "Not as bad as I hurt him." There's pride in her voice, and I smile in spite of the anger still simmering through my veins.

"You got a pretty good shot in, Al. I'm impressed." I take a deep breath, trying to calm the jealous rage coursing through my veins. My gaze falls to where I cradle her arm, the sight of the angry marks amping me right back up. "I should have come back here with you."

Al slides free of my grip. "I came back here to get away from you."

My eyes jump to her face. "To get away from me?"

Her hand rubs over her bicep. Not the area that's bruising, but the spot where I touched her. "I *know* you didn't forget the shit you said to me on Christmas."

There's a hint of hurt in her voice and it cuts into me, digging deep enough to let out an admission I've been trying to bury forever. "I was jealous."

Her brows lift, like I've surprised her. "Of Dillon?"

I grit my teeth, trying to keep the rest of my shame in, but fail yet again. "Of anyone who's ever touched you."

Her eyes widen a little more, then she confesses, "Dillon hasn't touched me."

"But he wants to." I creep closer to the soft curves of

her body. A body I had my hands all over not so long ago. "And it makes me lose my goddamned mind when I think about it."

Her lips part as she stares up at me. "Why?" The question whispers between her plush lips.

"You know why, Al." I clench my fists. "Because I'm the one who should be touching you." Shifting on my feet, I let the movement drag my chest across the nipples teasing me through the fabric between us. Leaning down, I brace one hand on the wall as my lips tease against her ear. "Maybe you should let me touch you now." I breathe deep against her skin as I palm the plush curve of her hip with the hand not sticky from that fucker's hair gel, nearly groaning as the tips of my fingers dig into the softness there.

She gasps as I find the hem of her shorts and tease the skin beneath it, tracing along the top of her thigh. "Would you let me touch you now?"

I hold my breath, knowing there's a good chance she might tell me to get fucked. I wouldn't blame her. I screwed up. Epically.

Her eyes fix on my face, pupils dilated in the dim light of the hall. "Are you going to be an ass again?"

I want to tell her no. I want to believe I can get past the bullshit bestowed on me by years of listening to my old man spew nonsense and vitriol.

More than that, I want to tell her about him. I want her to know why I was really at her house all the time growing up. The reason I spend holidays with her family and not mine.

But not here.

"I can't make any promises, Al. Some shit runs deep." It's the most I can give her right now, but it's more than I've told anyone else. Even her brother.

Al's head falls back against the wall behind her and she lets out a resigned sigh. "Fine."

The way she seems almost irritated by my offer to get her off makes me chuckle—lightening the weight of my mood—because it's so like her. "Don't sound so excited, Al." I let my lips drag down the line of her neck, tracing her soft skin with my tongue and teeth as my touch moves higher, finding the dip where her leg meets her body and following it like a path. "I might surprise you."

"I've seen your surprises." She's a little breathless now. "I'd rather you not do it again. I don't want to spend all night trying to clean this outfit."

The tips of my fingers brush across her mound, teasing the trimmed crop of hair there. "I promise to keep my jizz to myself this time."

"Such a gentlema—"

The last word cuts off as I press against the seam of her body, delving into the soft, slippery skin it hides. "Fuck, Al." I slide deeper. "You're so wet." I groan as I stroke along her flesh. "Is this all for me?"

"Stop talking." The retort is sharp.

I hum against her skin, smiling at this new discovery. "Make me."

Her clit is already hard and swollen and I trace slow circles around it, pinning her body in place with mine when her legs start to wobble. I make a tsk-ing sound as I continue teasing the nub at the apex of her pillowy pussy lips. "You aren't about to come already, are you?"

Alexis shudders against me with a gasp and a whimper, a fresh gush of wetness coating my hand. I can't resist letting my fingers slide through it before sinking into the tight heat of her body. "I was just getting warmed up, Al." I slide in and out of her, wishing I could watch what I'm doing. "You should take me home with you. Let me show you how sorry I am for the way I acted."

I'm pushing my luck, I know it. But I don't care. I don't care about anything but spending more time with Alexis. Even though it's a terrible fucking idea since the more I'm with her, the more of her I want. But I'm weak when it comes to her. And stupid.

Her eyes are unfocused as she stares up at me, looking flushed and dazed and only half as boneless as I want her to be. She glances toward the noisy bar, making me think she's going to turn me down and return to her friends.

But then she nods. "Yeah. Let's get the fuck out of here."

17

Big Man in a Little Car

I'VE DUCKED OUT early on my friends before, but it's never gone as smoothly as it is tonight. As Gavin leads me out the same door he tossed Tanner through less than ten minutes ago, I fire off a text to the group chat, expecting to hear endless shit about my sudden departure.

Instead, I'm met with understanding and offers to meet up for lunch soon.

"Weird." I stare at my phone as Gavin directs me to where my car is parked.

"What's wrong?" He scans the lot, tugging me closer.

"My friends aren't pissed I'm leaving." I frown down at the messages, disappointed. Part of me was hoping they'd talk me out of whatever temporary insanity is possessing me.

No such luck.

"Good." Gavin urges me to the passenger's side of my small SUV and holds out his hand. "Keys."

I frown at him. "Why do you get to drive?"

"Because I watched you suck down a drink less than half an hour ago."

Normally Gavin is laid back and easygoing. Full of jokes and jabs. Not tonight. Tonight he's being bossy, and I'm not sure how I feel about it.

"Now give me your keys."

I unhook my fob from the small bag I brought and pass it over. "If you put a single scratch on her, I will murder you."

"You can try." He presses the unlock button and opens the door, one big hand coming to rest against my back as he urges me inside. "Actually, I might really enjoy that."

He pinches my apartment key between his fingers and makes like he's going to drag it down the side of my car.

"You better fucking not." I swing at him and he easily dodges my second assault attempt of the evening, laughing as he catches my wrist and uses the hold to fold me back into the seat.

"I will be careful with your car, Al. I promise." His eyes move over me, gaze heated as it lingers on my tits. "You, on the other hand..."

The speed with which he goes from teasing to eye fucking would give me whiplash if my body wasn't so happy to be along for the ride.

Gavin leans in, coming so close I can feel the heat radiating off his skin. One finger traces the line of my jaw. "You, I will be *very* careful with."

He straightens and closes the door, leaving me panting.

I'm still lightheaded when he opens the driver's door. After leaning in to slide the seat back as far as it will go, he crams himself behind the wheel, looking both hot as hell and ridiculous as fuck at the same time. I snort, unable to stop myself from laughing as he tries to get situated.

Gavin angles a dark brow at me as he starts the engine. "You think something's funny, Al?"

I nod, high on whiskey and endorphins. "You look hilarious."

"Yeah?" He backs out of the spot, angling the wheel to take us toward the exit.

Once we're moving forward, his hand slides against my thigh, fingers tucking under the fabric of my romper to part my pussy and tease against my clit. I'm still embarrassingly wet from what happened in the hall, so his touch glides against me easily, strangling a little moan through my lips.

Gavin shoots me a smirk. "Still hilarious?"

I don't know how I went from being pissed at him to letting him finger me as he drives us home, and I don't really care.

Not at this moment anyway.

But then, just as I'm about to tip over the edge for a

second time, he pulls his hand out of my shorts, clamping the width of his palm over my pussy, making it impossible for me to finish what he started.

"You dick." I grip his wrist, trying to move his hand, but the man is unbudgeable. "You're making me regret my life choices."

His hand flexes, teasing me with just enough pressure to keep me on edge. "I don't think so."

I scoff, frustrated and, honestly, a little confused. "You're awfully cocky for a guy who—"

"Sullied your Christmas dress?" His gaze drags down my front as we come to a stop at a light. "Careful or I'll ruin that thing too."

"You better not." I wrap my arms across my outfit, like I need to protect it from sudden soiling. "I'll shave your head while you sleep."

He slowly smirks. "Is that your way of inviting me to spend the night again?"

I start to sputter. "What? No—"

"I accept." Gavin turns away as the light changes to green.

Soon we're pulling into a spot directly in front of my building. I lead him to the elevator, each second feeling more and more surreal as we step inside and the doors slide closed.

What am I doing? Have I lost my whole mind? I can't bring Gavin back to my apartment and...

And...

I peek at where he stands beside me, my eyes sliding

down to rest on the sizeable bulge attempting to break through the front of his jeans.

I mean... Would it really hurt anything at this point if I slept with him? We've already made things weird between us. I might as well get as much out of it as I can, right?

"I see you looking at my dick, Al." Gavin's voice is a low rumble but I still jump, eyes snapping to the elevator doors.

The fucking reflective elevator doors.

They part as we arrive on my floor, taking the image of my beet red face with them. I march out, making a beeline to my door, completely forgetting I am no longer in possession of my keys.

Again, Gavin smirks, like he's enjoying seeing me off balance. Flipping through the keys on the ring, he holds one up, angling his brow in question.

I snatch it away, sliding the correctly guessed key into the lock and opening the deadbolt, going straight in. I pause to take off my shoes, carrying them with me as I try to acclimate to the sight in front of me.

I didn't expect to have Gavin in my apartment again and it feels odd. Almost as odd as everything else about this night has been. I started the evening pissed at him for being a dick, and now I'm considering letting him fuck me.

I'm *still* pissed at him, I'm just willing to overlook it for a little while since I know from experience it will be worth the temporary lapse.

Gavin toes off his own shoes, leaving them right beside the door before slowly ambling through the open floor plan. "You took down your Christmas decorations."

His dark eyes move over the items I've collected since moving out of my parents' home, and I pause, wondering what he thinks of my place now that it's not covered in lights and tinsel.

"It's January." The explanation stands for itself, so I don't elaborate. I also can't elaborate because I'm not breathing so well. Especially not when Gavin's eyes come my way. I shift from foot to foot, shoes still dangling from the tips of my fingers as his gaze slides down my body.

He lowers to sit on the sofa, draping both long arms across the back. Lifting his chin, he says, "Come here."

I hesitate, but only because the gravelly sound of his voice shoots straight between my thighs, reigniting the flame of lust he stoked on the way here. Once my legs are willing to move again, I slowly make my way toward him, eyes fixed on his face. There's no missing the heat in his gaze and it has my belly doing a little flip-flop. No one has ever looked at me like they want to devour me whole, and I'm a little discombobulated over Gavin being the first one to do it.

My heart rate picks up with every step I take. Beating faster and faster until I'm concerned I might pass out the second I reach him.

And that would be a tragedy.

Forcing air into my lungs so I can maintain consciousness, I quietly pad across the thick rug covering the laminate flooring. I reach his side and stand there, because I'm not sure exactly what to do. Both times before, things between us were fast and furious, not giving me much of an opportunity to think through what was happening. Now, it's going slower. Quieter. Providing lots of space for doubt and second-guessing.

For a few seconds, Gavin takes me in, his assessing gaze starting at the top of my head and inching down until he finally reaches my bare feet. Normally, I would be worried he would find me lacking, but thanks to his confession at the bar, I know Gavin likes what he sees. He has to if he wants to be the only one touching it, right?

My breath catches as he leans forward, the muscles of his chest and stomach flexing under his fitted T-shirt as he reaches for my shoes, setting them on the coffee table. Then he leans back again, arms resuming their position along the top of the cushions. His eyes meet mine as he says, "Undress."

The command makes my pussy throb and I squeeze my thighs together, trying to ease the ache forming there. Swallowing hard, I hook a finger into the V-neck of my romper, working it over one shoulder and down my arm before repeating the process with the other side. Once it's pushed down to my waist, I reach behind my back to unhook my bra.

Gavin's eyes fuse to my tits as the lacy black fabric goes slack. He watches intently, nostrils flaring, as I peel it away and toss it to the floor. Going back to my romper, I shimmy my hips a little, making my boobs sway as I wiggle the garment to the floor. I do it on purpose. I know he's a tit man and it's fun to taunt him.

Once I'm naked, I straighten, standing completely bare for his perusal.

I've been naked in front of him before, but not like this. Never have I displayed myself so openly. I wouldn't have been brave enough to offer myself up for assessment with anyone but him.

Because I already know he likes what he sees.

Gavin's jaw clenches as he takes me in, body completely still while his gaze rakes over my curves. When his eyes finally come back to mine, I suck in a breath. Making eye contact with him while I'm naked brings a level of intimacy I wasn't expecting. It's raw and a little scary.

"You are so fucking perfect, Al." His focus dips again, resting on my tits before sinking lower. "Look at how pretty you are."

I preen a little, standing straighter, the scarily strong connection I felt a second ago easing as his eyes leave mine. The warmth that was initially localized between my thighs has spread, and now every inch of me is flushed and primed for whatever comes next.

"Come here." Gavin repeats one of his earlier

requests, but this time I'm not really sure what he means by it.

So I inch closer, trying to figure out if he wants me to just stand in front of him, or maybe sit beside him. I pause for a second when my shins bump the couch. I start to lower my ass to the cushions, but before my butt touches the upholstery, Gavin grips me by the hips.

"No." He hauls my body across his lap, letting my knees fall on either side of his hips. "Come *here*."

My short little legs can barely straddle the width of his body, so my spread pussy is pressed right against the front of his jeans. I glance down, horrified to see a slight bit of discoloration where the moisture of my body is sinking into the denim. "I'm going to get your pants wet." I try to move away, but his fingers press into my flesh, dragging me closer.

"Good. I hope you fucking soak them." Gavin growls the words before clamping his mouth over one of my nipples. I was so distracted by my position and what it would mean for his Levi's, that I hadn't noticed my tits were right in his face. Now, with the heat of his mouth pulling at one, and the pads of his fingers plucking at the other, I have to think that was by design.

Gavin's eyes lift to my face as his lips drag off my nipple, the slight rasp of his short beard teasing against my skin. His hand slides to the back of my neck, pulling me in until his mouth seals over mine. His kiss isn't hesitant or sweet. It's a little rough. A little demanding.

And a lot hot.

I whimper as his tongue strokes against mine, feeling way more drunk than alcohol has ever made me as he pulls me closer, enveloping my body in his arms. He's so big and warm and strong and—

I yelp as the room turns sideways and I'm flipped onto my back, arms and legs and titties flopping around because of the unexpected position change. When I land on my back against the cushions, one foot is hooked over the back of the couch, the other dangles off one side. My hair is everywhere, and I think the remote is jabbing into my kidney.

Swiping at the strands tangled across my face, I try to work myself into a more comfortable position. As I yank the television controller out from under my lower back, Gavin grips my thighs, spreading them far enough apart he can wedge his wide shoulders between them.

Then his thumbs part my pussy, and he blows a steady stream of air right at my clit. The shock of cool is almost as palpable as a touch and my back bows off the cushion. What the fucking fuck is that?

And why did I not know it was a thing until this moment?

18

Don't Cross Chihuahuas

ALEXIS GOES COMPLETELY still, and I pause, a little worried I'm doing something she doesn't like. Lifting my eyes to her face, I find her staring at me.

"What the fuck was that?" She's breathless, and doesn't seem put off, but I want to be sure.

"Like it?" My mouth is watering and I'm desperate to have her on my tongue, but I want her to enjoy everything about tonight. I need to make up for what I said. I need to show her how fucking sorry I am. That I'm better than that.

Even though I'm not sure I am.

Alexis nods, eyes wide. "Like it."

I love how she's not shy. How she stood in front of me, naked and proud. Like she was daring me to find her lacking.

As if that would ever fucking happen.

I haven't always looked at her that way though. For

years she was just Leo's little sister. Someone to annoy and aggravate. Then she grew up and went to college and started dating some pecker who wasn't good enough for her. She was so far out of Huge-nose's league, they weren't even playing the same game.

When he came around, it took everything I had not to punch him in his smug, weak-jawed face and throw him out on the lawn. I might have read more into it if Leo hadn't felt the same. Since he hated Huge-nose as much as I did, it was easy to convince myself I was just feeling protective because Alexis was like a sister to me.

Obviously that was delusional bullshit. Just like me thinking I could stay away from her. I can't. And I'm sick of trying.

"What about this?" I drag the flat of my tongue up her slit, stopping to flick against her clit before lifting my eyes to her face. "Like?"

I don't really need to ask that question. I know she likes it, but I want to hear her say it. To me. To herself. I want Alexis to admit she likes what I do to her.

Because I want her to keep asking me to do it. I don't want her going to assholes like Huge-nose or Dill-hole. I want her to come to me.

To come for me.

Alexis gives me a jerky nod, her blue eyes fused to mine. "Like." Her thighs jerk as I tongue her again. "Like a lot."

It's exactly what I want to hear. What my pride and

the jealous streak I've worked so hard to suppress *need* to hear. So I reward her.

Sealing my lips against her heated, slick flesh, I work her up quickly, hoping to prove myself. Determined to give her a reason to forgive me.

With her hands fisted in my hair, back arching to press those glorious tits higher in the air, my dick jerks in my pants, threatening to send me over the edge with her. But then my name erupts from her lips and the need to come is replaced with a different sort of satisfaction.

I'm the one who gave her that and she knows it.

Alexis slumps against the cushions, eyes glassy and dazed, limbs askew and boneless. Her full lips are parted as she fights to catch her breath, giving me time to offer the thighs just clamped at my ears a little attention. Her skin is soft and smooth against my tongue as I nip and tease my way toward her knees, kneading her muscles as I go.

"That was..." Alexis blinks a few times, still staring at me. "That was..."

"Amazing?" I'm happy to help her finish the sentence. "Fantastic?" My lips curve as I offer one more option. "Something you want to do again very soon?"

Alexis gives me a sly smile, lifting one shoulder. "I could be persuaded."

"Then I guess it's good I can be persuasive." I want to keep touching her, kissing her, but she straightens, pulling herself from my grip as the soft, satiated expression on her face shifts to something that has my stomach clenching with dread.

"But I feel like we should have a conversation before things get too..." Again, she fails to finish the sentence.

This time, I'm not helping her out. Not when I'm afraid I know where she's headed.

"Complicated."

The upset trying to squirm through my insides stalls out. That's not what I was expecting her to say. I was expecting something more like *serious* or *involved*. A word that would remind me this thing between us isn't a thing at all.

Complicated is different. *Complicated* I can work with.

"We passed complicated the night you climbed into that treehouse, Al." I run my hands over her skin, memorizing the curve of her hips. "Simplicity was gone the minute I touched you."

Alexis pinches her lower lip between her teeth, watching the path of my touch as it slides past the dip of her waist up to lift the weight of her tits. "Is that why you were jealous of Dillon?"

If her fingers weren't tangled in my T-shirt, pulling me closer, the sound of that prick's name on her lips when she's like this—naked and flushed—would have me jerking my dick until her skin was painted in my cum. In *me*.

Proving she will never be his.

But there's no judgment in Al's tone. The expression

on her face is soft and gentle, devoid of the hostility I expected to receive over the way I acted. It makes me want to believe she could understand me. To believe that once again Alexis will prove herself to be as different as I think she is.

I shake my head. "No." Wincing, I amend the statement. "It's not the *only* reason I'm jealous of him."

Alexis rubs her lips together, studying me for a minute. Then she tries to straighten away. "I feel like I should get dressed for this conversation."

I don't want her to walk away. I don't want to give myself time to think over what I'm about to do. I'll change my mind and go back to burying my shame. "Wait." I shuck my shirt, immediately dragging it over her head. "You can wear this." The solution solves two problems. It keeps her from giving me space I will fully take advantage of, and seeing her wearing something of mine soothes a little of the jealousy I need to explain.

Gently, I work the curls of her blonde hair free of the neckline, letting my fingers linger on the skin of her face. "You're so beautiful."

Al's lips twist, making me hold my breath as I wait to see where they'll end up. I never know with her. She's as likely to smile as she is to frown, but the expression on her face doesn't always go with what she feels. I've seen her scowl and roll her eyes over something I know damn well she found hilarious. I've also seen her smile when everything else on her face says she's contemplating murder.

But this time, it all matches up when her full mouth tips into a hint of a smile. "Thank you."

"Don't thank me. Thank yourself." I shift off my knees, pushing up onto the couch beside her. "I've seen your bathroom. I know all the work you put into looking the way you do." I can't resist lifting my hand to her face again, curving a section of hair behind the shell of one delicate ear. "But to be fair, you look just as good without all that."

One of her eyebrows angles and the hint of a smile teasing at me flattens into a serious line. I know she's pleased with my compliment, but Alexis gushing out emotion isn't ever going to happen. She's reserved. Serious.

Al's eyes narrow. "You're stalling."

She's also not afraid to call me out, but she's calm when she does it. Collected. Nonreactive. She doesn't feed the beast that lives inside me.

My chin tips in acknowledgment and agreement. "I am." Letting out a long breath, I lean back against the sofa, scrubbing one hand over my face. "I don't like to talk about this shit."

Alexis tucks one leg up, turning to angle her body in my direction before resting the side of her face against the cushion next to me. "What shit?"

I swallow hard. "My parents."

Al's eyes move over my face for a few seconds, reading whatever she sees there before responding. "I always wondered why we never met them."

My jaw tries to clench but I force it to relax. "You never met them because they're not like your family." I huff out a bitter laugh at the understatement of the century. "At all."

"Yeah, well." Alexis gives me a sad smile. "Right now my family isn't much like my family either."

I slide one hand onto her bare knee, giving it a gentle squeeze. "It'll be okay. You guys love each other and everyone in the situation has good intentions."

Again, Alexis studies me before responding. "Does that mean your parents didn't have good intentions?"

That's putting it lightly. "My parents were pretty much always out for themselves." For a while, I didn't see it. Not with my dad at least. I thought he was trying to help me through a shitty situation. Offering support and an explanation for the unraveling happening around me.

But his reasons for taking me under his wing were completely self-serving. He wanted me on his side. Wanted someone to tell him his words and actions were all justified and understandable. More than that, he wanted a kindred spirit. Someone who felt and thought exactly as he did.

"My parents were never happy together. I don't know if they ever even liked each other. I think they only got married because of me."

Alexis scoots a little closer, bringing her bent leg to rest against my thigh. "Is that why you were always over at our house? To get away from them?"

"Pretty much." My free hand toys with her hair, giving me something else to focus on as I lay out the framework of my shame. "By the time I was a teenager, my mom had fully checked out. She was done with my dad and acted like she was single."

Al's eyes widen. "Your mom cheated on your dad?"

My fingers tighten around her knee and I force them to relax, pulling in a slow breath. "All the time, and it made him lose his fucking mind."

One of Al's hands comes to rest over mine. "I can imagine."

She can't though, and I wish I could promise she never would.

"The more she did it, the worse he got." I close my eyes against the memory of how entrenched I became in their misery. "When I was learning to drive, he would take me out at night and we would go past all the places she liked to hang out." I don't want to continue, but I have to. Alexis deserves to know why I am the way I am. "Then we started following her. I knew it was wrong, but he was my dad, and he was so fucking miserable. I thought I was helping, but I wasn't. I was just feeding it."

And I'd continued feeding it for years. Yeah, it happened less and less, but it still happened. Every time I saw him, I would indulge his ranting. Listen as he spewed. Never once did I tell him he was wrong. Not a single time did I cut him off or tell him what a fucking embarrassment he was.

Because deep down, I knew chances were high I was exactly the same.

"Oh my God." Al's brows pinch as she stares at me, finally grasping just how fucked-up my formative years were. "That's awful."

I let her words sink in. Let them remind me why this can never be what I want it to be. "I shouldn't have done it. I know that."

Al's head bobs back, eyes widening. "What? You aren't the one at fault here." There's a hint of anger in her voice. "You were a kid. Your dad was taking advantage of that and using you for his own unhinged purposes." She leans close to me, the soft curve of one tit pressing into my bicep as her fingers wrap around my hand, gripping it tight. "Your dad should never have put you in that position. It wasn't fair. It wasn't right. And you probably did the best thing by never bringing him around, because if I knew what he'd done..." Her nostrils flare, eyes flashing. "Well," she scowls, "I probably would've told my mom, because she's way better at violence than I am."

The scenario she's suggesting easily plays out in my head. I can only imagine my dad's face if Babs ever went after him. "She can be pretty vicious, can't she?"

While Alexis has never paid much attention at our matches, her mother does, and I've witnessed Dan holding Babs back after a ref made a call she didn't agree with. I've seen her take on high school wrestling coaches and parents from the opposing team who got a little too mouthy.

Alexis smiles, the expression filled with fondness. "She's kinda like a Chihuahua when she's mad. More likely than not to bite you, and she will absolutely tear your ankles up." Her expression hardens. "And if she knew what your dad was doing, she would have taken his down to a nub."

19

She Does What She Wants

I'M TRYING TO reconcile the Gavin from my high school memories with the information he's giving me now, but it's not easy. The overgrown boy I remember was always smiling and easy-going. Not once did he give any hint that he was suffering.

And I hate that. I hate that shame and embarrassment forced him to hide his pain.

"Do you talk to either of your parents much now?" It takes a lot of work to keep my voice from showing how angry I am. I know myself well enough to recognize my face is probably giving me away, but I control what I can, and my face... That bitch does what she wants.

Gavin's eyes drop to where my hand holds his. "I just had dinner with my dad a few weeks ago. Up until now I've been taking him out for his birthday and Easter and Christmas."

There's something off in the way he said that—how he prefaced it. "Up until now?"

Gavin takes a breath so deep it lifts his shoulders and expands his already broad chest. As he lets it out, he turns his palm so it meets mine, our fingers lacing together. "I love him, but he's just so fucking miserable." Gavin lets his head drop back against the sofa. "The most fucked-up part is, I think he likes it." His voice lowers. "And I think he wants me to be just as miserable."

Again, I have to rein in my reaction, because what kind of shit-ass parent would want their child to be miserable? "That's fucked up."

Ok, so maybe I'm not great at reining in my reactions.

Gavin's eyes lift to mine. "It is, isn't it?"

I scoot a little closer, wanting to comfort him. "What he did was awful, and unfair." I hook one leg across his knee. "My parents are pissed as hell at Leo over Maddie Miller, but they would never want him to be unhappy. Even Christmas morning in the kitchen, they would have fought anyone who tried to hurt him." I huff out a little laugh. "And that probably includes Maddie Miller's ex-husband."

Sure, it would've gone against everything they were upset about, but my parents have always fought for us, and they always will. That's what parents do.

Some parents. Obviously not all. And that breaks my heart for Gavin. Makes my chest ache and my throat tight. But I know something that might make us both feel a little better. A fact he may not have fully internalized. "My parents would fight for you too."

Gavin takes another one of those deep, shoulder shifting breaths, the devastation I was hoping might dissipate lingering on his handsome face. "I know they would." His hand grips mine a little tighter. "That's why this thing we're doing should probably stop."

That has me mentally stumbling, but before my brain can even hit the metaphorical ground, I get pissed. "Are you saying you think I would push you out of my family?" I scoff, offended and irked and insulted. "What kind of an asshole do you think I am?"

"*No.*" The word jumps out of his mouth, loud and sharp. "That's not what I'm saying at all." His eyes move over mine like he's searching for something. "I don't think you would do that. That's not how you are." His hand comes to my face, smoothing across my skin then down my hair. "It's me. I'm the problem."

I'm trying to follow along, but I'm not picking up what he's putting down. "How are you the problem?"

His jaw clenches tight, a muscle in the side of his face twitching from the pressure. "I'm just like my dad, Al. If we did this and then it went wrong..." He pauses, voice dropping low when he says, "I can't trust myself to be around you after that."

He's giving me bits and pieces and I'm doing my best to put them together, but it almost seems like he's trying to say— "So you think you're jealous of Dillon because you're just like your dad?"

Gavin's expression doesn't change, but I can see a shift in his eyes. A pain that wasn't there before. One he's hidden so well I never suspected a thing. "If that's how I act now, can you imagine how I would be a month down the road? A year?"

I rub my lips together, because I'm messy enough that thinking about Gavin being jealous over me has my insides doing somersaults. "How would you be?" The question comes out breathy and soft, giving away how questionable my wants and desires are.

A flash of heat and possessiveness flares across his face and I fucking love it. I also hate it. I saw how devastated Gavin was at the prospect of being like his father. But, while I may not know much about that ass, I do know a lot about Gavin. More than enough to say with almost complete certainty he could never be like him.

One day he'll figure that out, but for now, maybe I can make things a little easier. Make him feel a little better.

"Then it's probably a good thing I couldn't be less attracted to Dillon." I wiggle around, dropping down to sit across his thighs, my knees braced at his hips. "I made the terrible mistake of going out with him once." Leaning close, I brace my hands against his shoulders and let my lips brush against his ear. "And let me assure you, he doesn't hold a candle to you."

Gavin sucks in a breath when I nip at the lobe of his

ear. His big hands grip my ass, palming it through the fabric of his shirt as he groans. "Al."

His voice is strained, and I smile against his skin as I leave a trail of wet kisses down his thick neck. "He is so far beneath you, there's no comparison." Letting my fingers slide down the front of his chest, I seek out the fly of his jeans and work it open. "I've never touched him, and he never touched me." I'm a little braver this time and I get his pants open pretty quickly. Fast enough Gavin doesn't seem to see what's coming. I slide one leg off the couch, planting my foot on the floor for balance as I drop to my knees between his feet, eyes on his face as I say, "I definitely would never have done this for him."

"*Al.*"

I've always hated that nickname, but that was because I thought it was a joke to him. But now— hearing it pass through his lips all ragged and rough—it might be my new favorite thing.

At least it is until I drag my tongue up the length of his cock, root to tip. That's when Gavin lets out a deep, rumbling groan, and *it* becomes my new favorite thing. So much so that my goal is figuring out how to get him to do it again.

And again.

Keeping my eyes on his face, I lean forward, parting my lips and slipping them over the flared head of his thick cock. The skin there is silky smooth and burning hot. Almost as hot as the smolder in Gavin's gaze as he stares down at me, fingers lacing in my hair to keep it out of my face as I swallow him down. He's a little too big for me to take as much of him as I want, but I keep trying, relaxing my throat as I bob over him, using the hand encircling his base to cover all the territory my mouth can't reach.

"Fuck, Alexis." His thumb traces the stretched line of my mouth, slicking through the spit easing my way. "Your lips look so pretty wrapped around my dick." His nostrils flare as he continues watching me. "I want to do so many things to you." One of his hands comes to wrap around mine, squeezing my grip tighter. "Fill every part of you."

A whimper works free at that, nearly smothered out by the mouthful of dick I'm navigating.

"Do you like the thought of that, Al?" Gavin leans closer, voice lowering. "Me being inside you?"

Holy mother of God. I like that Gavin moans. The sexy rumble when he groans. That he's vocal during moments like this. But the level of dirty talk he's bringing now?

I'm not sure I'll be able to keep from passing out if this is how he plans to be moving forward.

Gavin's hand slides to cradle the back of my head as the other keeps working the base of his dick with me. "Because that's what I'm gonna do if you don't stop me. I'm gonna spend every day trying to fill every part of you I can." His fingers fist in my hair, holding tight but not pulling. "Over and over again."

If I hadn't already gotten off twice tonight, that threat might have sent me over the edge.

And that's what it was. A threat.

Too bad I'm not scared of Gavin. He's big and he's strong and, yeah, he maybe has a little bit of a jealous streak.

But I will never be afraid of him. *Never*.

He's not capable of being the kind of man his father is. I know that.

Even if he doesn't.

"Fuck, Al." His fingers flex against my head as his cock twitches in my mouth. He tries to pull me off of him in spite of all his claims, but I don't let him.

"Sweetheart," his voice has a frantic edge, "you need to back off or I'm going to—"

I sink over him again, hollowing my cheeks to add a little more suction. That's all it takes, and the first hot splash of cum hits my tongue the same second Gavin lets out one of those deeply masculine groans I love so much. I keep working him, swallowing down everything he gives me. With one final lick, I pull free, a proud smile curving my lips as he gazes at me, dazed.

Gavin's silent for a minute, staring at me like he can't believe what just happened. Then he's pulling me close, tucking my body across his lap, cradling me against his chest. His breathing slowly returns to normal as he strokes my arms, my hair, my legs.

After a few, quiet minutes, Gavin pulls in a breath and dishes out what he likely thinks is another threat.

"You're never gonna get rid of me now, Al."

I smile up at him. "Don't threaten me with a good time." I can think of way worse things than having Gavin in my life. And maybe that's the best thing for him.

Because I clearly see what he doesn't.

20

Don't Drag David Bowie Into This

"THIS IS SO fucking good." I shovel in another helping of the lasagna Alexis ordered me from her favorite restaurant. "I can't believe I've never tried this place."

"I can't either." She stretches one leg across the couch so she can poke my thigh with her toe. "I'm honestly kind of disappointed in you." Alexis takes a bite of her own pasta, one hand coming to shield her mouth as she continues. "You live like, two blocks away from Bella Gusto. If I was that close, I'd be in a continuous carb coma."

I lift a brow. "How do you know where I live?"

Al's lips press tight together and a pink flush creeps over her cheeks. "My mom probably mentioned it."

I slide my takeout container onto the coffee table and scoot closer. "That sounds a little suspect, Al."

Her blue eyes widen. "You know where I live. Why shouldn't I know where you live?"

"I know where you live because I helped move your shit in." I slowly smile. "You know where I live because you're nosy."

Alexis sputters. "I'm not nosy."

My smile turns to a smirk because she walked right into what I say next. "Why else would you want to know where I live?" I hook one arm around her waist, pulling her body to mine. "Maybe because you had a crush on me?" I'm teasing her. Sliding back into the way things were when we were younger.

But the way her skin goes from pink to beet red as she tries to wiggle away makes me pause.

I stare in shock as she squirms free. "Wait. *Did* you have a crush on me?"

Her head snaps my way, eyes narrowed. "Like you didn't know."

Holy fuck. I stand, needing to be on my feet for this conversation. "Are you serious?" I'm not sure how I feel about this revelation.

What it means.

"Ugh." Alexis turns away from me, going to her kitchen. "Don't let it go to your head. I was sixteen and also in love with David Bowie."

My brows pinch together. "He's dead." I glance down my front, comparing my physique to the androgynous rocker's. "And scrawny."

"Two more reasons you shouldn't let it go to your head." Al collects the container of cream cake from the counter. "Obviously my standards are extremely flexible."

"I—" My words are cut off when my cell starts to ring in my pocket. I pull it out and my stomach drops at the name displayed across the screen. I don't want to answer it, but if I don't, it'll just keep ringing.

Bracing, I swipe across the screen then press it to my ear. "Hey, Leo."

Al's eyes widen and her skin pales.

I get it.

"Seems like someone found another way home." Leo's tone is gloating. "You're welcome for that. I told you going out was a great fucking idea."

I doubt he'd be thanking me if he knew who took me home.

Leo's a good guy. A great friend. He wants me to be happy. But there are limits, and I have to guess fucking his little sister is a hard line. Not that I've fucked Alexis.

Yet.

"Sorry to disappear on you guys. Something came up." I rake one hand through my hair, torn between guilt and shame. "Everyone get home okay?"

"They're all in their beds, safe and sound." Leo snorts. "And jealous as fuck of you."

"Not you?" I know more than a few of the guys on our team are itching for something beyond the one-night stands I'm famous for. Something more permanent. And all signs are pointing to Leo and Maddie Miller having something permanent.

211

"My personal life is none of their business," Leo snaps. "The less people know about me and Maddie's relationship, the safer she'll be."

I've never seen Leo like this over a woman, and it takes me aback. It also worries me. "Has something else happened with her husband?"

"*Ex*-fucking-husband." Leo practically yells through the line. He's loud enough Alexis hears and her brows climb her forehead in response.

Seems like she's as surprised as I am over Leo's outburst.

"Last night he started calling every five minutes. Maddie turned her phone off, and when she checked it this morning her voicemail was full." Leo's words are sharp. "If I ever get my hands on him again—"

"I think you should work on making sure that doesn't happen." I'm starting to see just how in over his head Leo is. Why Dan and Babs are so upset. "You should probably be as uninvolved in that mess as possible."

Leo scoffs. "Are you fucking kidding me?" His voice amps up—both in pitch and in volume. "You're supposed to be on my side, man."

"I am on your side." I keep my tone calm, like I'm placating a toddler. "I just know how easy it is to get tunnel vision when you care about someone." My eyes drift to where Alexis stands, watching me with an odd look on her face. "It can lead to stupid decisions."

I have zero room to judge him. Hell, I might as well

be living in a glass house because I'm making my share of stupid decisions. And—like Leo—I can't seem to stop.

"Keeping Maddie safe from that bastard will never be a stupid decision." Leo sounds disgusted, but I don't know if it's with me or Maddie's ex. "I gotta go." He doesn't say goodbye, just hangs up.

So he was disgusted with me then.

I release a slow breath, letting my head fall back. As if I hadn't already fucked up enough, now I've made Leo feel even more alone.

"You didn't say anything wrong." Al's words are gentle. Soft. "I know he feels like everyone's against him, but he'll figure out we're not soon enough." Alexis rests one hand in the center of my chest. "Give him some time to cool down. Once he does, he'll realize you really are on his side."

I drop my eyes to where Alexis stands in front of me. "Am I?" I motion around her apartment. "Because it looks a whole hell of a lot like I'm fucking around with his sister behind his back." I scrub one hand over my face, as frustrated with myself and my situation as I am with Leo and his. "And he's so wound up he's going to lose his shit when he finds out." The words are out of my mouth before I fully comprehend what I'm saying.

I didn't say *if*. I said *when*. Like there is some sort of scenario where Leo can discover what's going on. Like there's some way I can have it all. The family I've claimed as my own. My best friend.

And Alexis.

I don't think it's possible. Especially not now.

But Alexis doesn't seem bothered the way I am. She lifts one shoulder and lets it drop. "Like he said. What goes on in someone's personal life is no one else's business." Her chin tips higher, making her look stunningly defiant. "And that includes us."

Could it really be that simple? Can Alexis and I do what we want and keep it between us? "He did say that, didn't he?"

Al's lips curve into a slow smile. "Yes, he did." Her smile turns into a snarl. "But I am kinda with him on wanting to get my hands on Maddie's ex-husband. I've only met her a time or two, but she always seemed really sweet. I can't imagine what sort of douche canoe would threaten someone like her." Her eyes narrow, nostrils flaring. "I probably couldn't do much, but I'm pretty sure I could stab at least one eyeball out."

I start to chuckle, the vision of Alexis as a whirlwind of rage and violence way cuter than I will ever admit to her, but then my stomach drops.

Because I fucking forgot there's a one-eyed lizard trapped in my bathroom.

"I gotta go." This happens every fucking time. I get my hands on Alexis and everything else falls out of my fucking brain. All I see is her. All I want is her. All I think about is her. It's hazardous for my health, my friendships, and now, my newly remodeled bathroom.

Alexis follows behind me, face filled with concern. "What's wrong?"

I pause, turning to her so I can cradle her face in my hands. "It's a long story, but there's a five-foot long, one-eyed lizard in my bathroom, and I need to go take care of it."

Al blinks at me a second, then she starts to laugh, wiping at the corner of one watering eye. After a few seconds, she sobers, brows pinching. "Oh my God. You're serious."

"Unfortunately, I am." I lean in, catching her lips with mine in a kiss that escalates quickly. It takes everything I have to pull away, but it has to happen. Al and I might be able to keep this thing between us, but staying the night will still have very real consequences. As much as I want to hold her close and wake up to her sleepy face, I can't leave Cilantro alone with Popeye the one-eyed dinosaur that long. Not when it could chew through the door for all I know.

But—

"You could come with me." The offer slides free, and once it's out there I hold my breath, anticipation and fear fighting for the upper hand.

So far it's always been me coming to Alexis. Me showing up on her doorstep. Me seeking her out in the bar.

This would be her coming to me. With me. To my home.

To my bed.

Alexis blinks at me a few times, lips parted, blonde brows pinched in confusion. "You want me to come home with you?"

There's too much surprise in her voice. It makes me wonder how she views this thing we've got going on. "I do."

Alexis nibbles on her lower lip, uncertainty replacing the confusion that pinched her pretty face. "I'm not sure how I feel about dealing with your lizard."

Al is a serious person. Has been forever. She's not one to joke around, but she's great at accidentally setting me up to tease her, and I've never been good at resisting it. Even now. "You don't have to deal with my lizard. Promise." I reach for her, pulling her close. "We can just cuddle."

It takes a couple beats for her to get it, but then she snorts, rolling her eyes. It's as amused as she gets, and after years of women fake laughing at anything I say, I soak up her honest reaction.

Then I can't help but ask, "Is that a yes?"

Alexis shakes her head, but the exasperated look on her face tells me this is another contradictory reaction. "Fine." She smooths one hand over the front of my shirt. "But I'm bringing a change of clothes." Her eyes level on my face, a hint of a smile tipping her lips. "Just in case you get trigger happy."

I let her go but flatten my palm at the small of her back to urge her in the direction of the bedroom. "You're never going to let me live that down, are you?"

Alexis gives me an indignant look over one shoulder. "That dress was brand-new."

I chuckle. "I guess I should have aimed for your scarf then since that thing is old as hell."

Al's steps come to a halt, her body stiffening the tiniest bit. Something I said was wrong, but I'm not sure how. "What's the matter?"

Alexis peeks at me again over one shoulder, but this time she shakes her head. "Nothing."

She's shutting me out. It's there in her closed-off expression. The flat line of her lips. Al's reactions might not always be easy to read, but they do give her up eventually. Some faster than others.

This time they outed her at record speed.

I move toward her, not willing to accept her words. "Tell me." It seems like Alexis likes to withhold information—like how she had a crush on me—and I don't want secrets between us.

I don't know if I could handle it.

She blows out a dramatic sigh, eyes lifting to the ceiling. "Fine."

She crosses her arms in a way some people might read as irritation, but the hint of vulnerability that flashes across her face reveals the truth.

"My Grandma Dorothy made me that scarf." She scowls at me. "So you better keep your fluids away from it."

21

Confession Equals Connection

I DON'T TALK about my Grandma Dot very much. Not because I didn't love her—I worshiped her.

I don't talk about her because she's gone and I will never get another memory with her, so I guard them. Keep them to myself. For myself. But I've accidentally opened that can of worms and Gavin doesn't seem interested in letting me snap the lid back in place.

He gives me a slow nod. "Yeah, I'm going to go ahead and agree that is the plan of action we should take, because Granny D would come back to life and murder me for daring to deface something she made you."

My throat goes tight when Gavin says the nickname he gave her. She pretended like she hated it, but I knew the truth. My grandma always had a soft spot for him. I can't blame her. She and I were so much alike, and it seems our fondness for giant goofy rugby players is yet another similarity between us.

Gavin reaches up, sliding his fingers through my hair as he pushes it behind my shoulders. "Did you know Granny D is the reason I can cook?" His lips curve into a tender smile. "My parents were wrapped up in their own shit, so I was on my own in a lot of ways. When your grandma found out about the home ec fire incident, she made it her personal mission to teach me."

I hold my breath as he continues offering me the most precious gift anyone's ever given me. More of the woman I loved with my entire heart.

"I went over there once a week my whole junior year, and she taught me how to make all kinds of shit." His voice softens as he studies my face. "She was fucking awesome."

I nod, swallowing hard around the lump in my throat. "She was."

Grandma Dot was the only person who ever really understood me. She never expected me to be more than I was. Never got confused when I didn't react to things a certain way or enjoy certain activities. That's probably because she was just like me, or I was just like her. We were two peas in an introverted pod surrounded by a loud, outgoing family.

Gavin's eyes move over my face, one thumb coming to swipe at a tear I didn't notice had dropped free. "You should come home with me, Al." His voice is soft and tender. "I've got something I think you'll want to see."

This time I agree easily. Not because I want to see whatever it is Gavin wants to show me, but because for the first time in a long time, I feel understood. Appreciated.

Safe.

My mother loved my grandmother—I know that. But she never understood her—never understood me. I'm starting to think Gavin does, and that's a rare thing for me. "Okay."

Gavin gives me a tender smile before turning me toward my room, giving my ass a little swat, and telling me to hurry.

I grab a bag and get to work. I changed into my pajamas while we were waiting for dinner, so all I need is some clothes for tomorrow. After adding a few toiletries and my toothbrush, I come out to the living room to find him holding something that confirms my suspicions.

Gavin comes to stand in front of me, gently winding my most prized possession around my neck. His big hands stroke over the thinning weave of the yarn with an almost reverent touch. "Now I see why you were less than impressed with the scarf I got you."

"The scarf you gave me is beautiful." I defend his gift immediately. Not just because it's cashmere and gorgeous, but because he put thought into it. Chose something he knew I would like.

"Anyone can buy a scarf off the rack, Al." His big hands are still gently holding the scarf my grandma

221

made me. "It takes a lot of love for someone to spend hours of their life making a gift."

Again Gavin hits the nail on the head. Seems to understand exactly why the scarf is so important to me. It's not simply because it came from my grandma, but because it is a physical embodiment of her love for me.

He tips his head to the door. "You ready to go?"

My eyes are burning again, and my throat is still tight, so I just smile, giving the surprisingly sentimental man in front of me a little nod.

Gavin takes my bag, hooking the floral printed overnight tote onto one shoulder, then slips his hand around mine. After snagging my keys off the counter, he opens the door. I start to follow him out, but then stop.

"Hang on." I turn, rushing back to collect the rest of our dinner and dessert, stacking the foam boxes into the paper bag they came in before hurrying back to his side. This time I'm the one taking his hand, and Gavin looks down at where my fingers weave between his, studying them for a second before tugging me out into the hall.

When we reach my car, he doesn't even ask, just loads me into the passenger side then drops my bag into the back seat and climbs behind the wheel. The sight of him in my small crossover is still hilarious, and I huff out a little laugh over it.

"Yeah, yeah. I know." He turns out of the parking lot. "I'm sure everyone thinks I bought my Hummer because it's flashy, but I just wanted to drive without getting a fucking leg cramp and a crick in my neck."

I tip my head his direction, offering a disbelieving look. "You can admit you also like that it's flashy." My stern expression melts into a smile. I can't help it. "Especially to me, because we both know I like pretty things."

Gavin glances my way, giving me a slow grin. "You *are* a pretty thing, Al." He turns back to the road before confessing, "And I do kinda like that it's flashy."

I look over where he sits in the driver's seat, wondering. "Do I get to drive your car since you get to drive mine?"

Gavin barks out a laugh, and it has me expecting him to say no. But—like he's in the habit of doing—Gavin surprises me. "I would love to see you behind the wheel of my Hummer, Al." He gives my body the same appraising look I just gave his. "You might need a booster seat though."

I scoff in mock outrage. "I'm not that short."

"To me, everyone is that short." Gavin's tone is teasing, and it's hard for me to remember how much I used to hate it.

"That's because you're an overgrown beast." I'm terrible at teasing him back, but I give it a try even though it still comes off serious and dry.

Gavin sits up as straight as my small crossover will allow, giving me a wink. "Flattery will get you everywhere with me."

"Only you would take that as a compliment."

"Not true." Gavin's eyes come my way again. "Your brother would too."

The reminder of Leo sobers me a little. "I'm worried about him."

Gavin's jaw sets. "It's none of Leo's business what we do."

"I didn't mean that way. I don't give a shit what Leo thinks about my personal life." I gave that up back in college when he was so clearly against Hugo. Now I know he wasn't the only one. "I'm talking about him and Maddie Miller."

A little of the tension bleeds from Gavin's body, his shoulders easing down. "I'm worried too." He gives me a sidelong glance but doesn't fully look my way. "I know how crazy men can get over the women they care about." Gavin's frame stiffens. Like he's waiting to see how I respond.

I can admit, I don't know a whole lot about fucked-up relationships. My parents have a great marriage. The one boyfriend I had didn't treat me badly, just indifferent. But I do know a thing or two about human nature. I'm not a big talker, but I am a big listener. And I people watch better than anyone I know.

"Leo's situation is very different from the one your parents had, but feeling insecure can bring out the worst in people." I think back to the guy at the bar and his knee-jerk response to being shut down. "Leo's probably not worried about Maddie dumping him, but he is scared he'll lose her. Just in a different way." One that's way more terrifying than a simple breakup.

"I know I pissed him off tonight, but I wanted him to think this through. Reacting is easy. Deciding how to handle shit is hard." Gavin's hands flex against the steering wheel. "I can't judge him for what he's doing, though, because I don't think a lot of shit through either."

"You mean like inviting me for a sleepover?" I try to make it sound like sarcasm but fail epically. Even when I'm joking I sound serious, but this time I'm not making an attempt at teasing.

It's actually insecurity running my mouth. Gavin's a player. I knew that going into this and was fine with it. But Gavin doesn't seem to be playing, and I don't know what to do with that.

"I've spent way too much time imagining you in my bed to claim I haven't thought this through, Al." Gavin's gaze swings my way, devouring me as we wait at the light to turn onto the road where he lives. "It might be the first thing I've thought through in a long fucking time."

My belly flips at the sincerity in his tone, fluttering around my insides as his dark eyes hold mine. I've been ignoring the connection pulling us closer and closer. Pretending this was only some fun little fling. Just a couple of people making each other feel good. Scratching itches.

But it's not. And as the light switches to green and

we start moving, my little SUV slowing as we reach our destination, I have to consider my brother might not be the only one in over his head.

It's dark enough outside I don't get a great look at Gavin's building, but it doesn't take more than a glimpse to tell it's nice. I knew where it was located, but since it's on a dead-end road, the multi-story structure isn't in a spot I'd need to pass. And, even though I was curious about the place Gavin called home, I had the willpower and self-restraint to keep my nosy ass to myself.

It seems like that's the extent of what I possess where Gavin is concerned though, considering I always end up naked when we're alone together.

We pull into the underground garage before I see much more than the sleek reflection of giant windows spanning the six or seven floors. Gavin slides my SUV into the spot next to his Hummer, then shuts off the engine.

He turns to me. "Ready to face the dinosaur?"

"Uhh." I glance toward the elevator. "I thought you had something you wanted to show me." My eyes narrow. "It's not just your damn lizard, is it?"

"It's not just my lizard. I really do have something to show you, but we need to secure the premises first." Gavin gives me a wink as he opens his door. "Don't worry. I'll keep you safe."

I trust him—really I do—but the dinosaur comment has me... Concerned.

By the time we're standing in front of his door my

stomach is in knots. My parents aren't really pet people, so I haven't spent much time around the cute cuddlies most people have in their lives.

Let alone the ones with scales.

"I'll go in first." Gavin punches a code into the fancy keypad on the door. "Stay behind me."

I balk. "I thought you said it was locked in the bathroom?"

As much as I want to see Gavin's home—and take him up on that cuddling offer—I'm regretting my decision to tag along.

"It should be." Gavin gives me zero time to prepare before opening the door.

Fear has me latching onto the back of his shirt, using him as a shield as I follow him inside. My eyes dart around the space, but I'm not really seeing anything. Not when I'm worried a freaking *dinosaur* is going to jump out at me any second.

I stick to Gavin like glue, white knuckling the cotton fabric stretched across his broad back. When we come to a stop, I peek around him. My stomach clenches at the sight of what must be the door to the bathroom in question.

"Ready?" Gavin lifts a brow at me.

"No."

I don't have to think about it. When my friends find out I willingly came within ten feet of a lizard, they're going to take me to the hospital, sure I've been concussed.

Gavin grins. "Too bad." He opens the door without doing a countdown or anything, and I get my first glimpse of his dinosaur.

"Holy shit." The thing is almost as long as I am, but way better at climbing, because it's currently perched on the shower curtain rod. Its head turns our way, revealing a scarred mess where one eyeball should be. A collection of additional scars are scattered across its muddy green hide. "Was it in a fight?"

Gavin slowly walks into the room and I have no choice but to follow. "I think it was someone's pet and got too big so they set it free. It's probably been on its own for a while, and there's no telling what happened to it."

"Awe." A pang of sympathy hits me for the huge green monstrosity watching us with a squinted eye. "Why would someone do that?"

"People suck, Al." Gavin stops in front of the tub/shower combo. "They bite off more than they can chew and walk away when it gets to be too much."

I gasp when the lizard reaches one taloned hand toward Gavin. Then I gasp again when Gavin reaches back, gently collecting the reptile into his arms.

"Should you be holding it?"

Gavin runs one big hand down the lizard's back, flattening out the pokey things growing along its spine. "He seems to like it."

Gavin seems to know what he's talking about. The lizard leans into his touch, eye closing as he soaks up the affection. "He does kinda seem like he's used to being handled."

Gavin turns away from the shower, scanning the room. "That's why I thought he was probably someone's pet." He pauses to look over the counter, peering into the two bowls sitting on the granite surface. "You ate everything I gave you, didn't you, buddy?"

I swallow hard, afraid to look in the bowl because there might be remnants of the lizard's meal. "What did you feed him?" I give the giant beast in Gavin's arms a sidelong glance. "He looks like he could eat me."

Gavin's mouth slides into a slow smile, his voice dropping dangerously low when he says, "I'm the only one who gets to eat you, Al."

22

She's Not For Everyone

AL'S FLUSHED SKIN has my dick hard in a flash, as all sorts of dirty thoughts race through my head. Thoughts that involve her sprawled across my mattress, watching me with those wide eyes, her cheeks pink as I bury myself to the hilt in her warm, welcoming body.

That's got to be why I don't notice Cilantro strolling into the bathroom. It's also why the sound of my cat's low growl doesn't immediately register. Now that I've finally given in, I'm so wrapped up in the possibility of Alexis being mine, it's not until the iguana in my arms jumps to the floor that I notice there's a problem.

Al's shrill scream fills the bathroom as she backs away, practically climbing up onto the double vanity as the lizard takes off after my cat. I have no choice but to follow them out, uncertain which of the two I'll have to save. My money is on Cilantro getting the upper hand.

Paw? But then again, I haven't seen all the lizard brings to the table. He might be a scrappy bastard.

Cilantro darts across the hall and into my bedroom, nothing but a black blur as she screeches at the top of her lungs. The iguana is shockingly fast for as old as it looks, long claws scratching against the floor as it scurries after her.

"Was that your cat?"

I turn to find Alexis behind me, her small body tucked behind my back, fingers once again fisted in my shirt. Having her use me for protection is embarrassingly satisfying and sends my chest puffing. "Yeah. She's pretty feral."

Al's brows lift and her head tips to one side. "Honestly, that's probably gonna work in her favor."

She's right. Cilantro can likely take care of herself, but I'll feel like a complete asshole if she mauls a lizard who's already been torn up a few times in its life.

Al's grip on me suddenly tightens and she screams again, her short frame scrambling up my back until her arms are wrapped around my neck so tight I can barely breathe. I press one hand against her ass, hefting her higher just as Cilantro races out of the bedroom and between my legs, lizard still in pursuit.

I pivot, following them down the hall, but only make it a few steps into the living room where they disappeared before my front door flies open and my neighbor races in, an umbrella gripped in one hand and his wife shoved behind his back with the other. "What the bloody hell is going on in here?" Fynn's wild eyes snap around my apartment before finally coming to rest on where Alexis clings to my back, her short legs hooked at my waist. His dark brows lift and the arm holding the umbrella drops. "Have we interrupted?"

I'd laugh if I wasn't worried there was about to be bloodshed in my condo. "This isn't a sex thing, asshole." I go back to my task of catching the iguana. "That little problem I handled for you earlier is about to get its face scratched off by my cat."

Alexis clings to me, squealing a little as I drop to my hands and knees so I can see under the furniture. "It's not your cat you're worried about?" Her sweet voice in my ear and the press of her tits against my back threatens to distract me, but somehow I manage to stay focused.

I deserve a fucking award for that.

"Cilantro is pretty good at taking care of herself." The sound of my cat's slow growl sends me crawling toward the sofa. "I'll feel bad if she hurts that fucking lizard though."

Guilt makes me move faster, the slight weight of Alexis barely slowing me down as I reach the couch. Working quickly, I grip the arm with one hand and shove it away from the wall. There, standing face-to-face, are my cat and the lizard. Both are completely still, but I know it's only a matter of time before one of them makes a move.

"Al, I'm gonna need your help on this one."

Alexis shakes her head, arms tightening at my neck. "Nope. Not happening."

"Do you want to witness a bloodbath?" I lean to one side, trying to slip her off. "Because if we don't get these two apart, that's what's gonna happen."

Alexis hits the floor with a little grunt and huffs out a breath. "Fine. But I get the cat."

"Trust me when I tell you the lizard is the lesser of two evils." I inch closer to the face-off. "If you try to grab Cilantro, you're going to be the one involved in a bloodbath."

Alexis pushes up on her knees, full lips pressing into a confused frown. "Why is your cat named Cilantro?"

As cute as Alexis looks with her hair wild and her brows pinched, I cannot take my focus off my cat. "Because she's not for everyone."

She snorts. "That's actually kinda brilliant." After a very loud, very dramatic sigh, Alexis finally scoots behind me in the general direction of the lizard. "If this thing bites me, I'm going to kill you."

"If it bites you, I will let you kill me." I'm now within grabbing distance of Cilantro, but I'm afraid if I scoop her up, the lizard will leap. I need Alexis to grab the lizard the same time I grab the cat. "On the count of three."

"How about ten?" Alexis wiggles her fingers, cringing as she prepares.

"One. Two." I risk taking my eyes off Cilantro to give Alexis an encouraging smile before I say, "three."

To my surprise, Alexis doesn't hesitate. She scoops up the lizard and spins away, shuffling across the wood floor on her knees. I tuck Cilantro into one arm, smoothing along her head as I try to calm her down. "I'm sorry. I should have been more careful."

Alexis makes a little squeaking sound and I hurry her way. She's propped against one of my recliners, legs out in front of her, eyes wide, with the lizard stretched up her middle and its head resting on her shoulder. Almost the same way most people hold a baby.

She cringes, mouth tight and teeth clenched, as she awkwardly pats it on the back. "There, there."

"Uhhhh." Valerie looks from me to Alexis. "I'm still confused."

I didn't expect to be introducing Alexis to my neighbors yet. I was hoping for a little time to ease them into my new situation. Not because I didn't want them to know. I just didn't want them to be weird about it in front of Alexis. And considering this is the first time they've actually seen me with a woman, they're gonna be weird about it.

Fynn slowly smiles. "I'm not." He hooks one arm around Valerie's shoulders. "Come on, Darling. You can meet Gavin's new friend some other time."

My neighbor leads his wife out of my condo, and I breathe out a sigh of relief when the door closes behind them. I'm going to owe him a beer. Or five.

"I'm guessing those are your neighbors?" Alexis gives the lizard another pet. "It's nice that they were ready to defend you."

"Fynn's a good guy. He and I have been friends for a while." I carry Cilantro to the spare bedroom, setting her inside before shutting her in. It's basically her room, so her food and water and litter box are already inside. She's not used to having the door closed, but she'll be fine until I figure out what in the heck to do with old one-eye.

I come back to the living room to find Alexis on her feet, looking comically overwhelmed by the gigantic lizard in her arms. "You want me to take him?"

Alexis tucks her chin to peek down at the beast. "I think he's asleep."

"Yeah. He fell asleep on me earlier. I think he's had a rough go of it." I recount the events of my afternoon, filling Alexis in on how I came to be in possession of a green iguana. When I tell her how it got into Fynn and Val's condo, her eyes immediately jump to my own balcony.

"It's locked." I move in and gently take the lizard from her arms. "I think I'm going to put him back in the bathroom for tonight." If Cilantro's locked up, he has to be locked up too. It's only fair.

Alexis follows behind me, still looking confused by the whole situation. "So why didn't Valerie call a lizard catcher or something? They have to exist. There's all kinds of weird reptiles in Florida."

After settling the sleeping iguana onto the rug in front of the sink, I close the door. "She did, and they said green iguanas are an invasive species, so they would kill it."

Al's eyes fix on the bathroom door, her expression somber. "Well that's not very nice."

"It's not." I rest one palm against her back, directing her to the living room. "That's why Valerie came to me."

Al's head snaps my way, brows jumping up. "Because she thinks you *are* nice?" If I didn't know Alexis so well, I wouldn't notice the slight softening of her lips or the hint of a sparkle in her eyes. I would think she was being a bitch. And I hate to think how many men have had that same exact thought about her. Then again, it's likely the only thing that kept me from having to look at more pricks like Huge-nose. Hating their existence. Sick at the sight of them with her because I know they're not good enough.

I'm not good enough either, but at least I know it.

"I'm nice enough I didn't eat your Italian cream cake even though it's my favorite." I pull Alexis close, running my hands down the curved lines of her small frame. "Thank you for braving my lizard."

The twinkle of mischief in her eyes grows. "I don't mind at all." She angles an eyebrow at me. "This lizard was way more agreeable than the other one I had to deal with. Plus, it didn't ruin my clothes."

"If you're going to keep holding that over my head, I might as well go around ruining everything you own." I press my hips against her so she can feel the rigid line of my dick. "I might start with these pajamas."

Al's eyes widen. "You better not."

The threat in her tone makes me think Alexis is more like her mother than she realizes. Not so much in personality, but temperament. I'm willing to wager that given the right set of circumstances, Alexis would be just as vicious as the woman who raised her.

"I should probably behave myself since now you know all it takes is a couple screams to make my neighbors take advantage of the keycode I gave them."

Alexis narrows her eyes. "I'm a little concerned there hasn't been screaming in your condo before now." She tips her head. "It's making me reconsider my decision to spend the night."

A bark of laughter breaks free, a level of happiness I've never experienced consuming me. I didn't know how much it bothered me that I couldn't tease Alexis anymore. Having her not only allow my teasing, but also dish out some of her own, is fucking amazing.

Almost as amazing as it's going to be having her in my bed tonight.

Even though I have no plans for any more screaming.

I scoop her up, carrying her down the hall. "Too late to change your mind now." I bump the door to my bedroom open wider, going straight to the king-sized bed lined against one wall and dumping her into the center of the mattress.

Alexis lets out a little squeal as she flails around. "You can't just throw me around."

"I can. I think I've proven that." Grabbing the covers, I yank them back, shucking my clothes before sliding beneath the blankets in nothing but my briefs. "Now get your cute ass under here so we can cuddle."

23

The Cuddle Conundrum

CUDDLE?

Gavin really only wants to *cuddle*?

I'm thrown off enough by his request that I auto-matically wiggle my way beneath the light layer of blanket and sheet covering his bed. I'm barely in place before he hooks one thick arm around my waist and pulls me into his side, tucking my body tight against his and planting a kiss on my forehead.

Huh. I guess he does just want to cuddle. I'm not sure how I feel about that.

Messing around is one thing. Scratching itches and fulfilling needs can be only that. Just two people helping each other find physical release. Cuddling is a whole different ball game. One that is way more dangerous than rugby could ever be.

When he spent the night at my apartment, I was

nearly comatose as he tucked me into bed, and we both pretty much stayed on our respective sides.

That does not seem to be in the plans for tonight.

Gavin's thick arm keeps me close as he grabs the remote from his nightstand and switches on the giant television mounted to the wall across from us. It fills the room with a gentle glow and I finally have the chance to look around part of Gavin's home without worrying I'm about to be accosted by a lizard or feral cat.

It's pretty bare bones. There's no headboard or footboard on his bed, just a mattress, albeit a nice one. I splurged on my own bed, but it's still nowhere near as comfortable as the cloud of angel fluff Gavin owns. The sheets are just as nice. They're crisp and smooth and they smell fresh and clean.

Besides the amazing bed, there's only a chest of drawers and the humongous television to round out the room. He doesn't even have a rug covering the hardwood floor. There's also no blinds on the floor-to-ceiling windows lining one whole side of the room.

"What do you want to watch?" Gavin flips through the menu on the screen, stopping when he gets to a specific row of shows. "*Maid to Murder, The Santa Stalker, Killer in the Courthouse...*" He rattles off a few options as he continues down the line.

I crane my neck to look at him. "How did you know I liked to watch—"

"Creepy shit that would give most people nightmares?" He lifts an eyebrow at me. "I saw the 'recently watched' list on your bedroom TV." His lips quirk. "Kind of a weird way to wind down at night, but I have a one-eyed lizard in my bathroom, so I don't think I have room to judge anyone for anything."

———

WAKING UP NEXT to Gavin is just as strange the second time it happens. Both because he's basically wrapped around me, and because I'm not in my own bed.

"Morning." His voice is sleepy and soft in my ear. "How did you sleep?"

I peek at him from the corner of one eye. "I guess I know how my stuffed animals felt when I was a kid now."

Gavin chuckles, the deep sound reverberating through his chest and into my right side where he's pressed against me. "Funny."

"You're the only person who thinks so." No one has ever accused me of being funny. I don't try to be. I know it's not my skill set. Organization? Styling? Solving a cold case through a television screen? Those are things I'm good at.

"Most people just don't get your sense of humor."

I peek his way again, angling a brow. "And you do?"

Gavin shifts around, bracing one bent arm against the pillow before propping his head on his hand. "I do."

He sounds so confident. So certain of the very thing

that made me come here in the first place. Sure, the possibility of finally having sex with the man I've spent a good part of my life lusting after was a big draw too, but the real reason I agreed was because Gavin makes me feel understood.

And that doesn't happen for me much.

I'm not sure how to respond since I'm not faced with this scenario often, but it turns out I don't have to. Because a loud crash from somewhere else in the condo has both of us sitting up straight.

"What was that?"

"I'll give you two guesses." Gavin is off the bed before I can blink, the sight of him in nothing but his underwear making my belly flip because all of that man muscle was pressed against me all night long. Unfortunately none of it went inside me, but I guess you can't have it all.

Sliding off the mattress, I creep behind him, glancing around as I follow him down the hall. His condo is bigger than I initially thought, with a third bedroom right across from the master. It's set up as a super sparse office, with nothing but a bare desk and a cheap rolling chair. The door to the second bedroom is closed since it currently has a cat inside, and the full bathroom across the hall is the same, but because of a one-eyed lizard. I get a peek at the living room as we pause in front of the closed doors, and now that I'm not in a full panic chasing wild animals, I can see it is just as basic as everything else.

"Have you lived here for a long time?" I'm trying to remember when he moved in, but it must not be as long ago as I think. Surely Gavin would have bought a dining room table by now if he'd been here any length of time.

He shrugs. "A couple years, I guess."

That has my head bobbing back in surprise. "Two years?" I turn again to the large open area that should consist of the living room and a dining room space. All it has is a sofa, a couple recliners, and a giant television like the one in his bedroom. "Why don't you have more stuff?"

"Because I'm a guy, Al." Gavin cracks the door of the bathroom. "I don't know how to pick shit like that." He swings the door wider, stepping in.

I follow him in and find the bathroom looks exactly as it did last night. Not a thing is out of place, and there's an iguana on the shower curtain rod. "Looks like whatever happened is behind door number two."

Gavin turns, shooting me a smirk. "So I told you once you were funny and now you're going to be a comedian?"

I roll my eyes, smothering out a smile. "Fuck you."

Gavin reaches for me, pulling me close. "That doesn't sound like a bad idea, but we've got some shit to deal with right now, so you're going to have to wait."

For some reason that irritates me. "When have you ever made a woman wait to have sex with you?"

The minute the words clear my lips I feel bad. I really don't judge Gavin for what he's done before me.

I'm just starting to get a little bitter he hasn't also done it with me.

But Gavin doesn't seem offended by my outburst. His expression is soft and a little perplexed as he reaches up to run a finger along the line of my jaw, pausing under my chin to tip my face back. "Never. You are the first." He leans closer until his lips almost touch mine. "You have always been the exception, Al."

I'm holding my breath, ready to be kissed.

But then freaking Cilantro has to try to tear the building down with her own four paws again.

Gavin closes his eyes, letting out a slow breath. "I'm kind of afraid of what's behind that door."

"Yeah. It doesn't sound like Cilantro is a big fan of your new pet." I think through the entire situation. "Or me. Either way, she's pretty pissed off about someone else being in her house."

"She's used to having me all to herself." He gives me a slow, sexy smile. "Luckily, there's a lot of me to go around."

From the other bedroom, Cilantro lets out a blood curdling scream and then there's another crash. "I believe she disagrees strongly."

"That's her entire personality in a nutshell." After another deep breath, Gavin turns to the door and cracks it open. It's barely ajar when a pink nose shoves in the gap, pushing it wider so a skinny, sleek body can wiggle out.

I take a step back, just in case I'm the one his cat's

pissed at. Cilantro races past Gavin, tossing a hiss his direction, before winding her way around my ankles. I freeze, scared she'll suddenly use her danger mittens to climb me like a tree so she can scratch my eyeballs out, leaving me looking like the lizard one room over.

But she doesn't. Cilantro just tips her head back, looks at me with wide golden eyes and lets out the sweetest sounding meow.

I sense a trap. The minute I reach for her she's going to go all Jekyll and Hyde on me. I know it.

But then she starts to purr, rubbing her little face against my shin, and I feel bad. She was locked in that room all night, and is probably used to sleeping next to Gavin.

I wonder if he uses her like a teddy bear too.

A pang of something shoots through my gut, making me press a hand to my middle. What the fuck? Am I jealous of a cat?

Cilantro gives me another sweet meow, and I bend down, intending to just pat her head. But the second I get close, she stretches up, paws resting against my thigh like she's reaching for me. Like she wants me to hold her.

And I'm a dumbass sucker, because I do it. I pick up the feral cat named after dish soap herbs.

I am smart enough to close my eyes, though. Just in case.

But Cilantro doesn't attack me. Nope. She cuddles close, continuing to rub against me like I'm her new best friend. Like I'm her favorite person in the world. Like everyone else is garbage.

That's when it hits me. "Holy shit. She is so pissed at you she's willing to be nice to me to make you mad."

Gavin chuckles, seeming pleased at his cat's manipulative tactics. "She's a funny—" He reaches out, like he's gonna pet her, and Cilantro's head swivels his way, mouth opening wide in a fang bearing hiss.

"You be nice." I gently chastise the cat, pulling her away just in case she decides to lunge. "He can't help it if his fancy British neighbor couldn't handle a lizard."

"To be fair," Gavin flips on the bedroom light, "Fynn wasn't there when the iguana broke in." He scans the room Cilantro tried to single pawdedly dismantle, looking over the boxes stacked inside. "I don't think she broke anything. Just knocked over everything she could."

I lean down to look Cilantro in the eyes. "You're not too mad then, are you? If you were really mad, you would have shredded everything he owned."

She answers me with a loud purr and a quick lick on the tip of my thumb.

Gavin rakes one hand through his hair, looking around the room then at the closed bathroom door. "I guess I've got to figure out what to do with the iguana."

"Good luck with that. I don't have a clue..." Wait. "I might actually know someone who can help." I carry Cilantro into the bedroom, letting her go when she starts to wiggle free. She jumps up and circles the unmade bed, dropping down into a spot and kneading the sheets with her paws as I collect my cell and open up my contacts. "My boss has a giant snake, so he might know what to do." I'm about to press Grant's number when it starts to ring in my hand.

And my stomach hits the floor.

My eyes snap to Gavin. "It's Leo."

He stills. "You've gotta answer it."

Holding one finger in front of my lips like Gavin doesn't already know to keep his mouth shut, I connect the call. "Hello?"

"I need to talk to you about something. I'm on my way over."

I clamp one hand over my mouth to stifle the panicked yelp that tries to sneak free. I'm an adult. Gavin's an adult. We can do what we want. But Leo is already in a delicate state. I'm not sure how he might react to finding out I've seen his best friend naked, and I'm not so much in the mood to find out.

Plus, now that I know a little more about Gavin's life, I don't want to risk him being shut out by my brother over something ridiculous. And, given how reactive Leo's been lately, there's a good chance that might happen.

"Umm. Can you give me a little bit?" My brain races, trying to come up with a reason Leo would take seriously. "I'm waxing my butt crack."

The. Fuck?

Of all the things I could have claimed, why—WHY —is that the one I chose?

Gavin's brows jump high on his forehead as my face heats in embarrassment.

"Fuck, Alexis. You coulda kept that to yourself." Leo blows out a sigh. "How about an hour? Does that give you time to put your ass crack away?"

"Yup. Thanks." I'm barely paying attention as my brother hangs up because I'm too busy trying not to die of mortification.

I slide my phone into the pocket of my pajama pants, looking everywhere but Gavin's face. "So, I'm gonna go." I start backing toward the hall. "I hope you get the whole iguana situation figured out." I spin and practically run for the door, snatching my bag and keys off the counter, face on fire as I continue my escape.

"Al." Gavin says my name but I'm already turning toward the door, desperate to get the heck out of here before I go up in flames.

"*Alexis.*" This time he's louder, but I keep going, managing to get the door part way open before a big hand slams against it, closing the steel slab with a bang that sends me jumping back.

Gavin props into place, leaning a shoulder on the frame as he lifts an eyebrow, staring at me expectantly. I try to step back, but his hand comes to grip my hip, pulling me closer to him. "Where are you going?"

I swallow hard, already getting distracted by his closeness. "I'm leaving. Leo's coming to my place."

"Mmmhmm." Gavin's eyes move over my face. "And you were just gonna walk out without giving me a kiss goodbye or telling me when I get to see you again?"

"Well..." I run out of words, because what he's describing doesn't sound like the situation this started as. It sounds more like a relationship. And I'm not sure how to unpack the baggage I'm carrying for that.

Gavin leans down, pressing a sweet, soft kiss to my lips. He stays so close his nose nearly touches mine and says, "I'll see you tonight. I've still got something I want to show you."

"Kay." I don't know what else to say, and I can't trust my idiot mouth to handle itself with any sort of respectability.

He leans back, turns me toward the door, then opens it. I'm in the hall when he says my name once again.

"Alexis."

Pausing, I turn to find him relaxing against the opening, lips tipped up in a smirk.

His eyes run down my frame before coming back to my face. "For the record, I'm not concerned about the state of your butt crack. At all."

24

Drawing Lines and Cutting Ties

I STAND IN the doorway like the simp I am, watching Al's ass as she walks down the hall to the elevator. It takes an amazing amount of restraint to stay put when she turns and gives me a sweet smile. I haven't been angry at Leo much in the years we've known each other, but I could kick his ass for dragging her away from me.

Alexis lifts one hand, offering a small wave as the bell dings, signifying the elevator's arrival. I'm still returning her wave as she starts to step in. An odd expression flashes over her pretty features as she side-steps through the open doors, the smile she offered me flattening into something akin to a scowl.

When I see what caused both the look on her face and her maneuvering, my stomach sinks.

My dad steps out of the cab, turning back to stare between the doors as they close. Once Alexis is sealed in, he faces me, brows lifted. "I take it you're a tit man?"

He chuckles. "Cause that little thing had one hell of a rack on her."

I'm used to my dad objectifying women. Trashing or talking them down with nearly every word that comes out of his mouth.

But this time it isn't women. This time it's Al. And it has my hands clenching into fists as anger burns my gut.

"Don't fucking talk about her like that." I've never said a harsh word to my dad. Never told him how I really feel about his bullshit. I should have—I know that. It shouldn't have taken him turning his lewd opinions onto Alexis for me to draw the line.

But at least I'm drawing it now.

My dad stops short, hands lifting, palms facing me like he's innocent and I'm overreacting. "Don't get all bent out of shape about it. She's just a woman. There's a million more like her just waiting to tear you apart."

My molars grind together and the vein in my head starts to throb. "She's not like that."

My dad looks me over, hands dropping to rest on his hips as he snorts out a bitter laugh. "You said that about the last one too."

I'm not surprised he's bringing this up. He always does. "That was over a decade ago."

"Doesn't change the facts." My dad comes my way, slowly closing the distance between us. "You trusted a woman. Gave her your heart and your love and your time." He stops in front of me, dropping a heavy hand on my shoulder. "And she went and found someone else without so much as a fuck you."

I wait for it. Brace for the stab of pain to cut into that old wound. I've carried it for years and my dad has poked it at every opportunity, making sure it festered. Ensuring it dictated my actions and thoughts.

But the slicing sear of rejection and betrayal that kept me from ever letting—wanting—a woman close to me, doesn't come. Because it doesn't matter. Not anymore.

"I was a kid, Dad. So was she." The lens I've been viewing the world through is suddenly different. Clearer. "And even if she wasn't, who the fuck cares? It's not like I wish I was with her now."

For six months I've been trying to figure out what changed. Why my old ways no longer held the same appeal. Now I know.

It's me. I'm what's changed.

My dad's expression hardens. "Don't be stupid, son. Women can't be trusted, you know that. All they do is lie and cheat. They're just waiting to fuck you over and leave you behind."

"No. That's what Mom did to you." I look him over, new eyes casting him in a different light. "And I'm not sure I blame her. You're kind of an asshole." I back away. "I've gotta go. I have shit to do." I don't know why he's here and I don't care. I need space from him. Room to decide what I really think—what I really feel—without the poison of his influence.

After escaping into my condo, I close the door behind me, shutting out the last of my born-into family. The pain I couldn't find earlier finally shows up, and it cuts deep. I know I just hurt my dad, but he needed to hear the truth. Needed to be held accountable for his part in the bullshit he allows to dictate his life and tried to pour into mine.

I scrub a hand over my face before running it through my hair, resisting the almost overwhelming urge to open the door and apologize. To take back what I said—even though every bit of it was the truth—just to preserve the shitty relationship I have with him.

Instead, I force my feet away, crossing the open living and dining room as I make a beeline for the hall. I wasn't lying when I told him I had shit to get done. My to-do list is overflowing today, thank God. It'll provide a distraction I need.

After taking a quick shower and dressing, pausing a few seconds to again judge my closet and personal care routine, I grab my wallet and keys, along with my cell, and stalk down to the garage. After getting into my car, I seek out my first destination, entering it into the GPS before pulling out into the morning sunlight.

I've got a lot to get done while Alexis deals with Leo. Hopefully their conversation goes better than the one I just had.

25

The Beans are Spilled

I'VE NEVER SEEN my brother like this.

Leo paces through my apartment, pausing occasionally to rake one hand through his already messy hair. Each swipe sends it standing taller and taller, making my fingers itch with the need to repair the damage he's done. But the bags under his eyes and the tight line of his mouth make me think the style of his hair is the least of his worries.

"Do you want to sit down?" I point to the sofa and immediately regret it. I know what's transpired there, and I can't imagine Leo would be thrilled to find out he'd parked his ass in the exact spot my thighs were against his best friend's ears.

"No. I can't stay long." He completes another pass, turning to face me when he reaches the front wall. "I need your help with Maddie."

That has my brows lifting. "My help?" I'm not sure

how useful I would be against a violent ex-husband, and I'm also not sure how entangled I want to be in the rift between Leo and my parents. Especially since I can understand both sides. "In what way?"

"She's so fucking alone, Alexis." Leo's big shoulders sag. "I want to be everything she needs, but I can't."

"What about her parents? I thought they were a close family?" I don't know the Millers well. Like the rest of my parents' friends, I always did my best to avoid them so I didn't get dragged into some long-winded—and exceedingly boring—conversation about the weather, or—God forbid—sports.

"They are, but it's not the same." Leo comes my way, reaching me in two long strides. "She doesn't have any friends. When she was married, he did his best to cut her off from everyone, and now she doesn't have anyone to talk to about what's going on." He grabs both my hands, holding tight. "I thought maybe you and your friends could sort of take her in. Be like a tribe or something for her."

My heart squeezes for Maddie. I know how important my friends have been to me. They've helped me through things I couldn't—or didn't want to—discuss with my family, so I see where Leo's coming from.

Still.

"Maddie might not want you trying to force friends on her." I stop short of pointing out that while he might be well-intentioned, this is just another form of controlling her friends.

Leo starts shaking his head immediately. "I wouldn't do that. I told her about you and your friends and asked if it was okay for me to talk to you." His expression hardens the smallest bit. "I know you and Mom and Dad think I'm fucking everything up, but I really am just trying to take care of her and keep her safe."

"I know you are." I keep my tone gentle. "And Mom and Dad know that too."

No one thinks Leo's trying to cause problems for Maddie. And it bothers me that he thinks we do. Makes me think Maddie isn't the only one feeling a little alone.

He snorts. "*Right.*" The sarcastic cut of the single word is sharp. "Honestly, I don't give a shit what you think of me as long as you'll be there for Maddie."

I hold his gaze, guilt making me wish there was more I could do about the mess he's in. "Of course. I'm more than happy to help Maddie in any way I can."

Leo jerks his head in a nod. "Thank you." He releases my hands and digs his phone from his pocket. He taps across the screen and a second later my own phone vibrates. "I just sent you her number."

"I'll reach out to her today." Looks like my plans of relaxing on my couch and trying to wrap my brain around the fact I spent the night with Gavin again are shot all to hell.

In a surprising move, Leo grabs me, squeezing me in a genuine hug instead of the bone crushing, done only to annoy me, variety I'm usually subjected to. "Thank

261

you." He releases me and backs toward the door. "I owe you one."

I manage a weak smile, because I'm afraid the one he's going to owe me might cause just as much turmoil as his relationship with Maddie Miller. "Okay."

Leo lets himself out and I stand there for a minute, putting off the inevitable as long as I can.

Then I open my phone and begin my least favorite thing.

A flipping group text.

———

"THANK YOU SO much for offering your house up." I drop down into one of the stools surrounding Hazel's kitchen island. "I figured going out in public was probably not a great idea, all things considered."

Hazel's eyes widen and she shakes her head. "It sounds like she's been through some wild shit, and I can understand not feeling safe." My friend tips wine into a glass and offers it up. "I wouldn't want to risk him figuring out where she was and showing up." She gives me a wicked little smile. "But it would be kind of fun to watch Isla murder him with her bare hands."

"Honestly, that would solve a lot of problems." I blow out a breath as I lift my glass. "It's so scary to think someone can be like that. I can't imagine what she must be going through."

"Right?" Hazel shakes her head. "I've dated my fair

share of assholes, but none of them has ever threatened to kill me."

"Exactly." It's unfathomable to me. Impossible to wrap my mind around why anyone would do something like that. "She's a few years older than us, so I didn't really know her well growing up, but she's always been nice to me. It's hard to imagine anyone hating her enough to threaten her."

"It's not about hate." Hazel's lips flatten. "Shit like that is always about control."

The doorbell rings and I take a deep breath, hoping I can pull off what Leo wants from me. I haven't had to make a new friend in years, and I'm a little concerned I lack the skill set to actually be of any help to Maddie.

Setting down my glass, I force on a smile. "Here goes nothing, I guess."

I follow Hazel down the hall, smile frozen on my face as she opens the door. Leo texted me a few minutes ago letting me know they were on their way, so I'm expecting to see Maddie outside. And she is out there.

But so are the rest of my friends. Seeing them all huddled around her, offering compliments and the warmth I lack, makes me so fucking proud to be a part of our little girl gang.

Even though they love a good group text.

Hazel takes a sip of the wine she carried to the door as she eyes the crowd on her doorstep. "You guys might want to give her some breathing room."

For sure. Thankfully, Maddie doesn't look irritated,

but she does seem somewhat shell shocked by my friends' overbearing nature. I tried to warn Leo that once the girls found out about Maddie's ex-husband problem, they would go into support mode. And while I love the shit out of them, their support mode can be a lot.

Wren has one long arm looped over Maddie's shoulders. "She might as well get used to it now. We don't want her to think we're all as reserved as Alexis." She gives me a wink to soften the statement.

I angle a brow at her. "Someone has to be reserved. Can you imagine what would happen if I wasn't around to be the voice of reason?"

Hazel wrinkles her nose, stepping back so everyone can come inside. "Then I would be the only one who has any chill, and there's no way I can keep you guys in line all by myself."

Isla is at Maddie's other side, a wild look in her eyes. "Maybe we should kick you and Alexis out. Just for a week so we can get a little unhinged." She tips her head not-so-discreetly at Maddie. "Take care of a few things."

I roll my eyes Hazel's way. "I think staying in was probably a good idea."

She snorts, closing the front door behind everyone. "Agreed."

We all move together, following the hallway to the back of the house before collecting around the island like we always do. Since our little meet-up was pretty impromptu and no one had time to make anything, I placed an order at our favorite sushi restaurant and picked it up on my way over. Rolls of all kinds line the counter, and everyone chats as they begin plowing through rice and fish.

I've just popped a California roll into my mouth when my cell phone buzzes where I left it face down on the island. I discreetly lift it, peeking at the screen.

> What do you think?

The message is accompanied by a photo of a large wire and wood enclosure. There's a glowing light in one top corner and what look like branches zigzagging from side to side.

> Looks great. I'm glad Grant knew someone who could help.

After Leo left my house, I texted Gavin, letting him know I was going to be busy most of the day and evening. I expected him to reply back with a simple acknowledgment, but it's almost like I opened the floodgates. Gavin has been texting me all day. Nothing emotionally deep or overbearing, just little tidbits of what he's been doing since I left his place.

And it seems like he's had as interesting of a Saturday as I have.

"What are you doing?" Isla creeps in at my side, bumping my hip with hers.

I shove my phone into the pocket of my wide-leg

jeans before reaching for another piece of sushi. "Nothing."

"That smile on your face does not say *nothing*." She waggles her brows at me. "That smile says you just got a text from a certain long-haired rugby player."

My stomach drops as my eyes flash to where Maddie sits, hoping she's not paying attention to me or Isla. Sadly, the widening of her dark eyes as they meet mine crushes any hope I have that my entanglement with my brother's best friend will stay on the down-low.

Isla continues on, oblivious to the mess she's spilling. "You went home with Gavin last night, didn't you?" She leans closer, lowering her voice. "Did you have to leave because he nutted on your dress again?"

My stomach drops as shit keeps getting worse and worse. "I..." This is not how I want my brother to find out what's going on between me and his best friend. I wanted to wait for a while. Let this whole thing with Maddie blow over before explaining the overlap in our personal lives.

And I sure as shit don't want him to find out from someone other than me.

My loudest, and most oblivious, friend finally seems to notice everyone has gotten very quiet. Isla's brown eyes go wide, her skin paling as she realizes what she's done. "Oh fuck." She looks from me to Maddie, then back to me again. "I sorta forgot we had a new addition here."

I don't know what to say. How to fix this. I know Isla

didn't mean to spill the tea about me and Gavin, but I still want to throttle her. Just a little.

The silence drags out until finally someone breaks it.

"I guess it's a good thing I didn't hear a single word you said then." Maddie gives me a cautious smile. "But if I did, the only thing I would have to say is good for you."

Isla's shoulders drop as she lets out a loud sigh of relief. "Thank God."

I look my redheaded friend over. "I'm still mad at you."

Isla grins at me. "No you're not. That's just how your face looks." She turns to Maddie, leaning an elbow on the counter. "Well, since we can't talk about Alexis, and no one else here is getting laid, why don't you tell us how you and Leo got together."

Maddie presses her lips together, eyes flicking to me before darting away. "Leo and I have known each other for a while. Our parents are friends."

My phone buzzes in my pocket again, and I pull it out, keeping it below the top of the island so no one else can see.

> You were right. Your boss knew exactly who I should talk to.

I tap out the response before refocusing on Maddie as she talks about how great my brother is.

"Never in a million years did I think I would want to have another relationship. Especially so soon." She gives me another quick glance before looking away. "But it just sort of happened."

Her explanation makes me huff out a little laugh. "I understand completely."

I'd left my teenage dream of being with Gavin behind a long time ago. Even when we started messing around, I still didn't see it as anything long term. I figured it would just be a quick little fling. Enough to sate my curiosity and fulfill a fantasy.

My cell phone buzzes again, and my eyes drop to the screen to find a picture of Gavin holding the iguana in one arm and Cilantro in the other. Another text pops up almost immediately.

> I think they might be starting to like each other.

Normally, getting a steady stream of text messages starts to annoy me. Makes me feel overwhelmed and inundated. But every single one of the peeks into Gavin's adventures today has left me with a smile on my face.

They've also left me a little... Perplexed. Off-balance. Uncertain.

I feel like I bought vanilla ice cream and got home to discover I actually had peanut butter fudge ripple. Way more than I expected and planned for.

It's not at all what I anticipated. But it might be even better.

As long as I'm brave enough to take a bite.

26

Granny D Approved

"FUCK." I TIP my head back, taking a deep breath before returning my attention to the project in my hands. "This shit was not made for someone my size."

Cilantro tilts her head, yellow eyes wide as she watches me struggle, and offers a meow of commiseration. Or maybe she's trying to tell me to give up so she can have her wicked way with the yarn I'm fighting.

"Not happening." I scoot the bundle closer, just in case she doesn't want to take no for an answer. "This isn't for you."

It may not be for anyone if I can't figure out how in the hell to make more than just the repeating single loop the chick on YouTube calls a chain stitch.

Again, I attempt to turn and dig into the second row, pausing every two seconds to restart the video tutorial, making sure I'm following the instructions correctly. But again, the stitches end up too tight, the circle of yarn strangling the metal hook that's so small I struggle to maneuver it.

"For the love of—" I toss the barely started project onto the couch cushion beside me, abandoning it for the hundredth time. "There has to be an easier way." I don't know what sort of magic was in Granny D's old lady hands, but it's clearly not in mine.

Leaning forward, I focus on my laptop. After opening a new search window, I type in a prompt.

Easiest way to make a scarf

All the Google selected options populate the screen in front of me and I scroll, bypassing the sewing tutorials in search of a new yarn-based alternative. I saw the way Alexis responded to the cashmere scarf I bought her, so I'm not giving up on that part of this whole endeavor.

My gaze snags on a thumbnail and I click the link so I can inspect it better. What pops up might be the solution to my problem. Instead of using a teeny tiny hook to freestyle loop the yarn together, this new method requires some sort of plastic apparatus with pegs sticking up off it. The process appears to simply be winding the yarn around the pegs and then using a hook to pull one over the other. I deflate a little when I see a hook is still required, but it doesn't look like I'll have to gymnastic the mother fucker in all sorts of ways. Just one single maneuver.

I think I can do that.

I order the plastic thing and add on expedited shipping. Once that's handled, I pack up the cashmere yarn I spent an hour in a specialty fiber shop selecting. I didn't want to give Alexis another red and white scarf, so I ended up choosing the crimson and gray of the Swamp Cat branding. It's still a little similar to the others, but hopefully different enough.

Plus, I really fucking like the thought of Alexis in the stands wearing a scarf I made her, watching me do what I do best.

Because crocheting is certainly not what I do best.

Once I know the expensive yarn is hidden safely away from Cilantro, I go to check on the iguana. I wasn't able to get a perfect setup today, but thanks to Al's boss, I found a temporary enclosure and ordered a custom unit that should be ready in a couple of weeks.

I set up the wood and wire space in the corner of the spare bedroom where Cilantro's litter box is. It made the most sense to keep all the pet shit in one space.

And I'm pretty certain the iguana is now my pet.

The lizard looks happy enough, basking in the glow of its new heat lamp. I'm checking the temperature to make sure it's within the recommended span when my cell phone buzzes in my pocket. After less than one day, I've already got a fucking trained response to the vibration, and my stomach clenches in anticipation.

Alexis and I have been messaging each other all afternoon. I worried she would get sick of the constant communication, but she's reached out to me as much as I've reached out to her, and it has my brain thinking all sorts of things. Good things.

And also bad.

Swiping across the screen, I see the three words I've been waiting for.

On my way.

I give the iguana a last look. "It's show time."

It's been a busy day, and I think all my effort is about to pay off. At least I hope it is.

Going into the kitchen, I flip on the oven light, checking the contents before going to the fridge. After pulling out the first of many surprises I have for Alexis, I go to work setting everything up. My heart races faster and faster, driven by anticipation, excitement, and a little fear. Fear that I don't know what the fuck I'm doing.

Fear that this is all going to be too much.

Fear that maybe—as much as I don't want to consider it—my dad will be right. Maybe I am just setting myself up to have my heart broken again.

I scrub one hand over my face, forcing the thought away. That's not how Alexis is. She would never hurt me the way my dad hurt my mom, or even the way my high school girlfriend did me.

But Alexis is only half the equation. And I'm not sure my half is as trustworthy as hers. I don't know how

I'm going to handle being close to her. Don't know if I'll be able to keep the jealous, possessive side of me in check.

Thankfully, a light knock stops my spiraling thoughts. I practically run to the door. There's no sense hiding my eagerness to see her. There's going to be no missing it as soon as she comes inside, might as well put it out there from the beginning.

My heart nearly stutters to a stop when I see her on my doorstep. I expected her to be all decked out like she usually is, but instead Al is wearing a pair of flannel pants and a hoodie. Her face is makeup free and her blonde hair is pulled up into a messy bun at the top of her head. She looks fucking fantastic.

Even better, she looks like she's planning to sleep over.

"Hey." Words fail me. Seeing Alexis here—like this —eases a little of the worry I've been carrying about my plans for our evening.

She gives me a soft smile. "Hey."

Even though we've been communicating all day, this moment feels a little awkward. Different. Because now things are different. And it's about to get a whole lot worse.

I step back, holding the door wide. "How was your girls' night?"

Alexis seems to relax a little at the question. "It was actually really good. My friends loved Maddie and it seemed like she liked them." Her eyes drift to my kitchen. "Are you making food?"

I tip my head in a nod, uncertainty gnawing at my excitement. "I am."

She lets out a long breath, shoulders relaxing even more as her overnight bag slides down one arm. "Thank God. I didn't come close to ordering enough sushi, and I'm starving."

"I'm pretty sure there's no such thing as enough sushi." I take her bag, setting it at the end of the long island separating the main living area from the kitchen. "I can eat my body weight in that shit and still be hungry an hour later."

Alexis looks me up and down, gaze lingering on my chest and shoulders before coming back to my face. "That's a lot of sushi."

"It is, and I'm positive you didn't come close to eating that much, so come sit down before you pass out from starvation." I press one palm against the small of her back, directing Alexis to one of the counter-height stools I've never used before since I usually eat on the couch in front of the television.

Alexis slides onto the seat, her gaze immediately falling to the plate I pulled from the refrigerator. Her brows pinch together as she reaches out to hook a finger at the rim, pulling it close. "Is this..." She doesn't finish and I feel like that's a bad sign.

"Granny D's cheese ball." I pass her a butter knife. "I

don't have one of those fancy spreaders like she did, but I think this will work."

Alexis stares at the appetizer, her pretty face still tight with confusion. "How do you know how to make this?"

"Like I said, your grandma is who taught me how to cook." I round the island on my way to the oven. After grabbing a couple hot mitts, I start pulling out our dinner. "And she told me all her secrets." I settle the dish of scalloped potatoes onto the counter before going back to retrieve the meatloaf. Once it's in place, I peel the mitts away, take a deep breath, and lift my eyes to Al's face, bracing for her reaction.

Her eyes move from the meatloaf, to the potatoes, to the cheeseball and crackers, before finally coming my way. "You made all this?"

Her tone gives nothing away. Doesn't hint at whether she's happy or I've come on too strong.

"I just thought since you fed me last night, it was only right that I feed you tonight. And I know you loved your grandma, so..." I run out of shit to say. Out of explanation to give. All I can do is wait and hope I haven't fucked up already.

Alexis stares at me a second before once again looking over the meal I made. Silently, she slides off the stool and rounds the island, stopping at my side. For a few more torturously long seconds, she stares at the meatloaf and potatoes.

Then she jumps at me, arms locking around my

neck as she squeezes tight, her face buried in my neck. "This is amazing." It's not until she sniffs, her breath hitching, that it registers that Al's crying.

"No, no, no, no." I wrap my arms around her, hugging tight. "Don't cry. I didn't mean to upset you. I just thought you might like eating some of Granny D's favorite recipes."

Alexis tips her head back, watery eyes moving over mine.

Something just changed. I see it in the way she's looking at me. It's like she's seeing too much, and it has me gently setting Alexis on her feet before turning away, needing some space from whatever just happened between us.

"I have something else for you." I'm working on autopilot, going through the motions of what I had planned, unable to think of anything besides the way she just looked at me. "It's what I wanted to show you last night."

I open a drawer and pull out one of my most prized possessions. I've carried this thing with me for over a decade, but I think Alexis needs it more than I do.

Turning to face her, I pull in as much air as I can manage and hold the item out between us.

"What's that?" Her voice is barely a whisper.

"Granny D wasn't confident in my ability to remember all the shit she taught me, so she made me a little book with all her recipes in it." I move it closer to Alexis. "I think you should have it."

For a second, I think I've fucked up again. Gone too far. Done too much.

But then Al takes it, her delicate, tiny fingers reverently sliding over each page as she silently flips through the small, handwritten notebook.

"I spilled some stuff on a few of the pages." I would have been more careful with it if I'd known one day I'd be giving it to Alexis. I would have kept it fucking pristine. "I always wiped it off but you can still tell."

"I can't believe she gave this to you." She says it so softly I barely hear it. "She didn't even give my mom her recipes."

My chest goes tight. I've treasured the hell out of that book, but hearing I'm the only person she gave those to?

"I didn't know that." My head drops, dragged down by guilt. "I would have given it to you sooner if—"

"Shut up." Al's demand is sharp.

Sharp enough to snap my head up and bring my eyes to her face. "What?"

"I said stop talking." She carefully slides the notebook onto the counter and takes a step toward me. Her lips are pressed into a thin line, as she lifts her chin, coming closer until the full swell of her tits presses against my stomach. "Get your dick in me." Her nostrils flare as pink races across her cheeks. "Now."

27
Houdini

Alexis

BEING SHORT HAS its disadvantages, but it also has its perks. Like how it forces you to be a good climber. I never filed that under the perk category before, but it's there now, because it prepared me for Gavin.

And he is one hell of a jungle gym.

Between leverage, years of practice, and sheer determination, I manage to arrange myself so we're eye to eye, my ass perched on the edge of the counter and my thighs hooked tight at his waist.

Gavin's voice is hoarse when he asks, "Right here?" He glances at the dishes lined down the granite next to me. "In front of Granny D's meatloaf?"

I grab at his T-shirt, more desperate to fuck than I have ever been in my whole life. "Right here in front of Granny D's meatloaf."

I don't think she would mind. In fact, in light of all the new information I've recently gathered regarding my grandmother and her obvious affection for the man still gaping at me, I think she would wholeheartedly approve.

Gavin still hesitates. That's fine. It gives me more time to get my hands on as much of him as possible. Shoving his shirt higher, I tighten my legs so I can keep my balance, using him to stay steady as I bark out another demand. "Lift your arms."

Gavin does as I ask, but before his shirt even hits the floor, he's gripping me tight, one arm at my back and one hand planted against my ass as he pulls me off the counter. "I can't fuck you with that meatloaf staring at me, Al." He turns, completely unhindered by my added weight as he carries me out of the kitchen.

The ease with which he supports me is just as hot as everything else about him, and it only works me into more of a frenzy. I tangle my hands in his hair, rubbing myself against him as I suck on the spot where his neck and shoulder meet, raking my teeth over his skin.

A sharp slap hits my ass cheek, making me gasp as it reverberates between my thighs.

"*Behave*." Gavin's request is clipped and commanding.

And—like everything else he seems to do—it amps up my lust exponentially.

I lean back, knowing he won't let me fall as I run a hand down his chest. "Why?"

Gavin growls when I tweak his nipple, eyes dark as they flash to my face. "You know why, Al."

He's right. I do know why, and it's a heady feeling—seeing the way I affect him.

Gavin. My brother's irritating best friend and rugby's biggest star. The man who uses my grandma's recipes and remembers what my Christmas scarf looks like. The guy who takes in stray iguanas and feral cats.

Never in a million years would I have expected to be here now.

Falling for him.

Literally.

Because a second later, I'm sailing through the air, tossed onto his bed like I weigh nothing. My body is still bouncing from the impact when he crawls over me, big and broad and looking a little feral himself.

Because of me.

"I think you like trying to make me mess up your clothes, Al." Gavin grips the bottom of my hoodie and starts pulling it up, but I get tangled and I'm not in the mood for delays.

I lean up a little so I can wrestle the sweatshirt off, then I fall back against the blankets, ready to pick up where we left off.

But Gavin goes still, his eyes dragging over my chest. I take that as a hint to get rid of the T-shirt too, so I grab it next, desperate to get naked and stuffed full of his cock. I'm ready to have Gavin as close as I can get him. I'm ready to know how good sex can really be, and there's not a doubt in my mind he can show me.

"Don't you dare take that off." One big hand grabs

the front of the T-shirt, stopping me from peeling it away. A deep sound rumbles through his chest as he continues staring. "You're wearing my shirt."

I swallow hard. I told myself it wasn't a big deal when I put it on. Figured Gavin probably wouldn't even notice it.

I was wrong.

"You left it at my apartment so I figured it was fair game."

And by 'left it', I mean I'd hidden it away after he walked out Christmas morning. When I saw it in my closet as I was getting ready to come over here, I couldn't stop myself from picking it up and tugging it over my head. "You can have it back."

"I don't want it back." He almost sounds angry. "I want you to wear it every fucking night." Gavin's eyes come to my face. "While you're sleeping next to me."

"Oh." All the air rushes from my lungs on the single syllable.

"Yeah. *Oh*." Gavin's expression hardens even more. "I've spent years making sure I never wanted anyone, Al. Making sure I'd never end up proving I'm like my dad." His dark gaze slides down my body. "And now I can't stop myself from trying to get everything I can from you." The set of his jaw softens the smallest bit. "From trying to give everything I can *to* you."

I can't pretend I don't like what I'm hearing—the blatant way he lays out what he wants—even if it looks like the revelation makes him anything but happy. I want to ease a little of the worry drawing a line between his brows. A little of the self-doubt I don't want to taint this moment. Now would be a great time to make a joke. Lighten the mood.

Swallowing hard, I try my best to bring a teasing tone to my next words. "I know something you can give me." Instead of coming out the way I intended, the sentence is laced with suggestion. And maybe a little impatience.

Gavin's head tips back as his eyes snap to mine. Surprise lifts his brows as one corner of his full lips tilts up. "Yeah?" His large frame settles over mine. "What's that?"

My mouth goes dry because I think he's expecting me to follow up my little foray into dirty talk, and I'm probably going to be just as terrible at that as I am at teasing and sarcasm.

But what's the worst that could happen? I suck? Who cares? It's not like it'll ruin his outfit.

Taking a deep breath, I dig around my brain for all the less than chaste thoughts I've had about Gavin recently, then I lift one hand, tracing his lips with a finger. "You can give me your mouth." I slide down, drawing a line over his chin, along his neck, past his chest, lower until I cup the hard line of his length. "And you can give me your dick." I give it a little stroke through his jeans, my breath hitching when his nostrils flare.

It's enough to keep me going. Keep the words flowing from my increasingly filthy mouth.

"I want you to be so deep inside me you might not get back out." My thighs clench. "Can you do that for me?"

Gavin's hand grips my hip, fingers sinking into my softness as he groans. "Fuck, Al. You could have eased me into that shit."

I open my mouth, ready to keep going. Ready to get more of the endorphin rush that comes with seeing the effect I have on him. Instead, Gavin leans in and catches my lower lip between his teeth, giving it a gentle nip, pulling just a little before releasing it.

"I think that's enough of that." His hand slides from my hip to my waist, continuing its upward trajectory. "For now."

I pout, disappointed. "You're no fun."

"I'm planning to change that opinion." The width of his palm slides under the baggy cotton of the T-shirt he wouldn't let me take off. "A few times."

I suck in a breath as his calloused hand tickles against my belly. "That will be tricky if you won't let me take my clothes off."

"I didn't say your clothes weren't coming off." His hand changes trajectory, sliding behind my back to deftly unhook my bra, the soft squishiness of his luxurious mattress giving him more than enough wiggle room to slide it free. "Just the shirt." In a move I didn't think men understood, Gavin reaches into the armholes of my—his—shirt, sliding the straps down before tugging the entire garment through one. He flashes me a grin and a wiggle of his dark brows as he tosses it away.

"Impressive." I can't help but return his grin. "You're like Houdini."

Gavin's smile widens. "Wait till you see what else I can do."

I lift my brows. "How long do I have to wait, because I feel like I gave you very specific directions forever ago and your dick is still in your pants."

"You're an impatient little thing, aren't you?" Gavin's voice lowers, but still carries a teasing edge. "Probably because you've been thinking about this since high school."

I shoot him a glare. "I never should have told you that."

Gavin chuckles, the sound deep and rich. "It's only fair I get something to hold over your head since you're never gonna let me live down ruining your Christmas dress."

"Let's make a deal. I promise to stop bringing it up if you promise to hurry up and ruin more of me."

I'm not sure I've ever asked for sex in my life. With Hugo, it was just what we did. A natural development of a long term relationship. It wasn't that I felt obligated, I just never felt eager. Not like I do now.

Gavin doesn't hesitate. "Deal." His big hands hook

into the waist of my joggers, dragging them and my panties down in one quick move, whisking away both—along with my socks and slip-on shoes—before dumping it all over the side of the bed. Then, before I can fully process what's coming, he grips me behind the knees, spreads my legs wide, and plants his mouth right between them.

Like he's starving.

The shock of the wet heat of his mouth sends me arching off the bed, gasping as the tip of his tongue flicks my clit in that teasing motion that drives me freaking wild.

Gavin works me up fast, but to be fair, I was already halfway there anyway. In what feels like seconds, I'm coming, writhing against his blankets and grabbing at his hair.

Before I've even fully come down, he's kissing his way up my body, wet lips sliding over my belly as he shoves up my T-shirt, baring my tits. He sucks one nipple hard, movements jerky as he frees himself from his jeans and briefs with one hand, kicking them away almost violently.

Gavin releases my breast, the wide width of his body spreading my thighs even more as he settles between them. His teeth drag across the lobe of my ear, voice ragged as he says, "I know that was fast, Al. I just don't think I can wait anymore to feel how tight you're gonna squeeze my dick."

My earlier orgasm dulled the flames licking across my skin, but they flare right back to life at his admission. I totally understand the appeal of dirty talk now, and Gavin seemed to like when I did it earlier, so I decide to do a little more myself.

"I can't wait either." My breathing quickens as he reaches to grab a condom from his nightstand, aggressively tearing the packet before fisting it down his substantial length. "Your dick is going to feel so good. It's going to fill me so full." I wiggle around, impatience and need making it hard to stay still. "I'm going to come so hard it will ruin me. I won't want anyone else but you."

Gavin's eyes snap to my face as he notches the flared head of his cock against me. "Say that again."

"I won't want anyone but you." It's too easy to say and even easier to think.

Gavin catches one of my hands with his, lacing our fingers together before pressing them against the pillows above my head. "Again."

The intensity in his stare is doing all sorts of crazy things to my insides, and I can't stop myself from minorly adjusting the words. "I don't want anyone but you."

"Good." Gavin's nostrils flare as he finds my other hand, joining our fingers like before then lifting it to the pillows. "I plan to keep it that way."

His eyes fuse to mine as he presses into me slowly.

He's maddeningly careful, and part of me wants to tell him to just get it in there already. I'm not breakable.

But a bigger part of me wants this moment to drag out. Wants to commit every second to memory. Wants to soak it all in.

Because I can't help but feel like this is something big. Possibly monumental. That it might change everything. Not just for Gavin, but for me.

When he's finally fully seated, Gavin lets out a long, ragged breath as his forehead drops to mine, eyes tightly shut. He stays like that as the seconds tick by, face taunt, body strung with tension.

I want him to move. Need him to shift just a little, because I feel like I've been pinned to a corkboard. "Gavin, I—"

"Stop wiggling, Al." One hand releases mine to grip my hip, holding me still. "I just need a minute."

My skin flushes, but not in embarrassment. "What's wrong?"

"You know what's wrong." He grits the words out, lids finally lifting to meet my gaze. "I don't want this to be a Christmas party repeat."

His confirmation of my suspicions has the air rushing from my lungs. "Oh." My eyes drop down to where our bodies are joined, and I can't stop myself from asking. "Does this happen a lot?"

Gavin's lips quirk, like he's amused instead of insulted by my question. "Are you asking if I'm normally a two-pump chump?" He shakes his head, not waiting for my answer. "No. Not even close." He leans in, rubbing his nose against mine. "You seem to bring out the best in me."

I can't put into words how much I like what he's saying. What it does to me to hear what I do to him. It makes me realize everything actually changed a long time ago. Not tonight. Nothing was ever going to be the same between us from the second he walked into my old playhouse. "Then stop worrying about it." I hook my legs around his, trying to encourage him. "I don't mind."

Gavin's eyes narrow. "I mind. I'm not getting off unless you get off with me."

His heart's in the right place and I very much appreciate it, but— "That's an awful lot of pressure put on yourself, big guy."

Gavin's serious expression holds. "I'm used to playing under pressure, Al." He inhales deeply. "I just need a second." He lets the breath out and then finally starts to move.

And barely makes it through one stroke before he goes still again.

I roll my eyes, because this is kind of ridiculous. "Stubborn man." Bringing my free hand between our bodies, I slick my fingers alongside my clit. "Let me help."

Gavin's eyes drop to where I touch myself, and he lets out a low growl. "Fuck, Al." He pushes up so he can have a better view. "I'm not sure if you're helping or hurting."

Since the only boyfriend I had never managed to get me off, I'm well practiced in the art of self-pleasure, so I'm already breathless and throbbing. "Do you want me to stop?"

Gavin doesn't look at me, but his grip on my hip tightens. "I didn't say that."

"That's good, because I wasn't planning to." I move away from my clit for just a second, sliding back to feel where I'm stretched tight around the thickness of his cock. "Holy shit." I trace around our joined bodies. "That's so fucking hot."

"You like that?" Gavin's hand moves from my hip, taking over the task I abandoned, his thumb gently strumming. "You like feeling how well you take me?" His eyes stay fused to where my hand and his are side-by-side. "It's like I was fucking made for you."

Why is it so sexy that he said it that way? Not that I was made for him.

He was made for *me*.

The hand above my head clenches his, gripping tight as his words and touch ripple through me, pushing me closer to a peak I didn't think was possible. "Gavin." His name rushes through my lips as his thumb sends me faster and faster toward the edge.

"That's right, Al." His body rocks into mine, each stroke slow and purposeful. "It's me." Gavin's dark gaze lifts to rest on mine. "It's always gonna be me."

The moment steals my breath. The strength of his hand in mine. The possessive look in his eyes. The feel of his cock deep inside me. It's too much.

And yet exactly enough.

The orgasm he refused to deny slams into me, ripping a wail from my throat as every muscle I have clenches tight.

Gavin groans but doesn't look away from my face. "That's it, Al. Milk me dry with that perfect little pussy."

Is it possible to come while coming? I vote yes, because I swear a second jolt flashes through my insides, stealing another savage sound from me.

I'm so wrapped up in what's happening to me, that I barely notice when Gavin buries himself to the hilt, sealing our bodies together as my name passes through his lips.

When my senses decide to return to the premises, our faces are still aligned. Our hands are still entwined. I'm still full of Gavin and he's still staring at me.

A hint of awkwardness—and maybe a little worry—tries to creep in. I came into this knowing who Gavin was. His history with women. I was fine with it. But somewhere along the way I started to think this would be different. That *I* was different.

Maybe I'm not. Maybe he can't get over the fears he has about his dad's influence. Maybe this will be the end. Maybe—

"I think we need to discuss something, Al." Gavin's words stab into my aching heart.

Is this it already? While we're still naked and pressed against each other? While we're—

"I meant it when I said no one but me." He brushes a kiss against my lips. "Because from now on, it's no one but you."

28

As Long as it's Not Liver

"I SWEAR TO God." Leo bends at the waist, sucking in air as he tries to catch his breath. "I don't know what you've been eating, but you've got to stop."

I grin in spite of myself. I can't help it. "You don't want to know what I've been eating." And I'm not telling him. Not yet. Not when he's so clearly hanging on by a thread.

"It's liver, isn't it?" Leo grimaces as he straightens, face slanting toward the clear sky. "I knew it would be fucking liver."

I tip back a water bottle, squirting a steady stream into my mouth, trying to replace some of what I've sweat out over the past couple of hours. After swallowing down as much as I'm comfortable putting in my stomach, I pass it off to my friend. "Maybe you should try relaxing. You've been wound up for weeks now. That shit would wear anyone out."

Leo takes the bottle. "I can't help it." He downs a quick drink. "You don't know what it's like worrying about what could happen every time she leaves the house." He pours more water into his open mouth, then wipes the sweat off his face with the hem of his shirt. "It's killing me that I have to leave her for the weekend."

I can see the worry etched on his face. The tension bunching his shoulders and clenching his teeth. "You've got to try to relax, man. You're going to drive yourself crazy."

Leo shakes his head, huffing out an odd sounding laugh. "I can't relax." He meets my gaze. "I fucking love her."

The admission stuns me. "What?"

"I love her." Leo repeats himself, sounding even more convicted than he did the first time. "And before you try to tell me it's too soon, it's not."

Was I going to try to tell him that? I've spent a lot of time over the past month attempting to convince him he needs to give Maddie the space to deal with what she's facing, but I knew he'd never do it. I guess on some level I expected this. Recognized he was already too far gone to turn back.

And I understand. Completely.

But it puts a wrench in my plan to tell him about me and Alexis. Pushes back that timeline indefinitely. I know how Leo would have reacted before, but now? Now finding out his sister's sleeping in my bed almost every night might make him lose his shit. And he doesn't have much to spare.

"Do you think she loves you back?"

Leo's brows lift, like he hasn't considered the possibility. After a few beats he slowly nods. "I think she does."

I hope like hell he's right, but I'm not sure it matters either way. Even if Maddie broke up with him tomorrow, he would take care of her. Still look out for her. Still do whatever he could to keep her safe.

It's one of many reasons Leo's been my best friend since the day we met. His feelings are what they are. They don't change based on circumstance. Or someone else's opinions or actions.

I've always hoped he'd rub off on me. That I wouldn't spend my whole life being reactive. Wouldn't allow someone else to dictate my thoughts and emotions. But I'm pretty sure that's not how that works.

I drop a hand onto his shoulder, giving it a squeeze. "Then I'm glad she found you. No one in this world will take care of her the way you will."

Leo's mouth tips up in a half smile. "I'm glad someone's finally on my side."

Guilt stabs my gut. Guilt that I've made him feel unsupported and alone. Guilt that he's thought everyone was against him.

And guilt that I've had his sister under me every night for the past two weeks and he has no fucking idea.

The sharp trill of a whistle signifies the end of our

break and sends us going our separate ways for the rest of the morning.

Like always, I'm fucking spent when practice is over, and I drag my ass into the showers to wash away the sweat and dirt. I come out to find Owen giving Leo shit.

"You're telling me you can't even come out for an hour?" Owen shakes his head, running one hand over his buzzed scalp. "You're fucking pussy-whipped, man."

Leo grabs his bag. "Yup." He slings the duffel over one shoulder, giving Owen a smirk. "And you're a jealous asshat."

Normally, any mention of jealousy sends me into a spiral, reminding me of everything I can never have. Of what I'll become if I'm not careful.

And today is no exception.

The panic of fucking shit up with Alexis starts twisting my gut almost instantly, sloshing around the water I chugged before my shower.

"Jealous of being locked down?" Owen shakes his head. "No fucking way." His lip curls. "I'm not done playing the pitch." He shoots me a grin, wiggling his brows. "You see what I did there?"

"You're a fucking wordsmith," I deadpan as I pull on my clothes, trying to look unhurried even though I'm itching to get out of here so I can see Alexis. Talk to her. Hear about her day then occupy her night. Prove to myself I can do this. That I'm better than my old man.

Better than the old me.

Owen turns his attention from Leo, focusing on

where I stand. "What about you? You up for a little drinky drinky?"

"Not tonight." I wrestle my T-shirt over my still damp skin. "I've got to take care of my iguana."

Owen's nose wrinkles. "Is that code for jacking off? Because if it is, then you should definitely come out and find someone else to handle that shit for you."

I finish dressing and shove both feet into my runners. "And how's that working out for you?"

Owen grins. "Not well."

That's the thing with Owen. He doesn't take much outside of rugby seriously. That includes himself. "Then one more night of taking matters into your own hand won't kill you."

My winger buddy's face lights up. "Does that mean you'll come out tomorrow?"

I glance at Leo's retreating figure. He's sure as shit not gonna go out, and I know Owen's not going to shut up until he gets what he wants. "Sure. I'll go out tomorrow."

I don't plan to stay out, but I didn't really stay out even before Alexis. I always managed to find a reason— a pretty one—to skip out early. So no one will be surprised if I do it again.

Hell, they might even celebrate it. They've all been giving me shit about my sudden and lingering celibacy. I don't have any intention of telling them that streak has ended.

Like Leo said, my personal life is no one's business.

"I knew *you* wouldn't let me down." Owen slaps me on the shoulder. "I'm gonna go find us some company."

I shake my head as he walks away, hoping Alexis won't give me too much shit over making plans for tomorrow. Going out isn't her favorite thing. She hates the crowds and the noise and the general overstimulation that comes with many of the bars in Sweet Side.

Which reminds me. I should have a package to pick up at home.

After collecting my shit, I pile into my Hummer and head out. Sure enough, when I get home, there's a delivery waiting on me. I drop the noise reducing earplugs I ordered for Alexis onto the counter before going to check on Cilantro and the iguana Al dubbed Scary Terry, even though the thing is about as far from frightening as it gets.

I reload the lizard's food and water, making sure the temperature in his enclosure is within the right range, then grab Cilantro and carry her into the living room. She purrs on the sofa next to me, kneading the cushion as I add a few rows to the scarf I've been secretly working on when Al's not around.

Which isn't often.

We've spent nearly every evening together for the past two and a half weeks, and it's been fucking magical. Since we're still early in the pre-season, I'm usually finished with practice before she gets off work, so I make us dinner, adding a few rows to the scarf I plan to give her the day of our first home match while it cooks.

Then she comes over, we eat and watch television and talk and joke.

Then we go to bed and fuck like animals.

I'm just finishing up a row when my cell starts to ring. I grab it, expecting to see Leo's name across the screen. Instead, it's Alexis calling me.

She's never called me before and my stomach clenches in excitement at this new development. This new level of connection.

I quickly swipe across the screen. There's no hiding my eagerness to talk to her, even if I wanted to, so I don't bother pretending her call isn't the most important thing at this moment. "Hey."

Alexis lets out a relieved sounding sigh. "You answered."

"Of course I answered." There's something off in her tone and it has me standing. "What's wrong?"

She groans. "My freaking car won't start."

A slow smile spreads across my face. Not because I'm happy about her car—I don't like that it left her stranded. But I *am* happy that I'm the one she called. The one she counted on.

"I'm on my way." I have my keys in my hand before she can say another word. "Are you still at work?"

"Ugh. Yes." She blows out another loud sigh. "I would be way less pissy about it if I could wait in the comfort of my own apartment. Instead I'm stuck standing here in the parking garage."

"Go back up to the office and hang out there." I

don't like the thought of her being uncomfortable while she waits for me. "I'll come up when I get there."

"Yeah? You don't mind?" She sounds skeptical and it makes me regret not kicking Big-Nose's ass even more. Then again, he's clearly set the bar low as hell.

"Of course I don't mind, Al. What kind of man would want you to wait for him in a hot car?" I know what kind. I just want to make sure she sees the difference between me and anyone who came before.

"What kind of man indeed." There's a hint of a smile in her voice and I can picture the way it's trying to twist her full lips. "How long do you think it will take you to get here?"

"I'm already in the elevator." I punch the button to close the door. "My phone might cut out."

"I'll let you go then." She pauses. "Be careful."

My chest warms at her concern and I press a hand over the spot. "Always."

I'm still smiling as I climb behind the wheel and whip out of the garage, unable to stop myself from pushing the limits as I speed toward the building where Alexis works. I can't wait to see her. Can't wait to show her how right she was by calling me. By trusting me to take care of her.

Because I'm starting to think I might want to do it forever. I know it's early for that, but I can't imagine not having her in my life. Smiling at me every morning and eating dinner with me every night.

I get to her work in record time, but it still feels like

it takes forever and, after parking it in the vacant spot next to her little crossover, I practically jump out of my Hummer. The elevator moves maddeningly slow as it carries me to her floor and I rush out the second the doors open, like the eager bastard I am.

I haven't been to Al's office before, but I've sent her flowers a couple times, so I have the suite number memorized. When I reach it, I pull the door open, ready to be her knight in well-worn jeans.

And come face to face with the sight of her luscious body pressed against that fucker who came to her place Christmas morning.

29

Elevation Matters

I'M LEANED BACK in my office chair, bare feet kicked up on the top of my desk as I scroll through posts on my phone, sipping the tea I brewed up, when the door opens. I'm expecting Gavin, so I immediately straighten, my belly doing a little flip while I try to control the smile plastering itself across my face.

But instead of a giant hunk of rugby-playing man meat walking in, it's Dillon, and that smile I was fighting gets hella easy to smother. "What are you doing here?" The question comes out snarky. I'm fine with that.

My coworker's eyes drift around the darkened office as he tucks his keys into the front pocket of his expensive slacks. "I forgot my jacket." His gaze comes to me, lingering in a way that makes me want to squirm in my seat. "What are *you* doing here?"

I slide my phone and my tea onto the desk as I stuff

both feet into my pumps. "My car wouldn't start, so I'm waiting for someone to come get me." I stand, the added three inches still only brings me to Dillon's chin, but at least it gets us closer to a level playing field.

Dillon's narrowed gaze hardens. "You mean you're waiting for *Gavin* to come pick you up." His lip curls into a sneer. "You know you're just wasting your time with him, right?" Dillon begins to slowly stalk my way. "He's nothing but a fucking manwhore and he's just using you. When you get boring, he'll ditch you the same way he has every other woman he's fucked."

There was a time where I would have believed what he was saying. Easily. Now all Dillon's bullshit only pisses me off. Makes me want to defend Gavin in a violent and vicious way.

I know what Gavin was. But I also know why he was that way. I know there were probably plenty of girls who crossed his path that he wanted more from, but he avoided them, sure letting them close would only bring out the worst in him.

Just like Dillon is about to bring out the worst in me.

"And I still picked him over you, so what does that tell you?" I've never been good at diffusing a situation, and apparently I have no plans to start now. "So get your jacket and take your bitter, jealous ass home."

What the fuck did I ever see in this guy? How could I have possibly believed there was anything redeeming about him? Even his fashionable wardrobe and over-the-top grooming doesn't appeal to me anymore. Could

I appreciate some other man in a well-tailored, expensive suit? Probably.

But it still wouldn't be nearly as mouthwatering as Gavin in worn jeans and a broken-in T-shirt.

Dillon snorts. "Is that what you think? That I'm jealous?" His brows lift. "Of *him*?" He continues coming my way, each step looking more predatory than the last. "If anything, I'm grateful." There's a mean glint in his eyes now. "He's going to show you how fucking stupid you are and how big of a mistake you made."

I back up as he closes in, not liking the threatening vibe he's giving off. "Pretty sure only one of us is making mistakes, Dill-hole." I can't stop the little laugh that sneaks out over the way I've come full-circle. From hating Gavin's nicknames to loving—and using—them.

Dillon's expression turns murderous. "What the fuck are you laughing at?"

"You." Shit. My mouth is starting to be as big of a problem as my face.

He's coming at me before I can blink, the weight of his body hitting me hard enough to send me stepping backward in an attempt to stay on my feet. When Dillon's hand grips my throat, shoving me into the wall behind my desk, my whole body goes cold and my stomach drops.

I might have underestimated this guy. Definitely gave him more credit than he deserved by thinking he was just a twat.

"Don't fucking laugh at me, Alexis." His words come

out through clenched teeth. "You won't like what happens next."

Already there asshole. "I'm gonna give you two seconds to let me go, motherfucker."

This time it's Dillon laughing. "Or what?"

I don't know what, but it's gonna be messy. "One."

Dillon leans in until we're almost nose to nose. "Say it. I dare you."

"Two." Gavin's deep voice does the hard work for me as his big hand clamps around the wrist of the hand Dillon has on my neck. In the blink of an eye he wrenches it away from my body, twisting it hard enough something lets out a sickening pop.

Dillon's scream of pain cuts off abruptly when Gavin slams him into the wall beside me, using his hold on Dillon's arm to pin him in place, face smashed so hard he's got duck lips.

Gavin leans into Dillon's ear. "Apologize to her."

"I'm sorry." Dill-hole doesn't hesitate to squeak out the words.

But Gavin's not done yet.

"Now apologize to me." There's a downright deadly edge to his demand. One I don't doubt he's capable of backing up.

"To you?" Dillon's eyes are wide and filled with panic. "For what?"

Gavin's attention flicks to me for a split second, scanning my frame from head to toe before going back to Dillon. "For thinking you can put your hands on something that belongs to me."

I should be outraged by that claim, right? Pissed Gavin is acting like I'm nothing more than something he possesses.

But...

Gavin doesn't treat me like a possession. He doesn't act like he owns me. Gavin treats me like I'm a fucking gift. Like I'm the best thing in his life.

Like I'm what matters most to him in the world.

Dillon hesitates to give Gavin what he wants. Right up until my hero twists his already injured arm, making him squeal like the pig he is.

"I'm sorry. I'm sorry." Dillon starts to cry a little. "I shouldn't have touched her."

"And you won't touch her again." Gavin's voice drops lower. "If I find out you so much as breathe on her, I'm going to rip this arm off and shove it so far up your ass you'll be able to tickle your tonsils, got it?"

"Got it." Dillon's nodding along, head bobbing against the drywall.

"Good." Gavin hauls him away from the wall and away from me. "Get out before I decide to do it now."

Dillon doesn't look back. Doesn't get the coat he came for. Just scurries away, clutching his arm to his chest.

As soon as the door closes behind him, Gavin swings my way, hard expression gone completely and replaced with concern as his hands gently brush against my skin. "Did he hurt you?"

I shake my head as an odd sensation trickles down my limbs. "No."

Gavin lowers his head, bringing our eyes level. "I need you to breathe, Al." He sucks in air. "In." He slowly sets it free. "And out."

"I am breathing." Dots start to swim in front of my eyes and I try to blink them away, fighting to keep my body still as an aggressive trembling takes over.

"You aren't." A warm palm settles against my cheek. "You're freaking the fuck out and I don't have time to go find that piece of shit and murder him, so I need you to get some air into those lungs for me."

I try to stare at him, but he's all blurry. "I don't freak out." It's why my friends like me. I'm a little bitchy and a little boring, but I'm great in the clutch. I don't get wound up and I don't lose my cool.

"Then humor me so I don't freak out." Gavin's tone is soft but steady. "Breathe in." Another loud inhale.

And to humor him, I go along with it.

"Good girl." He blows warm air across my face. "And out."

I follow along as he continues, and the dots dancing around his face start to dissipate. Unfortunately, the shaking in my limbs only intensifies. "Why can't I hold still?"

"Probably adrenaline." Gavin grabs my phone and shoves it into my purse before slinging the bag over one shoulder. "Keep breathing, Al." He leans forward, and suddenly I'm off the floor, swept into his arms like a bride being carried across the threshold.

"You don't have to carry me. I can walk." It's weird, but I don't sound snarky at all. I actually sound a little wobbly.

"I'm not carrying you for you." Gavin easily bears my weight with one hand, using the other to open the door. "I'm carrying you for me." He pauses in the hall then swings my purse onto my lap. "Keys to lock the door."

My fingers don't want to work so it takes a few tries to fish them out. Once he has them, Gavin flips the deadbolt into place and then we're moving toward the elevator. He holds me the whole ride down to the parking garage, then all the way to his Hummer. After settling me into the passenger's seat, he buckles me in but remains close, once again checking me over. Like he needs to know I'm okay.

The tips of his fingers slide over the sensitive skin of my neck, gently inspecting the area Dillon manhandled. "I'm sorry for the way I acted, Al. When I walked in and saw his hands on you, I lost it."

My brows pinch together in confusion. "Why would you be sorry? You protected me from him."

Gavin's pale brown eyes lift to mine. "I said you belonged to me." His lips thin. "I should probably take it back, but I don't know if I can." His gaze falls, face tight with regret. "I knew this would happen. I knew I wouldn't be able to keep it together." He swallows, Adam's apple bobbing with the motion. "I understand if this changes shit between us."

I mean. It kinda did. Just not in the way I think he's expecting. "Can I ask you something?"

Gavin goes still, his whole body filled with tension as he brings his eyes to mine and offers a single nod.

I hate seeing him like this. Hate what his father's done to him. Hate the fear he carries from all the years of manipulation and bullshit. Hopefully I can help him start to pack a little of it up and ship it off.

"Do you belong to me?"

Gavin's eyes move over mine as he slowly says, "Every inch of me is yours, Al."

I'm still shaking and my stomach is starting to feel a little queasy, but it's remarkably easy to smile. "Good." I lean into him, breathing in the smell of his skin as I tuck my face into the crook of his neck. "Because I would probably also try to break a bitch's arm if I saw someone grabbing you the way Dillon was grabbing me."

Gavin seems to relax a little. "Are you calling Dill-hole a bitch?"

"Oh, for sure." I try to wiggle even closer, but the seatbelt keeps me in place. "He's a world class bitch."

"He's going to be an unemployed world class bitch once I tell Grant what happened." Gavin sighs, leaning back. His hand slides along my hair, smoothing out the tangles I collected during my altercation with Dillon. "We should probably make a police report too."

I groan, letting my head fall back against the seat. "Can't we just go home and have dinner and cuddle?"

A little more of the tension bleeds from Gavin's body as he continues petting me. "We can absolutely go home and eat and cuddle." But his expression turns serious. "As soon as we go to the station and report that fucker."

30

The Good, the Bad, and the Speedy

I'M STILL STRUGGLING when Alexis and I walk into my condo two hours later. I'm not sure how long it'll take me to get over the sight of that bastard threatening her, but it's going to be more than one evening.

If ever.

"It smells really good in here." Alexis pauses just inside the door to slip off her heels, the change immediately bringing her down to my mid chest, and reminding me how much worse tonight could have been.

She's so small. Yeah, she's fierce as hell, but it's hard to overcome size and strength with attitude and sass. What if I hadn't walked right out the door when she called? What if I hadn't rushed to the building? What if I'd had to wait on the elevator? There's no telling how far that piece of shit could have taken things in a few extra seconds.

There's also no telling what I would have done to him.

"I texted Val and had her come switch the oven to warm so our dinner didn't burn." I rake one hand through my hair, trying desperately to find a way to calm myself down. It doesn't work. I need a minute to breathe. A second to collect my shit before it falls everywhere.

I blindly motion to the couch as I turn. "You get comfortable. I'll be right back."

There's a pit in my stomach and I need to fill it. I need to comfort myself so I can comfort her.

I pause, the thought of caring for Alexis soothing the unrest crawling through my veins. Maybe I'm on the right track, but I have things in the wrong order.

We came straight from the police station, and I know that as much as Alexis likes all her pretty clothes, she loves being comfortable when she's at home. Going straight into my bedroom, I collect one of my T-shirts and a pair of the soft pants she keeps here. Over the past couple of weeks, more and more of her things have crept into my space, and it's still not enough.

I want to see her everywhere.

But, after tonight, I could be facing the opposite. It took everything I had not to do more damage than I did —to keep myself in check. And I still failed epically. Women don't like to be owned. They don't like to be possessed. They don't want to be controlled and they sure as hell don't want to be claimed. I get it. I don't blame them.

I'm just not sure I can keep myself from it. I *need* Alexis to be mine and mine alone. I'm more than willing to offer the same in return—whether she wants it or not. Hell, I might be willing to sign my soul over to her if she asked for it.

No. Not might. I would do it in a heartbeat.

Ready to do as much damage control as possible, I hurry back out of my room and down the hall. Then I stop short, my stomach bottoming out at the sight in front of me.

Alexis sits on my sofa with Cilantro curled up next to her. That part of this is pretty normal. I think my cat might like Alexis more than she likes me, and I don't blame her one bit.

The problem staring me in the face is, I was in such a hurry to get to Al when she needed me, I left my little craft project out in the open. Now she has it in her hands, her delicate fingers tracing the less-than-perfect bands of crimson and gray I've been linking together for the past couple of weeks.

I swallow hard, certain this is the moment Alexis decides I'm too much. That the kind of love I have to offer is beyond overwhelming.

Her pretty blue eyes slowly lift away from the scarf to rest on my face. "Is this for me?" The question is quiet. Soft.

"Everything is for you, Al." I don't bother trying to

hide the truth. It's too late now. There's no denying how far gone I am. How deep this goes.

She stares at me a second longer before her gaze returns to my subpar attempt at a craft Granny D mastered. She lifts the half-finished accessory and gently rubs it against her cheek. "This is cashmere."

I take a deep breath, knowing I have to plead my case and I have to do it well. "I thought it was what you liked best about the scarf I gave you, so I found a place that sold it and decided to see if I could make one myself." I fight the urge to step closer. "I'm not trying to replace the one your grandma made you." I know I could never do that and I wouldn't even try. Granny D would come back and haunt me. "I just figured you could work it into your rotation so the one Granny D made you would last longer."

Alexis continues stroking the sizable portion I've completed. "These are The Swamp Cats' colors."

I can't tell if the observation is a good thing or a bad thing, so I keep explaining. "I know most of our matches are when it's warm out, but I thought there might be a few you could wear it to." I shift on my feet. "If you want to. You don't have to wear it at all if you don't like it."

I'm rambling. It happens a lot when I'm around her, and I know it gives me away. Offers a peek at the insecurities I try to hold close. Try to hide. Because men like me aren't supposed to have them.

People think I'm always confident and sure. Always

in control. Only Alexis knows the truth. And that's because I meant what I said to her earlier. Every inch of me belongs to her. The good. The bad. The ugly.

"I love it." Alexis gently sets my project onto the coffee table and slowly rises from the couch. "You know, as a kid, I thought my parents had the best marriage. That it was exactly what I wanted when I grew up." She comes to stand in front of me, head tipped way back so her eyes stay on mine. "But then I dated Hugo and realized that while my parents seemed happy with the dynamics of their relationship, I would never be okay with a man sitting around waiting for me to bring him his dinner."

She reaches up to smooth a small hand down the center of my chest. "Then we started spending time together, and you're always the one taking care of me." Her pale brows pinch together. "You do all the cooking. You save me from assholes. You rescue me when my car doesn't start." Her head swivels toward the scarf. "Now you're spending hours making me a gift." Al's eyes come back to my face. "And it makes me afraid that I might still end up in a relationship like my parents, just with the roles reversed."

Alexis inches closer, bringing the full swell of her tits against my stomach. "I don't want you to think you have to wait on me, Gavin. I don't want you thinking you have to make up for something that doesn't exist." Her hands slide higher, curving over my shoulders. "I know you don't see it, but you are *nothing* like your dad.

Some jealousy and possessiveness is normal. Everyone feels that way about the person they're with."

Alexis pinches her lower lip between her teeth for a second as her eyes move over my face. "While we were waiting at the station to make the report, I thought about what I would have done if I walked in and saw another woman pressed against you."

I swallow hard, uncertain whether or not I want to know the answer to my next question. "What would you do?"

Alexis gives me a slow, sly smile. "Let's just say I'm pretty sure I would make my mother look docile." She scrunches her face adorably. "And I probably wouldn't have been nice enough to make her apologize to you, because I would have been busy ripping all her hair out."

I find myself smiling at her confession. "Yeah?"

Alexis nods. "I think it's fair to say jealousy and possessiveness exists on both sides."

Could it really be that simple? That the thing I've worked so hard to escape in my adult life is not only inescapable, it's normal? "I'm not sure everyone feels this way though, Al."

She gives me a little shrug. "Maybe not. But I bet way more people do than you think." She lifts her brows. "You think Leo doesn't feel that way over Maddie?"

That eases even more of my long-harbored fears. It also reminds me there's something I should tell her.

"Leo says he loves her." My allegiance has always been to my best friend, but that loyalty has somewhat shifted. Especially in this situation.

I love Leo. I will protect him and back him up in almost every situation. But there are going to be times where what I have with his sister trumps that. There will also be times where I tell his secrets for everyone's benefit. Now is one of those times.

I want Alexis to understand what her brother's going through. I don't want her to judge his reactions or question his motives, the same way she doesn't question mine.

But Alexis doesn't look shocked by the revelation that her brother loves Maddie Miller. "That doesn't surprise me." She rolls her eyes toward the ceiling. "He's never been this way over a woman before, so I kinda figured as much." She sighs. "I guess I'll have to get used to the idea of my brother being in love."

She's given me an opening, but the thought of taking it is terrifying. All I can hope is that I'm really not too much for her. "Leo's not the only one who's never been this way." I let my fingers trace along the soft curve of her cheek. "You should probably get used to the idea of me being in love with you too."

Alexis purses her lips and tips her head. "I could probably find it in me to get used to that." She lifts her brows. "Especially since I'm babysitting your crazy cat and Scary Terry this weekend." Her expression grows serious. "You kind of have to love me after that."

Never in my life did I expect to be in a relationship that was easy. Hell, I never expected to be in a relationship at all. But being with Alexis is so fucking simple.

Will there be tough moments? Absolutely. We've got to tell her brother and her parents at some point. But even that doesn't feel as terrifying as it once did. Because I know, no matter what, she has my back. We're in this together.

"I think that sounds like a deal I'm happy to make." I pull her closer. "How hungry are you?"

The smile Alexis gives me is wicked. "I could wait thirty seconds if you want to mess around."

"Ha ha." I bend at the waist, banding an arm around her back before hefting her small body up mine. "You're so fucking funny."

Al's head tips back on a laugh as her legs link around my waist. "You're still the only person who thinks that."

I give her bottom a swat as we turn toward my bedroom. "Good. You know I'm a jealous bastard, so let's keep it that way."

She continues laughing, and I chuckle along with her, filled with an odd sense of peace.

Tonight was a complete shit show. It could've gone wrong in so many ways. Instead, we're where we should be. Together. Teasing each other. Laughing at ourselves and each other.

Alexis stays latched onto my front as I crawl onto the bed, hauling both of us up to the top of the mattress. As soon as I reach the pillows, she drops, grinning up at me. Her cheeks are already flushed and pink, and I love seeing the effect I have on her. Knowing it's the same one she has on me.

She tries to drag me closer, but I hold my ground, angling a brow. "Sure you don't want to set a timer? You seemed pretty confident this was only going to take thirty seconds."

Alexis continues trying to get me closer, this time hooking one of her legs around me in an attempt to drag me to her. When it fails, she lets out an aggravated grunt. "If you don't get down here, I *will* set a timer." She fists the front of my shirt, eyes narrowing. "And I will say the filthiest shit you can imagine just to prove my estimate right."

She thinks she's getting one over on me, and I'm going to let her. "Deal." I fumble around. "Where's your phone?"

Alexis scoffs. "You're really going to make me set a timer?"

"Yup." I give up looking for her phone and grab mine from my back pocket, swiping across the screen. "*And* I'm going to make you follow through with that dirty talk offer."

31
Iguana Smuggling 101

"ARE YOU SURE Gavin won't mind me coming with you?" Maddie hesitates at the open door, chewing her lower lip as she peers into Gavin's condo.

"Positive." I crouch down to pick Cilantro up as she weaves around my legs. "He knows we're hanging out this weekend while they're out of town, so I'm sure he figures you're coming with me." I glance around the sparsely furnished condo. "Plus, his place is pretty boring, so it's not like he's got anything to hide."

Maddie follows the path of my gaze. "Fair enough." She steps in, letting the door close behind her. "I'm surprised you haven't helped him out with that yet."

"It's been a little crazy." I give Cilantro a few pets before setting her back on the floor. "But I definitely have plans."

I love Gavin's place. The view is amazing. It's a great

size and a great floorplan. I definitely wouldn't balk if he asked me to move in.

I would, however, make it less utilitarian.

"I can't wait to see what you do with it." Maddie gives me a little grin. "As soon as you figure out how to tell Leo about you two."

I let out a sigh that turns into a groan. "If you have any ideas on how to accomplish that without causing him a full menty B, let me know."

Maddie's expression falls immediately, sadness taking over her pretty features. "It's my fault." She says it quietly. "I feel like all my shit has turned him into a different person, and he doesn't deserve that." She gives me a sad smile. "He's amazing and should be with someone whose life is uncomplicated."

I don't like what I think she's getting at here, and I sure as hell don't want her feeling guilty. "We might have to agree to disagree on this, because Leo was an asshole to me plenty of times growing up, so I think he has some shit coming to him."

Maddie's smile lifts a tiny bit more, but she still looks despondent. "If it was just normal shit, I might be fine with it. But what I'm dealing with is so much more than that." She sucks in a breath, eyes lifting to the ceiling. "He's afraid to even leave me alone for the weekend because of my ex." Her eyes come to mine. "How is he going to focus on actual games when he can barely make it through a charity game without texting to make sure I'm okay?"

I lift one finger, hating that I have to correct her, but I don't want Maddie to make the same mistake I have. "They are actually called matches."

Maddie's smile turns a little more genuine. "See? I don't even know the proper terminology for his career." She deflates, blowing out a loud sigh. "He does so much for me, and I'm just a mess. It all feels so one-sided and unfair."

I feel a little of that myself. "It is kind of weird when you're used to men who do the bare minimum and then end up with a guy who just wants to take care of you, isn't it?"

Maddie's dark brows lift as she gives me a sly look. "It sounds like you're familiar with that problem."

I scrunch my face up. "Is it really a problem?" It's something I've been working through the past few days, and I've come to a realization or two. "Yes, Gavin cooks our dinners and brushes my hair and rubs my feet and would pretty much jump through any hoop I came up with, but I bring a lot to the table too." I stand taller, trying to let a little of my confidence rub off on my new friend. "I'm a great conversationalist, I babysit his pets, and I have amazing tits."

Maddie's eyes drop to her significantly flatter chest. "I'm probably screwed then, because my brain won't shut up long enough for me to be a great conversation-alist, your brother doesn't have any pets, and I don't have much more than nipples on skin."

I can't do anything to help her with the conversation thing. She's going through a lot, so her poor little brain doesn't need to be any more overwhelmed. I can do something about the other parts though. "Listen." I lean in, lowering my voice conspiratorially even though we're the only two here. "Boobs are all fucking amazing. And we could totally find Leo a pet for you to take care of when he's out of town."

Maddie twists her lips to one side, pursing them tight before saying, "Leo probably could use a pet."

I grin. "That's the spirit." I turn toward the hall. "So let's take care of *my* boyfriend's weird pets, and then we can go find *your* boyfriend a weird pet." Gavin told me where he adopted Cilantro, and I'm sure that place has a whole variety of crazy kitties to choose from.

Maddie follows behind me as I stride into the bedroom Cilantro and Terry share. She eyes the iguana's cage warily, lingering in the doorway as I move to refill the lizard's food and water. "Just so we're clear, I'm not getting Leo a lizard."

"Probably a good choice, because these things are high maintenance." I shoot her a grin. "They're even worse than I am."

I turn back to Scary Terry's enclosure and look him over, tipping my head at the odd color of his skin. I lean closer and it almost seems like he's breathing faster than normal. "Are you okay, buddy?" I reach in to give him a little pet, but he doesn't lean into my touch like normal. "*Oh* no." I shake my head and raise my voice. "You are not going to get sick and die on my watch."

"*Is* he sick?" Maddie's voice is right beside me, and I turn to find her peering in at Terry. "He doesn't look very good, does he?"

"Not at all." I inspect the food and water and it doesn't look like he's eaten anything since I was here last night. "Shit." I fish my cell phone from my pocket and dial the number of the only person who can possibly help me in this situation.

My boss picks up after a few rings. "Alexis? Is everything okay?" He's been a little jumpy since I had to call and tell him his newest employee assaulted me in the office.

"I'm taking care of Gavin's lizard while he's gone, and it doesn't look very good."

"Okay." He drags the word out. "How does it look?"

I tip my head, trying to come up with a word to describe what I'm seeing. "Peaked?" I check the food dish again, confirming it's as full as I remembered. "And I don't think he's eating. Is there like, a vet or something I can take him to? I don't want this thing to die while Gavin's out of town playing in a charity match."

"Understandable. Let me get you the number of the vet I use for Amidala." He goes quiet for a minute and then my phone buzzes in my hand, alerting me to the shared contact. "Try them. I'm pretty sure they take emergencies since they're the only exotic vet around."

"Awesome. Thank you so much." I offer a goodbye then dial the number he sent, filling the woman who answers in on the situation with Terry.

"I think you should bring him in. We can give him a look and make sure it's nothing serious." Unfortunately, the only opening she offers is in thirty minutes which will be cutting it close. I take the appointment and immediately go to work trying to maneuver the iguana out of its enclosure.

Maddie watches me closely but doesn't offer to help. "You are way braver than I am."

"I bet you would do this for Leo." I finally free Terry and adjust my grip so I'm sure I won't drop him.

Maddie gets an odd look on her face. "You're right." She looks at where I hold the iguana. "I would do anything for him."

"See?" I walk past her into the hall. "Come on. You have to drive because this thing is as big as I am."

———

"ARE YOU SURE you can't tell?" I adjust the blanket wrapped around my shoulders, tucking it tighter against my neck. "If the property manager sees this thing she'll probably evict me on the spot."

"You just look bundled up." Maddie reaches out to adjust the fleece hiding Terri then situates her own barely-noticeable bundle. "What about me?"

"I can hardly tell you have a fat-ass hairless weirdo hidden under there."

Maddie looks down. "You're talking about the cat, right?"

"Did you just make a joke?" I stare at her, a little shocked. Maddie is almost as serious as I am. "Super prouda you."

She perks up, giving me a smile. "Thanks."

The lump on her chest lets out a raspy meow and I glance around, making sure no one is close enough to hear. Who would have thought some ass would dump their cat on the vet's doorstep the same morning we decided my brother needed a pet? It was some sort of freaking kismet. "Come on, let's get these girls inside."

Maddie snorts as she follows me through the lot. "Gavin's going to shit when he finds out Terri's a chick."

I peer down though the tiny gap at the top of the blanket. "And a loose one at that."

"You don't know she's loose." Maddie shifts around the bags in her hands. "They said iguanas lay eggs even if they haven't gotten busy."

"That's too depressing to consider, so I'm going to choose to believe she got something out of this besides a full hysterectomy."

"Who knew iguanas could get egg-bound?" Maddie opens the door to my building, holding it while I go in.

"I guess we do now." I go straight to the elevator. "Not that it matters since she doesn't have any of her lady parts anymore."

As if Terri hadn't already been through enough in her life, she had to undergo emergency surgery to take out not just the eggs, but everything else that went along with them. It was a long freaking day of sitting at the vet's office, hoping they could save her.

The doors open and Maddie follows me in, pressing the button for my floor. "Are you sure we shouldn't take her back to Gavin's place?"

"She isn't supposed to be alone. And Gavin's televisions are great, but if I have to babysit a dinosaur, I'm going to do it in the comfort of my own home."

"Good point." Maddie leans back against the wall. "But what if Terri shits all over your apartment?"

"Terri is going to be sleeping her sedation off in the bathtub." The vet said she probably wouldn't move around much for the first twenty-four hours, and I'm really hoping he's right. I like Gavin's place, but it's not nearly as appealing when he's not there. "I'm more worried about Gillette there."

Maddie pauses, dark brows lifting in consideration. "That's actually not a bad name."

"Right?" I widen my eyes. "Because she's bald and Gillette makes razors."

"Yeah. I got it." Maddie shifts around when the cat meows again. "We might want to hurry. I think she's about to go rogue."

We pick up the pace, reaching the door to my apartment in record time. Maddie uses my keys to let us in, and the second the door's closed, Gill drops free, shaking off as if being covered in a blanket was the most offensive thing that ever happened to her.

I point at her. "Don't shit in my apartment." I narrow my eyes. "I mean it. You better hold that crap in until the Instacart guy shows up with your litter box."

Gill stares me down for a second, but finally meows, which I'm going to take as acquiescence.

Together, Maddie and I arrange some old towels into the tub and get the sleepy iguana settled in. I won't be taking a shower anytime soon, but it's worth being in my apartment so we can pile up on my couch with blankets and watch all the shit I have on DVR while we eat dinner.

As if she's thinking the same thing, Maddie's stomach growls.

"Agreed." I flip off the light, leaving just the glow of the wax warmer illuminating the space. "Let's order some food. I'm freaking starving."

We place an order then collapse onto my couch to wait for the delivery guy to arrive.

Maddie curls up, resting her cheek against the back cushion. "Thank you."

I snort. "Pretty sure I should be thanking you." I grab the remote. "I won't be offended if you decide to hang out with someone else the next time Leo goes out of town."

"I actually had fun today." Her nose wrinkles. "Outside of having to watch the vet try to manually unbind a lizard."

"I don't think anyone enjoyed that." I flip through the show selections. "Least of all Terri."

It gets quiet for a second, then Maddie softly says, "It's been a long time since I've had a friend."

I stop what I'm doing and turn to the woman beside me. "You want me to kill him for you? I'm pretty sure I could." I've been kind of wishing Gavin hadn't had such perfect timing the other night. It would have been so gratifying to punch Dillon right in his fucking face. I also would have been less disappointed at the freak-out I had afterward if I'd been able to get a shot in.

I bet killing Maddie's ass of an ex would make me feel way better. Her too.

Her expression turns thoughtful. "I appreciate the offer, but I think I'll pass." She pulls one of my blankets across her legs. "I'm sure he'll lose interest eventually."

"I hope so." I reach out to hold her hand in mine. "You deserve to be able to live your life without being afraid all the time."

She gives me a little smile. "Thanks."

My phone buzzes on the table, letting me know the delivery guy is outside. I give her hand a squeeze and jump up. "I'm gonna go grab our food. I'll be right back." I head for the door, pointing at the television as I pass. "Pick something to watch while I'm gone."

"You want me to come with you?" Maddie starts to stand.

"No way." I'm starting to understand why my brother feels the way he does about her. Maddie is sweet and kind and easy to be around. She's also got this delicateness about her that makes me want to wrap her up and keep her safe. "It'll only take a second. You relax." It's the least I can do after making her sit in a boring office on uncomfortable chairs all day.

I hustle to the elevator, quick stepping toward the exit once I reach the main floor. As I expected, there's a man outside with a big bag of garlicky gloriousness.

I'm so excited I even smile at him as I step out, letting the door close behind me. "Thank you so much." I reach for the bag, but before my hands can close around the plastic, he pulls it away.

That's when I notice I'm the only one who's smiling. His expression is hard. Angry.

A little scary.

Instead of me grabbing my dinner, he grabs me, one hand clamping down hard on my arm.

What the fuck is it with men lately? First Tan-the-Man, then Dill-hole, and now this ass?

"Let me go." I try to wrestle my arm free but he only holds on tighter.

"Not happening." He tugs me closer, leaning in. "Open the door."

My brain stumbles over the demand, trying to figure out what in the hell he wants. I can narrow it down to a few possibilities. All of them end badly. "No thanks."

"I wasn't asking." His fingers dig into my skin. "Open the door."

He's trying to intimidate me, but it's not going to

work. This time I'm going to prove how bad I would have fucked Dillon up if I'd gotten the chance. "Or what?"

A slow, sickening smile creeps onto his lips. "Or I take something from your brother, the same way he took something from me."

32
The Night's Young #2

LEO'S LEG BOUNCES so hard it rocks the whole vehicle as we sit at a stoplight.

"Maddie said she was fine." I've been reassuring him all day. Starting the second we woke up in the hotel, then during our match, and the entire flight home, but it doesn't seem to be working. He's still agitated and antsy, and it's starting to make me agitated and antsy.

"She didn't sound right." He rakes one hand through his hair. "She said everything was fine, but I could tell some thing's wrong."

I can't fault his argument. I can tell when something's wrong with Alexis. Even when I can't see her face.

Technically, I could call her and solve this little mystery, except Leo still doesn't know we're together.

And now is not the fucking time to tell him.

"I just want to get to her and make sure she's good."

My best friend shifts in his seat, leaning to look at the GPS on my phone. "Why does it say it's gonna take so long?"

"Fucking traffic, man." We landed not long ago after taking the earliest flight home possible. The rest of the team won't come back till tomorrow, but Leo was hell-bent he was getting home as soon as possible. And being the good friend I claim to be, I offered to accompany him.

Because, while I'm not worried about Al's safety, I don't fucking like being away from her. We've been together every day for weeks now, and last night in the hotel was awful. I hated every second of it. Instead of sleeping, I laid in bed trying to come up with ways to convince her to go with me to all my away matches.

Unfortunately, unless she quits her job, that's not possible, so I'm stuck suffering.

Speaking of suffering, my stomach growls as we pass an exit. "I'm guessing you don't want to stop for food."

Leo's head snaps my direction and he looks at me like I've lost it. "No, I don't want to fucking stop for food."

"Got it." I turn back to the road, keeping my focus there, because I honestly don't like thinking too hard about Leo's current state. He's almost become a different person lately, and I don't like it. I understand it, because I would be the same way—was the same way when Alexis was in danger.

I still don't like seeing my formerly laid-back, goofy friend like this.

The rest of the drive is silent, but the tension rolling off Leo speaks volumes. And what it's saying is that I might never be able to tell him I'm in love with his sister. I can't bring myself to add one more thing to his already overflowing plate. Six months ago, I could have anticipated his reaction. He might've been a little pissed. A little shocked. Maybe even grossed out. But he would've accepted it and eventually been happy enough to give me unending shit about it.

Now?

Now it might be the thing that pushes him over the edge. Especially if he discovers how long it's been going on behind his back.

The drive feels like it takes forever. Both because of my friend's silence, and because I can't wait to see Alexis. If Leo wasn't in the seat beside me, I could have called her. Checked in. Made sure everything was going okay and that she'd eaten. But, under the current circumstances, that's not possible, so I'm forced to wait.

By the time we're pulling into Al's complex, I'm practically crawling out of my skin with excitement. I don't know how the hell I'm going to hide it. The best I can hope for is that Leo's so distracted by Maddie, he doesn't notice what's going on around him.

Cutting through the parking lot, I go straight for Al's building, ready to park as close as possible so we can get inside as fast as possible.

Leo leans forward as I round the corner, one hand coming to grip the edge of the dash. "What the fuck?"

I follow his sight line and see what has him agitated. "The fuck?" I don't think, just throw the Hummer into park and jump out, feet hitting the blacktop hard. I take off, pushing my body to its limits, grateful for every ounce of speed I've managed to gain. Because I can't get to Alexis fast enough.

Even with as hard as I'm pushing, Leo manages to catch up to me, so he's right at my side as I close in, giving me zero time to choose who I want to get my hands on. Ultimately, he decides for me.

In the blink of an eye, Leo leaps, tackling the man gripping Al's arm and barely giving me enough time to sweep her away from the collision. She lets out a little yelp because the prick doesn't immediately let go. I clamp one hand around his forearm, squeezing hard enough I'm shocked I don't break bone. The instant I see his fingers relax, I spin her away, hauling her body up against mine.

My heart is racing, my breath coming fast as it saws in and out of my chest. I don't know what the fuck I just witnessed, but I don't ever want to see it again. This is twice in one week I've had to deal with the sight of another man putting his hands on her. It's like the universe is fucking testing me, and at some point, I'm going to fail.

Alexis latches on to me, her arms so tight around my neck it's hard to breathe. "Oh my God." She buries her face in my neck. "I was doing so good until I figured out who he was, and then I just froze."

I curve my palm against the back of her head, squeezing her even tighter. "You didn't do anything wrong, Al. You did just fine. Fucking perfect."

"No, I didn't." She almost sounds mad, which makes me relax a little. "How come I could punch that guy at the bar, but no one else?"

"You didn't know him." I take another step away before craning my neck to see what's going on behind me. Leo's got the other guy on the ground and is beating the complete and total shit out of him, making it relatively easy to deduce who the man is. "It's a hell of a lot easier to hit someone you don't know." I smooth down Al's hair, trying to calm her as much as I'm trying to calm myself. "Trust me."

"*Leo.*" The piercing sound of Maddie's wail makes me go still. "*Stop.*"

I want to run away with Alexis. Let everyone else figure this shit out on their own, but I can't.

Gently, I settle Al on her feet, cradling her face in my hands. "I'm gonna go make sure your brother doesn't kill him."

She gives me a jerky nod. "Please do that."

I have to force myself away from her, because I know she needs me, but Leo needs me more, whether he knows it or not. I'm at his side in two steps, hauling him away from the bruised and bleeding piece of shit who doesn't deserve this mercy. As I expect, Leo fights me, using all his strength to try to break free of my hold.

"Let me the fuck go." His voice is low and deadly, making it even less likely I'm going to give him what he wants.

"I can't do that, man. You know it." I keep backing away, putting more and more space between us and who I highly suspect is Maddie Miller's ex-husband. "I need you to think about this. About what will happen if you don't stop now."

Leo continues flailing, forcing me to hold tighter. "He deserves what he gets."

"He does, but you don't deserve what will happen if you're the one who gives it to him." I plant my feet, forcing us to turn so he's directly facing where Alexis is squeezing a sobbing Maddie. "And she doesn't deserve for you to be locked up either."

Leo's shoulders sag. I know using Maddie against him was low, but I also know it's the only thing that will work. My need to be close to Alexis and keep her safe trumps everything. Even my desire to fucking pummel anyone who hurts her. I know Leo is the same.

He tries to shake me off again. When I don't release him, he shoots me a glare. "I'm not going to touch him." He turns away from me, all his attention going to Maddie. "I need to make sure she's okay."

After hesitating just a second, I let him go, but stay ready to grab him again just in case. Thankfully, he goes straight to where Alexis and Maddie stand, pulling the brunette from his sister's arms before wrapping her in his.

Then he adds Alexis to the embrace.

I wait for the stab of jealousy I know is coming. He's her brother, but he's still offering comfort I should be giving. Support she should get from me.

But the dreaded emotion doesn't come. Not even close. All I feel when I watch Leo look Alexis over is gratitude. I'm grateful she has someone like him to care about her. Happy Alexis has more than just me to worry about her wellbeing. She deserves to be loved and appreciated by as many people as possible.

But I'll still kick Dill-hole's ass if he so much as looks at her again.

Once Leo's finished confirming his sister is okay, his full attention goes to a still sobbing Maddie. He tucks her against him as the sound of sirens reaches my ears. Thank God someone thought to call the cops, because it hadn't even crossed my mind.

Alexis steps back from where her brother holds Maddie and her eyes sweep my way. She barely hesitates before running straight at me and jumping into my arms. I catch her easily, lifting her off the ground as the first cruiser squeals into the lot, swerving around where I left my Hummer idling in the middle of the lane.

Maddie's ex is just trying to roll onto his stomach as the ambulance pulls in behind the squad car. I hold Al a little tighter as the medics rush to his side. "Did he hurt you?"

Her head rocks against my shoulder as she shakes it. "I'm okay." She sniffs. "He wanted me to let him in and I wasn't going to do it. If you hadn't gotten here when you did—" Her voice cracks.

"Then you would have figured something out." I breathe against her hair, relaxing a little more now that she's in my arms. "You should have looked at him the way you looked at me on the deck the night of your parents' Christmas party. That would have killed him on the spot."

Alexis leans back, expression pretty damn close to the one I'm referencing. "I thought you were being an asshole."

I lift my brows. "By giving you a cashmere scarf?" I scoff. "I'd like to know what you would consider me being nice."

Her expression softens as she glances back where Leo stands. "It was pretty nice of you to make sure my brother didn't end up charged with murder."

I lift my gaze to Leo and our eyes meet. My stomach clenches as he looks over where I stand, holding his sister in a way that is clearly more than just friendly. "The night's young, Al."

33
Thanks For the Warning

"YOU LOOK LIKE you're about to throw up." I squeeze Gavin's hand with mine. "It's going to be fine. I promise."

"I like how optimistic you are, but your brother throws a mean right hook, and I don't know that I want to be on the receiving end of it."

"I'll protect you." I practically drag Gavin up the front steps to my parents' house. "But I'm pretty sure he has more pressing things to worry about than us."

I hate how true it is. Of all the fucked-up things, Leo ended up being charged with assault over the whole incident outside my apartment. His lawyer says it will probably be dismissed, but still. It's bullshit since he was just protecting me.

Mostly.

Gavin scans the driveway and the street. "I'm actually surprised he and Maddie aren't already here."

"I'm sure they'll be here any second." Leo isn't usually late, but, it's not surprising he would be. Especially since my parents invited us all over to stage some sort of an intervention. Yet another reason I don't think Leo is going to be that concerned when he finds out about me and Gavin.

My mom opens the door as we reach the porch. Her smile is lukewarm at best, but I'm gonna chalk that up to all the shit that's been happening. Her eyes settle on my hand in Gavin's, one blonde brow slowly angling. "Well, this is an interesting development."

Gavin tenses beside me, likely bracing for my mother's disapproval. When her forced smile turns genuine and she reaches up to pat his cheek, I can see all the worry bleed from his body.

"Are you sure you want to do this, Gavin?" She tips her head my way, widening her eyes. "Alexis can be kind of a handful."

I don't think my mother could have said anything more perfect. I'm going to have to thank her for it later.

Even if it is a little insulting.

"That is actually a big part of the appeal." Gavin pulls me closer, wrapping one heavy arm around my shoulders to tuck me into his side. "She keeps me on my toes."

I roll my eyes, because I do no such thing. I'm as boring as it gets. Luckily, Gavin seems to like being boring. I'd always assumed he was just as outgoing and social as my parents and Leo, but I'm starting to think that was just something for him to hide behind. A way to avoid the kind of connections that terrified him.

"Well, if anyone can handle your crazy schedule, it's Alexis." My mom lowers her voice, leaning close to Gavin like I can't hear what she's about to say. "She'll have your whole life organized before you even know what hit you."

Gavin lowers his own voice conspiratorially. "I'm banking on it."

"Ugh." I wiggle out from under his arm and step past my mom into the house. "You two keep having your weirdo conversation. I need some fucking coffee and a scone."

Gavin chuckles behind me, unbothered by my little show of attitude, and I smile as I walk away. Right up until I see my dad's scowling face.

I walk over to where he sits at the kitchen island, likely waiting for my brother's arrival, and lean in to press a kiss on his cheek. "Hey, Dad."

His hard expression softens. "Hey, honey. How are you?"

"She's dating Gavin," my mother answers for me, and I'm not surprised. There's a good chance everyone we know will get a phone call before the day's over.

I warned Gavin that was going to happen, but he claims he's fine with it. The strange thing is, so am I. Normally, my mom's love of telling everyone everything she knows drives me crazy, but I don't mind who finds out Gavin belongs to me. She can shout it from the fucking rooftops if she wants.

My dad looks Gavin over as he follows my mom into the kitchen. His gaze is assessing and, honestly, a little unnerving. But then he says, "About damn time. You two have been dancing around this thing for years."

My mouth drops open. "What?"

Mom snorts. "You think we didn't notice you guys flirting all the time?"

My gaze swings to Gavin. "We weren't flirting."

He shrugs. "Maybe you weren't."

"At least one of my kids is making good choices." My dad scrubs one big hand over his face before downing half of his coffee. "Leo decided it wasn't enough to ruin Maddie's life, now he's decided to ruin his own too."

I take a deep breath. I knew this was coming, and I've been preparing for it. "Are you telling me you wouldn't have done the same thing if Mom had been coming out of a shitty marriage when you met?"

I've tried to stay out of this because I was worried I would make things worse. Now, it's clear things can't get any worse, so I might as well try.

After spending time with Maddie, I one hundred percent see why Leo adores her. I also understand why he's willing to do whatever it takes to protect her from her crazy-ass ex-husband.

My dad narrows his eyes as they slide from my mom to me. "I would have done what I needed to keep your mother safe, and if that meant leaving her alone, that's what would've happened."

"But how do you know leaving her alone would have kept her safe?" I look between my parents, meeting both of their gazes. "You haven't seen how her ex is. I have." My stomach twists at the memory of the look in his eyes. "And I'm not sure Maddie would be any safer without Leo in her life." I pause, thinking it over. "Actually, Leo probably gives him someone else to hate, so she's probably better off."

"Not anymore."

I spin at the sound of my brother's voice, taking a step back at his disheveled state.

Leo looks like shit. Not even warm shit. He looks like lukewarm shit that's been left out in the rain overnight.

"Maddie dumped me last night, so everybody can fucking celebrate. You got what you wanted." Leo moves to the island, snatching a scone off the countertop and biting it in half before continuing. "She said she wasn't going to let me destroy my life, and then she blocked me." He makes a sweeping motion with his arms. "So, congratulations. You win."

I'm stunned.

But also, not.

I learned a lot about Maddie while she and I hung out, and one of the biggest realizations was that she genuinely cares about my brother. Deeply. Apparently deep enough that she wants to protect him as much as he wants to protect her.

"Oh, honey." My mom goes to give Leo a hug, but he steps out of her attempted embrace. "Don't." He shakes his head. "Don't act like you're sorry, because I know you're not." He backs away. "I'm not staying. I just came to give you the good fucking news."

Leo storms out, and I follow right behind him, chasing him down the steps. "Leo, wait."

He stops so quickly, I nearly collide with his back, feet skidding across the sidewalk as he spins to face me.

"If you're here to apologize, you don't have to." His eyes flick toward our parents' house. "I wasn't talking to you in there."

"Maddie loves you, Leo." The words jump right out of my lips. "She didn't say it, but I could tell."

His brows lift. "You're an expert on love now because you fucking love Gavin?" There's an edge to his voice that makes me cringe.

"Kinda?" I don't know what the right answer is, but I feel like admitting I am madly in love with someone who is also madly in love with me would be rubbing salt into a wound. Especially since no one is trying to kill either of us.

I don't have to turn around to know Gavin steps in behind me. I can tell by the look on Leo's face. It's not anger or disappointment tightening his already tense expression. Instead, he almost looks...

Jealous.

And doesn't that fucking break my heart.

He holds Gavin's gaze for a few seconds before turning back to me. "Do me a favor and take care of Maddie." He drags one hand through his already messy hair. "She really likes you, and she needs all the support she can get."

"I really like her." And finding out she's willing to sacrifice her own happiness to protect my brother only makes me like her more. Makes me more determined to find my inner Babs so I can shred her lunatic of an ex-husband the next time our paths cross.

And I have a feeling they will be crossing.

I manage a little smile, hoping to ease some of Leo's worry. "If it makes you feel any better, she's pretty much stuck with me and my friends forever."

I'm shocked when he offers a flicker of a smile back. "That does make me feel better, actually." Leo takes a breath so deep it lifts his shoulders before turning to Gavin. "I'm still probably gonna kick your ass for fucking my sister."

To my surprise, Gavin grins. "Understood."

I watch as Leo goes to his car and drives away, then I look at the man beside me. "Why did you look so happy when Leo said he was going to kick your ass?"

"Because," Gavin hooks an arm at my waist, pulling me close, "if he was actually mad, he wouldn't have warned me."

34

Love Cuss

"HERE?" I TURN to lift a brow at Alexis, making sure I've got the sofa exactly where she wants it.

She taps a finger against her lips, tilting her head to one side as she assesses the new layout of my living room. "Maybe back where it was before."

I wait, trying to decipher the look on her face. "You're either constipated, or you're giving me shit."

Alexis scoffs, her mouth dropping open. "I don't look constipated."

I leave the couch where it is then head for where she stands next to the dining room table that was just delivered. "That means you're giving me shit then." I narrow my eyes. "Again."

She lifts a hand to the center of her chest, resting it against the tits I love so fucking much. "I would never do something like that."

A grin takes over my face because I love how awful

she is at teasing and sarcasm. "You'd never do it well, that's for sure."

Her hands drop to her sides. "You take that back."

"Nope."

I rush her, scooping Alexis up so fast she gasps. I seal my lips over hers, swallowing down the sound of surprise as I hike her higher on my body.

I've given her free reign over my place, and every week it looks more and more like a home. More and more like her. And that is exactly what I want. More of Al everywhere in my life.

Right now, I want more of her in my bedroom.

I'm halfway down the hall when someone knocks on my door, and I groan, letting my head tip back toward the ceiling.

"It's probably Val." Alexis wiggles her brows. "Bet she needs you to save another knocked-up dinosaur."

"No more pregnant lizards." I shoot Terri a grin where she's perched in her new, custom-made enclosure, so she knows I'm not really mad. "No pregnant anything."

For now.

Alexis and I are planning on moving her in as soon as her lease is up, and I have every intention of making that a lifelong sort of thing. One I hope will someday include kids. Never would I have expected to be in a relationship, let alone considering all the white picket fences I can find, but here I am.

All thanks to my best friend's little sister. The girl

who never treated me like The Wall. The woman who's always held her own special place in my mind.

And my heart.

Whoever's at my door knocks again and I sigh as I turn, carrying Alexis along with me. "This better be fucking important." I whip the door open and stare at the man on the other side in shock.

"Hello, son." My dad tips his head at Alexis. "Hi."

Al looks from me to my dad then back to me again. "Hi?" She lets her legs drop, wiggling her way down my body as I continue to stare. I didn't expect to see him again. Figured he'd have no use for me if I wasn't feeding into his dumbassery. But here he is. Looking fucking contrite.

I have no clue what to say to him so I just stand there, feeling farther from him—from the life we used to share—than ever before.

My dad shifts on his feet. "Can I come in?"

I start to tell him no. I don't want him near Alexis. Don't want him to taint what we're building.

But Al beats me to the punch. She angles a brow at my dad, giving him a look that could melt the paint off a car. "Are you going to be an asshat?"

Fucking hell. I love everything about Alexis, including her mouth's tendency to run all on its own, but if my dad says something shitty to her, I might end up like Leo did a few months ago, and it took forever to clean that mess up.

My dad rocks back on his heels, eyes coming to me

before going back to Alexis. "He told you about that, huh?"

Alexis crosses her arms, continuing to glare at him. "Which part are you referring to? The part where you told him to never trust a woman because we're nothing but lying whores? Or the part where you objectified me the first time our paths crossed?"

My dad's brows lift, climbing his forehead as Alexis continues to dress him down.

"If you're here to try to put more of your idiot opinions into his head, then you can turn your ass right around and crawl back into whatever pit you escaped from." Her chin lifts. "But, if you're here in an attempt to apologize, then you should probably start talking."

My dad blinks and I hold my breath, waiting to see how he reacts to the little ankle biter Alexis is becoming. He takes a breath, but instead of turning to me, his focus stays on Alexis. "I'm sorry for what I said about you. You didn't deserve that."

"It was gross." She doesn't back down. Doesn't give him an inch. "You shouldn't talk that way about any woman, much less one your son is with."

Another deep breath from my father. "You're right."

Alexis studies him for a second before tipping her head my way. "Now apologize to him."

If I wasn't already obsessed with the woman beside me, the way she's handling this situation would have put me there in record time. Seeing my dad again is a lot, and without her here, I would have simply slammed the door in his face.

My dad meets my eyes. "I'm sorry." He pauses, lifting his shoulders. "For everything."

Again, I don't know what to say. It's too much and not enough at the same time.

And again, Alexis steps in.

"That's a good start, but you know you're going to have to dig into the specifics if you really want to fix all the shit you fucked up, right?" She steps in front of me, eyes narrowing as she stares my dad down. "And just so you know, if you do anything to hurt him in any way, I will make sure you suffer."

My dad nods. "Understood."

Alexis lifts her chin high in the air. "Good." She turns to me, running one hand down the center of my chest. "I should go check on the stuff in the oven." She raises her brows in silent question, making it clear she won't leave me on my own with him unless I want her to.

"Good idea." I lean down to press a kiss to her lips. "Don't want your first attempt at making Granny D's butter cake to burn the building down."

Al scrunches her nose at me. "Funny."

"I'm hilarious, remember?" I kiss her wrinkled nose. "See you in a minute."

She gives my dad another glare before disappearing behind me, leaving us alone.

"She's real protective of you, isn't she?" There's

something akin to awe in my dad's voice. Like he can't believe what he's seeing.

"She is." I cross my arms and lean against the door frame. "And I'm real protective of her."

My dad nods and goes quiet for a minute. When he speaks again, his voice is softer. "I miss you, son." He glances down the hall before continuing. "I want to fix this."

"To fix this, you have to fix you." I still love my dad, but I won't let him be around Alexis if he's going to be the man I know him to be. He has to be different. Better.

"I know, and I'm trying." He scrubs one hand down the back of his neck. "I've had a lot of time to think about things, and I started to realize I might have fucked up as much as your mom did."

This is the first time I've ever heard my dad take accountability for anything. It's weird.

"Maybe I can take you and..." His eyes drift into my condo.

"Alexis."

"Maybe I can take you and Alexis out for dinner sometime." He peers around me, like he expects her to come back to lay into him again at any moment. "Or just coffee. Whatever you want."

It's funny how quickly he walked back from dinner, but it's hilarious that my little spitfire of a girlfriend is probably why he decided to offer something with a shorter time frame.

"I'll think about it." I'm not committing to anything. Not until I talk to Alexis. Not because I want to make sure she's okay with going—I know she will always support me—but because I need to figure out if *I'm* okay with going.

Things are so good between us. Fucking perfect. I won't risk that for anything.

Not even my dad.

"Fair enough." He gives me a tight smile. "Let me know what you decide."

"I will."

I watch as he leaves, waiting until he's in the elevator to go inside. I find Alexis sitting on the sofa with Cilantro, aggressively working on the project she's been fighting with for weeks.

"You might want to calm down before you start dropping stitches and get really pissed." I sit next to her, carefully taking the scarf she's torn apart and reworked more times than I can count. "You sure you don't want me to do this for you?"

"It's your scarf. The point of it is that I'm the one who makes it." She snags it from my hands and goes back to fighting the loops. "That way it's filled with all my love for you."

I squint. "Is it though? Because you're usually cussing at it."

"Listen." She all but throws the scarf onto the coffee table, nearly taking out the selection of candles and artfully arranged decorations that now line its surface. "I never promised my love didn't include cussing."

I grab Al, pulling her across my lap so her knees straddle my thighs. Raking both hands through her blonde hair I breathe in the soft scent of her skin. "Thank you."

Her expression softens. "Was I too mean to him?"

I shake my head. "You were just the right amount of mean."

Her lips curve. "I think I'm going to put that on a T-shirt."

I let my thumbs skim over her cheeks. "You don't think your face conveys it enough?"

Her eyes widen. "If it wasn't for this face, you would be beating every woman in Sweet Side off you when we go out."

I nod in agreement. "You are kinda scary."

"Damn right I am." Al leans in to press a kiss to my lips before leaning back to grab the scarf she launched seconds ago. "Now help me make this damn scarf of love so I can give it to you."

———

Made in the USA
Las Vegas, NV
19 December 2024

14824190R00213